Of Time and Light

Citizen J. Edwards

FIRST ORDER
PRESS

Of Time and Light

Library of Congress Control Number: 2025919581

Ebook ISBN: 979-8-9879991-1-0

Paperback ISBN: 979-8-9879991-3-4

Printed in the United States

*To my loving parents, who probably never thought
that this would happen in their lifetimes.*

Chapter One

A brilliant, beaming light burned at my back. In front of me, a veil of flickering gray and black particles flutters like curtains in a breeze. They shimmered and twisted, as if the air itself was breaking apart into waves of light and sound, looking as if a hologram was trying and failing to hold itself together.

Within the swirl, I could just make out the figure of a man. Shifting between static and chaos, his face would scramble then reappear, and his presence crackled in and out with urgency. Then came the man's voice—clear and haunting.

"Six! Six!"

He was calling for me. My name. Not Veronica—**Six**. Just like my Dad used to.

A chill danced up my spine as the particles began to collapse, breaking apart like ash in the wind.

"No! Wait!" My hands shot out, desperate to hold on, but the dream was already slipping away. Colors bled into gray, faded entirely into black. Panic clawed up my chest as if I should pull something loose.

"Six! Six!"

THE VOICE WAS different this time—sharper, real.

"Hey! You need to wake up, girl!"

My mom.

The sound of her dragged me back, yanking me out of the dream and into the crumpled heat of old bedsheets, the faint smell of dust and last night's air pressing in around me.

I groaned into my pillow, the cluttered walls of my tiny room coming into focus. I'd had that dream before—just pieces of it. Lately, however, it had been happening more and more.

"The bus will be here in 45 minutes," Mom called from the hallway.

I rolled over towards the wall, blonde hair in my eyes, and mumbled, "Ugh. Just ten more minutes?"

"Nope. I've got an early shift at the museum. You're on your own."

"Fine," I muttered, kicking off the sheets. My bare feet hit the moss-green carpet, and as I stretched, a Rubik's Cube tumbled from the edge of my nightstand— an old cardboard-topped milk crate near shelves made from cinder blocks and warped planks. A cockroach scurried across the carpet and vanished into a pile of clothes.

"Mom! Another roach!" I called out, in half-disgust, half-resigned.

"I'll call the landlord—again," she said, already sounding over it. "But maybe if you picked your stuff up once in a while, we wouldn't have roaches."

My room, or more of a nook, is mainly filled with scattered

clothes and books stacked like leaning towers on DIY cinder block shelves. A film of aged yellow pollen coats the window, giving a golden tint to the maps and charts of the Atlantic coast—some drawn on, others faded with age—curled on the wall like brittle scrolls. The whole apartment smelled of old wood and mold, as if it had been underwater at some point in its hundred-year history.

The place became too quiet, and the dream still spun in my head as some sort of warning. I'd been having those dreams since Dad disappeared eight years ago. And usually, afterward, I'd feel something. A shift. A disturbance no one else noticed.

I padded barefoot across the apartment to the living room and flicked on the TV. The old box crackled to life, static rolling across the screen like a ghost from the dream.

"—AMAZING video out of St. Augustine, Florida this week," the anchor said. His expression was too chipper for the morning. *"Several airport workers raced down the runway in a BMW with a sunroof. Watch as a mechanic stands through the roof and pulls down a stuck landing gear strut on a Piper aircraft flying just above their heads—"*

THE FOOTAGE WAS WILD.

"Mom! The St. Augustine Airport's on national news!"

"That's nice, dear," she called from the bathroom, not really listening. "Hey, how's that Earth Science project going?"

I grabbed the box of *Lucky Charms* and spoke with my mouth half full. "Ugh. Mr. Harrison is the worst. I'll be lucky to pass. I'm going to the library after school to work on it."

"Well, make it to the finals so I can see Ted—uh, Mr. Harrison," she said with a weird little smile.

"Ew. Barf. Mom! Everyone knows he has, like, extreme dandruff."

She kissed my cheek, grabbed her purse, and headed to the door. "Don't stay out all night at the library. I'll order pizza. Want me to rent a movie?"

Standing up on my toes, "Oh. See if *Passage to India* is in?"

She paused, then wrinkled her nose. "How about something fun? Maybe *Splash*?"

"Tom Hanks is so lame," I said, nearly spitting cereal as she shut the door behind her.

The apartment went quiet again, except for the hum of the TV and the creak of old pipes. I got dressed in jeans and a neon orange T-shirt before grabbing my backpack. The old wooden stairs groaned as I made my way down to the sand-dusted street. The March morning was cool, but I knew the Florida heat was just waiting to pounce. Sunlight poured over the palm trees, and a breeze from the Atlantic tugged at my shirt as I stood at the bus stop. The cracked sidewalk under my sneakers smelled faintly of damp concrete and moss.

THEN: the roar of the Camaro.

JENNY UNSNER and her perfect little clique, all glossy makeup and hair teased up with too much Aqua-Net hairspray, zipped by in her boyfriend's shiny black Camaro. *Billy Idol* blared so loud it rattled the street signs, and the girls whooped as if the world was their private concert. Jenny leaned halfway out the window, sunglasses flashing, her laugh sharp and confident.

Jenny lived on Lew Boulevard, in one of those waterfront houses where the dock lights glowed at night like runway beacons. She had a pool in the backyard, turquoise water glimmering in the Florida sun, the kind of place where every summer party ended with her holding court on a raft while everyone else orbited around her. I'd been there once, years ago, and the memory still clung to me like smelly chlorine on skin. An entire other universe just blocks from my own crumbling apartment.

Just before they disappeared around the corner, one of them shouted out the window:

"See ya in 2nd period—wouldn't wanna be ya!"

A loud honk followed, then wild laughter trailed behind them along with the car's exhaust.

My feet sank deeper into the sidewalk, as if the weight of the distance between Jenny's world and mine pressed down harder than the Florida sun ever could.

———

THE LOCKER ROOM REEKED—SWEAT, cheap deodorant, and bad attitudes. Lockers banged shut. Girls giggled in whispers sharp enough to shred any sense of self-esteem.

I ducked into a bathroom stall, gripping my gym clothes like armor.

The stall door latched, and I was safe.

Leaning against the metal door, I changed quickly, biting the edge of my shirt. I waited until the voices outside moved on before stepping out, praying I'd be invisible.

Once in the gym, we lined up for roll call.

"Veronica Ingram," Mrs. Hamstead droned, snapping me out of the dream replay in my head.

"Here," I mumbled.

"Move it, Six!" called a voice behind me—bold, brash, and impossible to miss.

Claire McKennon crashed into the line as if she owned the whole gym. Loud where I was quiet, wild where I was cautious. Red hair trailing behind her in a messy bun, sneakers squeaking across the polished floor, she leaned in close and whispered—just loud enough for half the class to hear—"Volleyball? Again? This is not how I want to die."

A few kids laughed. I tried not to smile, but failed.

We couldn't have been more different. Claire had a reckless kind of confidence, as if the world owed her something, and she intended to collect. She wore eyeliner to school in sixth grade and got into trouble for calling our creepy guidance counselor a total douchebag during freshman year.

I was meek little Veronica Ingram, who practically apologized for existing. I liked library corners and calm behavior. I didn't break the rules; I welcomed them.

But somehow, Claire picked me, and she stuck. Pulling me into her orbit with a force that felt equal parts thrilling and terrifying. She said things no one else would say. Did things no one else would do. She was a one-girl hurricane. Hurricane Claire.

I became the anchor when she drifted too far. And in return, she reminded me I didn't always have to be small. That I could shout sometimes, or say yes, even to things that frightened me.

And if I was being honest, I never really understood how Claire saw the world—but I was glad she saw me in it. I smiled despite myself. Claire always knew how to shake loose the tension. Or completely bulldoze through it.

Everyone knows me as Six. That's what my Dad called me: the Roman numerals, my initials: VI. I want to hold on to that.

I want to hold on to everything my dad left behind.

EVERYTHING.

Chapter Two

Mom and I cocoon together in our tiny apartment on Anastasia Island most Fridays. Pizza and movies. That was the routine, familiar and comforting. Tonight, Mom splurged and ordered delivery. I sink into the worn couch, the greasy, cheesy warmth of the pizza melting into me. The flickering TV glows in front of us, casting shadows on the peeling walls.

She's picked *Splash*—about a guy who falls for a mermaid. Classic Mom—romantic to the bone. My mom collects stories where love wins, as if they're proof that the world isn't as messy as it feels. I can't help but roll my eyes a little, even as I savor the salty, gooey slice. Like the pizza, the movie is cheesy, sure, but I get why she loves it. She keeps telling me how the movie's director, Ron Howard, had played little Opie on the old Andy Griffith Show. I always call it the "Andy Griffin Show," and Mom laughs, correcting me with a gentle shake of her head.

"It's Griffith, dear," she says, then begins whistling the theme, her voice warm with nostalgia. "A Griffin is a mythological beast— half lion, half eagle. Quite the creature, huh?"

I smirk, taking another bite. "Oh, Really? Then what about Merv-Merv Griffin?"

She chuckles, raising her hands. "Okay, you got me with Merv. Moving on." She leans back, gaze soft with affection. "So, how was school? Especially Science?"

I sigh, feeling that familiar sting. "Mr. Harrison went over the project for the competition. He didn't like my idea. Saying that it's not real science."

MOM TILTS HER HEAD, her voice gentle but firm. "Six, the Bermuda Triangle isn't science. It's just stories—nautical legends."

"Yeah, I know," I mutter, feeling that familiar frustration bubble up. "But I argued magnetic anomalies could be out there. He didn't buy it. Now I have to do boring solar energy."

She places her slice on the armrest of her faded chair, then scoots nearer, settling beside me on the battered couch. The quilt—my grandmother's gift—wraps around me like a hug I didn't know I needed. It still smells faintly like lavender, and I bury my face in it for a second, letting the warmth settle in my chest.

Mom's voice breaks the quiet. "Sweetheart..." She pauses, the word soft and careful, like she's walking onto thin ice. "I know you're still looking for answers about your Dad. Six, I get it. It's been seven long years. Long enough for everything to feel... final." Her voice catches, just a little. "His boat disappeared. No goodbye. No wreckage. Just... gone. Believe me, I know how much that hurts."

I don't answer. The TV flickers in front of me, playing something I'm not really watching. Everything blurs together. Mom's words hang there, in the space between us.

My eyes stay fixed on the screen. At the same time, my thoughts drift out across the water to the place where he vanished like a ghost. No storm. No distress signal. Just open sea and silence.

It should be enough to let go.

But I can't.

Hope can be fragile, useless, and stubborn at the same time. And no matter what anyone says, something deep in me still whispers:

He's not gone.

Not really.

I'd know if he was.

My voice cracks before I can stop it. "Mom, you can't just give up. Dad's not gone—he's out there. I know he is." Clenching my fists to steady the trembling, my voice remained steady and stubborn. "I feel it in my gut, Mom. He's waiting to be found."

Mom's eyes soften, but her expression stays gentle. "Six, I wish I could believe that. But sometimes, hope isn't enough," speaking softly.

That's when I stand up and lose it. "Mom! That's bullshit! Dad wouldn't just disappear. People don't just vanish into thin air. He's alive—I know it. I can feel him. We can't give up on him."

She sighs, a long, slow breath, and calls my name softly. "Six."

I STORM OUT. Tossing open the door, then slamming it behind me. Something feels off, everything seems to stop for a split second, and I end up nearly tripping down the rickety stairs, furious that she seems so calm about all of this. I guess she's learned to accept the silence, the waiting, but I haven't.

I wipe my eyes, tears blurring as the streetlights cast a hazy glow over the quiet neighborhood. The late hour hushes everything—only distant voices from televisions, a car or two, and the faint hum of the city. Shadows of old homes loom around me, their crooked shapes like silent witnesses to secrets buried deep.

I walk east along Magnolia Drive, sand sticking to my bare feet, gritty and cool. After living here for three years, I know every crack and shadow of this place. Turning onto Lighthouse Avenue, the sight of the lighthouse materializes through the mist—its beams slicing through the night sky, faint but steady. The fog made the lighthouse fade in and out of existence, as if it hadn't decided what century it belonged in.

A massive Live Oak's branches reach out, with tentacles similar to those of an ancient sea monster, its tree limbs twisting out and upward as if guarding the lighthouse. I pass a three-car garage, which has seen better days, with its paint peeling and the scent of mildew and decay hanging in the air.

The lighthouse itself is a relic, its faded black and white stripes worn down by salt and time. Its brick tower stands proud, although battered with several windows bricked over, and its tin roof rusted. It's a sad sight of neglect, but it still shines every night, unwavering.

To my left, the charred remains of the Lightkeeper's house. It burned down fifteen years ago. According to my Dad, the blaze occurred on the day I was born. There's always been this strange, sort of pull as if a part of me belongs in this space. The brick walls look solid, sure, but everything else is just missing or scorched black. The smoky smell is still there, too, hanging phantom-like in the air. It's all fenced off now, but sometimes, when no one's around, I creep up close and just stand there, imagining the way it probably looked a hundred years ago.

I TURN, ready to leave, when something shifted—just enough to raise the hair on my arms. A creaking sound, not the wind, so I freeze. The lighthouse door groans open—slow, deliberate. My heart pounds. Who would be inside on a Friday night? No cars are parked nearby. The shadows shift as someone moves cautiously. A tall figure, unkempt, with a hoodie pulled up obscuring his face, looking as if he belongs to the shadows. He's young—maybe a little older than me—lean, strong, with dark hair and sharp features. He steps forward, pulling back his hood to reveal a face that's both attractive and mysterious.

He doesn't see me at first, standing stock-still, breath caught in my throat. Then he notices me. Our eyes meet—mine wide with shock, his dark and intense. He stumbles back, startled, voice rising in surprise.

"My God!"

I yelp, instinct kicking in. I jump back, unsure of what's happening, and make ready to fight or run. Both of us are breathing hard, caught in that frozen moment. The man places a hand on his chest, eyes wide. "Wha... What are you doing here?"

Stepping back further, my voice trembling but defiant. "Same question. What about you?"

He looks me over—shorts, T-shirt, bare feet—and then his gaze drops to my fluorescent green, cheap imitation of a *Swatch* watch. He studies it, then looks back at me, calm but curious.

"What year is it?" he asks.

I glance at my watch. "Eleven twelve," I say, trying to keep my voice steady.

He shakes his head, patient. "No. The year—what's today's date?"

I hesitate, confused. "March sixteenth, 1985."

He nods slowly, then grins a little, eyes twinkling with some strange recognition. "If today is March sixteenth, 1985... then you must be Veronica."

My skin crawls at the sound of my name. A weird mix of fear and curiosity stirs inside me. I want to bolt. But his calm demeanor pulls me closer.

"Who are you?" I demand, voice broken. "How do you know my name?"

He exhales, almost as a laugh. "I thought so," he says, leaning against the fence. "I know about your father, Veronica."

My throat tightens. The cadence of my heart quickens. "What about him?" I whisper, trying to sound steady but failing.

He looks at the lighthouse, then at the charred keeper's house, meets my eyes again—so intense, so searching. "He's a time traveler," he says softly. "And we think you are too."

The words didn't register right away. They hung there, like smoke. Me? A what? Everything blurs—the world sharpens, then fades. My mind races—Dad's out there? A traveler? This isn't possible.

I inch closer to him, desperate. Smelling of sage and salt, both earthy and of the ocean. "A traveler? How?"

He hesitates, then says quietly, "I can't explain it all now. Not here. But back to your first question, my name is Dorian."

He pulls his hood up, but doesn't move. His eyes suddenly go wide and dart past me.

"Car!"

Without another word, he sprints toward a white building. Headlights crested the hill on Lighthouse Avenue, brightening the street behind me.

My body moved before I could make a decision. I chased after him, ducking into the shadows as we crouched behind weathered wooden walls. My heart thundered as the sound of the car engine crept closer.

The car rolled to a stop—a harsh beam of a spotlight cut across the property, sweeping back and forth toward the lighthouse.

Dorian's breath brushed my ear. "Police," he said. "Stay with me —we won't get caught."

I nodded, too breathless to answer.

The spotlight shifted, then flicked off. As the cruiser crawled forward, Dorian pulled me around the corner to stay hidden.

We crept along the side of the whitewashed building. He found a green door, tugged it open with a creak, and we slipped inside just as the engine faded into the night.

I leaned against the wall, lungs burning. "This is insane," I whispered.

Dorian stood, moving closer than before. His eyes held a strange mix of adrenaline and... something else. Conviction? Desperation?

"I know," he said calmly. "But try to trust me."

He rummaged through drawers in what appeared to be an old kitchen. A match flared and then an oil lantern flickered to life, casting long shadows across the room.

The place was a wreck: boxes were stacked everywhere, broken chairs, dust so thick it was almost tangible, and a peculiar, salty varnish smell. "What even is this?" I asked, tiptoeing around some ancient mop.

"Abandoned Coast Guard barracks from wartime." He ducked under a sagging shelf and waved me after him, past bins of bolts and creepy, rusty tools.

The next room was, if possible, even sadder—a couch with stuffing showing, folding chairs, and a table that looked allergic to cleaning. He plunked the lantern down and pulled out a chair. "We're safe here. Sit."

I sat, the cold metal biting my bare legs. My heart was still racing, and my mind spun with too many questions. "About my father. You need to start explaining," I said in an almost commanding tone.

Dorian leaned in, face lit by the warm flicker of the lamp.

"Everything I'm about to tell you will sound insane, Six. Can I call you that?"

My breath catches in the stale air, and I nod in silence.

"Your father thinks that you could be in danger, and I think so too." Dorian's voice is steady, urgent. "I came to find you before they do."

My stomach twists. Too much—so much I can't process. Still, a flicker of trust ignites. "Who's after me?"

He stares at me, then says softly, "A group called the Council of Chaos. They want to control time and travelers like us by creating... well, chaos."

"Like... Like us?" My mind spins—wait, I can do that? Time travel? It sounds totally radical, but also totally bogus, and my thoughts jumble—hope and fear, disbelief and curiosity.

He nods, serious, "You've felt it, haven't you? The disturbances? The weird vibe. You're likely gaining more sensitivity. No one's told you because they don't understand."

I nod slowly, remembering those strange moments—how time seemed to pause around me, how I felt strange vibrations inside. The moment I left the house, just 15 minutes ago, a shiver went down all my bones. One foot on the warped floorboard, the other hovering above the first cracked step of the decaying stairway. It all starts to make sense now.

Time seems to stop—not for long, maybe a millisecond—but in those slivers of nothingness, I feel it, like an echo rippling through the universe and somehow passing through *me*.

And now, standing here, it clicks. My body always knew. It wasn't a dream. It never has been. That flutter in my chest, that quake in my center—it's not fear. Not nerves.

It's something else.

Something waking up.

He leans back, studying me. "Your Dad wants to find a way back to you. But the Council of Chaos wants to control anyone with the gift."

Questions flood my mind. How? Why? What if I could really do this?

"Prove it," I demand suddenly. "Take me to him. Take me there."

Dorian's face softens, regretful. "I wish I could," he says quietly. "We travel on gravitational waves. Another wave won't reach us for weeks. So the next time it happens, we cannot miss our chance."

I stare at him in frustration. "Then why tell me all this now? When there's nothing that can be done?"

He looks at me, serious. "Because your father asked me to. Because you deserve to know."

The room suddenly feels too small, too tight. My mind begins to spin with all these weird ideas that I can't quite grasp. I stand up abruptly, needing space, and press my forehead against the cool glass of the window, staring up and out at the steady glow of the lighthouse. It's a beacon in the night—constant, unwavering. Like hope.

"How do I know you're not lying?" I whisper, fogging the glass.

"You don't," Dorian says softly, "I'm asking for a little faith until I can prove it all to you."

I turn to look at him, shadows flickering across his face. Is it a look of truth, sincerity, or something more dangerous?

Standing as the lantern's glow catches his features is an outline of hope, or possibly desperation.

"It's late," he murmurs gently. "Your mom's probably worried. Come on. I'll walk you home."

Chapter Three

When I finally opened my eyes, it was already 10:25 in the morning. A soft stripe of sunlight had inched across the room and landed on my pillow, warm against my cheek. I didn't move and just stared up at the ceiling, letting everything from the night before drift back in.

It all felt unreal now—like something half-remembered from a dream. The fog rolled in. The lighthouse glowing through it like a signal meant just for me. Dorian's voice echoes in the dark. The way he walked beside me afterward—quiet, steady—like he belonged out there, like the night recognized him.

But more than anything, I kept turning over one thing in my mind: the possibility that my dad might still be alive.

Dorian carried himself with quiet confidence, every word deliberate. He didn't seem much older than me, but there was something different about him—something unhurried and confident; he was always a step ahead of time itself. He seemed nothing at all like the guys at school, who either ignored me or tried too hard to be noticed. Dorian didn't have to try. He just *was*. And that made me want to know everything about him. Not just the time travel part. *Him.*

I sat up and looked all over, with fresh eyes, noticing how cluttered my room had become. Nautical charts, news clippings, books about vanishing ships and magnetic anomalies—my whole world mapped in ink and pinned to the walls. Part of me wanted to rip it all down. Maybe it would make Mom feel as though I was moving on, like I had finally accepted what the Coast Guard report said.

With a heavy sigh, I got out of bed and hitched the legs of my sweatpants around my calves. I moved toward the wall, fingers brushing the edges of a brittle chart. I started tearing it all down— each paper curling as it hit the floor, each one a quiet goodbye. Until I stepped up on the edge of a narrow wooden shelf to grasp a chart just beyond my reach, my weight shifted precariously, causing the entire structure to tilt slightly. The shelf jolted, toppling a cascade of objects, among them several dusty books and trinkets that tumbled onto the floor.

I found myself reaching for an old cigar box—beat-up and familiar. The corners were worn down, the lid chipped, the whole thing covered in scratches from being shoved around over the years. I hadn't seen it in forever. Back in grade school, it held my pencils, markers—probably a bunch of scratch-and-sniff stickers too.

When it hit the floor with a soft thud, the lid popped open, and everything spilled out in a messy little heap. Scraps of paper. A couple of faded photos. And something else—something I hadn't expected.

A brass compass.

It was tarnished now, dulled with age, but the second I saw it, something in me stilled.

I froze.

I hadn't seen Dad's compass since that camping trip to the Shenandoah Valley—our last vacation. I picked it up by the chain, letting it swing a little from my fingers. It felt heavier than I remembered, like the way his hand felt on my shoulder that final morning when he'd said, "Keep this safe for me."

My throat tightened. He'd never asked for it back.

When I touched the worn brass case, my fingertips recognized the small dent where he'd dropped it trying to teach me how to find true north in the rain. A faint vibration seemed to run through the metal—probably just my pulse, racing like it used to when we'd race to the top of those Virginia hills.

I tightened my grip, suddenly aware of how much my hands had grown since then. Seven years old with skinny wrists, now fifteen with nail polish he'd never see.

My thumb found the little latch—the one that always jammed unless you knew the trick. Press and lift, and not pull. Dad's directions still familiar in my head.

The latch resisted me, as always. I persevered, as he'd instructed. Then—click—the top opened.

I'd anticipated the old compass needle, his device for showing true north, for finding home. It wasn't there.

Spread across it was something weighty—a coin or a medallion. Massive designs etched its face, cut deep into metal.

I allowed it to drop into the cup of my palm. It rested there with easy assurance, as if it belonged there. As if in waiting.

For this instant. For me.

A warm glow crept across my fingers. Steady. Calming. Beneath that, an insistent vibration—a heartbeat perceived, felt rather than heard.

The surface shone golden as if dipped in sunlight.

One side was laced with intricate symbols. Precise. Geometric. Like tiny knives engraved on metal. In its center, a small hourglass was tilted on its side.

Damaged perhaps, or empty?

As if time had expired.

The other side was more chaotic—looping symbols I didn't recognize, arranged like constellations falling in on themselves. At the center, a sixteen-pointed star. Surrounding it were rings of writing—unfamiliar, shifting slightly when I tilted the coin in the light, as if it didn't want to be read too easily.

Like it had secrets to keep.

A SOFT KNOCK pulled me out of it.

"Come in," I said, still facing the box, carefully placing the coin back inside.

The door creaked open, and Mom stepped in. She looked tired. Her eyes moved from the clutter on the floor to my hands, still holding a thumbtack.

She crouched without a word, picked up a photo from the pile, and brushed the dust from one corner. Her hand trembled a little. Just enough for me to notice. When she stood, she stared down at the picture—me sitting on a cannon in the old plaza downtown, Dad's arms around me, steadying me so I wouldn't fall.

"Honey... about last night," she began. "I just don't want you to dwell on it forever. Hope is good—but there comes a time—"

"Mom, it's okay," I said gently, though my voice cracked. "I thought a lot on my walk. You're right. It's been eight years. I can't keep scanning every face in a crowd," I paused, tears stinging my eyes. "Wondering if he's out there, or imagining how different things would be if he never left."

She pulled me into a hug, her arms surrounding me tightly as my tears finally broke free. But the tears weren't for my father. They were for her because she might never know the truth, if it is all true. Not yet. Maybe not ever.

AFTER SHE LEFT for the laundromat, I slipped out too—needing to clear my head. The sun was high and sharp, the kind of brightness that makes you squint even with your eyes half-closed, but I didn't care.

I didn't really have a plan. Just walked. Hoping—yeah, maybe stupidly—that I'd somehow run into Dorian again. Like fate might feel generous today.

Without even meaning to, my feet took me back toward the lighthouse, back to the place where things had started to feel real.

The wide lane near the old barracks was no longer empty—just a few parked cars, sun-baked and still. A couple of women stepped out of the building Dorian and I had ducked into last night. They noticed me right away, their faces a mix of surprise and curiosity. But then one of them smiled, soft and polite, like she already knew I wasn't there to cause trouble.

"Hello there! Here to volunteer?" one asked.

"Not exactly. I was just wandering. Wanted to get a closer look at the lighthouse," I said—half-truth at best.

"We're wrapping up for the day, but we're always looking for help," she said warmly. "We meet here on Saturdays at eight in the morning. Yard work for now, mostly. I'm Doreen, and this is Cassandra and Natalie."

"I'm Veronica Ingram, and I live in the neighborhood—just a few blocks away," I said, feeling an unexpected flutter of shyness.

"Well, nice to meet you, Veronica. If you've got any free time Saturday mornings, we could always use an extra pair of hands," Doreen said, her smile easy and genuine. "That old brick house won't restore itself." She punctuated the offer with a quick wink.

As I walked on, a salty breeze tugged playfully at my hair, its coolness threading down the back of my neck. I let it guide me toward the quiet strip between the pier and the boat ramp.

The waves met the shore with unhurried laps, steady and rhythmic—as though the long cove was breathing. And for a moment, I breathed with it. The tide looked low, though I could never quite tell if it was going in or out. I climbed up onto a flat coquina rock, warm from the sun. Despite its rough surface poking my legs, it offered a sense of comfort, something rough yet steady. Nearby, a few people trickled into Navigator's Grill. I watched them as my gaze drifted to the end of the pier—and that's when I saw him. Dark hair. Tall. Confident stride.

Dorian?

I waved instinctively.

The boy paused, confusion flickering across his face.

Wait. Oh God. Oh no, it's not Dorian.

As he got closer, I could see the differences. Slightly older. Broader shoulders. A tattoo wrapped around one forearm—an intricate design like a compass tangled in an infinity symbol.

"Do I know you?" he asked, smiling.

Embarrassment hit me in a wave. "No—sorry. I thought you were someone else."

"No harm in that," he said, grinning. "I'm Bram. Just got into town."

"I'm Six—well, Veronica. Most people call me Six," I replied, stumbling over the words.

"Six? Not the sixth child, I hope?"

"Only child," I said. "It's complicated."

"You Catholic? Veronica is the sixth Station of the Cross," he said, glancing toward the lighthouse.

I laughed nervously. "No, not even close. You must be."

"Well, raised Catholic. Not practicing," he said with a shrug, like it wasn't anything worth unpacking. "So, Complicated Six—what do you know about the lighthouse?"

"Not much," I said. "Built in the 1870s, I think? It's all fenced off now—Coast Guard signs, 'U.S. Government, No Trespassing,' penalty of federal law stuff."

He raised an eyebrow. "You've *never* snuck in?"

The way he said it made me pause. I wasn't daring enough or often on the wrong side of any possible misadventure.

"No!" I laughed, though the idea no longer seemed entirely crazy. "It's locked up."

He gave a small smile. Then his gaze drifted toward the lighthouse, visible above the line of distant trees.

"Lighthouses are kind of my thing," he said, as if it were a confession. Something that he wouldn't tell just anyone.

"They're kind of strange, when you think about it... These old towers are scattered all over the world, built to shine beams of light through darkness. Being a guide to everyone out there. Merchants, refugees, anyone. Warnings. Guides. Sometimes both."

He glanced at me again, then back toward the lighthouse like it had just said something only he could hear.

"Each one has a unique flash pattern like a fingerprint. That way, sailors could tell which one they were looking at miles offshore. You couldn't just glance at the light," he said. "You had to learn it and feel its rhythm, its pulse. There's something really kind of beautiful about that."

Then he looked at me. Not with a smirk or some calculated charm. As if the quiet between us wasn't awkward at all, just honest.

There was something anchored about him. The way he spoke. How he carried himself. Almost as if you were standing next to a lighthouse yourself. As if he knew exactly who he was and didn't need to prove it.

I glanced away, heart ticking a little faster, caught in the silence he left behind. Then my eyes landed on the ink curling around his forearm—a sideways figure eight, fine lines looping into tiny stars and arcs. It looked like a chart, or a secret. Something made to be studied up close.

I found myself leaning in. Drawn to the tattoo's shape, I saw how it shifted slightly when he moved his arm to give me a better look. The warmth of his skin, the faint line of muscle underneath, the closeness, made heat creep into my cheeks.

"What is that?" I asked, my voice softer than before.

"It's an analemma," he answered, picking up on the curiosity of my tone. "It tracks the sun's position in the sky over the course of a year. Ancient sailors used it as a kind of chart for time and light."

"Time and light," I echoed, tracing the tattoo's lines across his tan arm with my eyes. Not really understanding, but willing to learn.

Then he shifted the topic like a fresh wave off the cove.

"My family travels by sailboat," he said. "The Ampoletta. We're docked downtown, right next to The Calypso: Jacques Cousteau's ship. You've seen it, right? I can't believe that it's actually here," he mentioned excitedly.

"Ampoletta," I said slowly, tasting each syllable. "Is that, like, a woman's name?"

He grinned. "Nope. It's Spanish for 'marine hourglass.' Back in the time of Columbus, sailors used them to track time at sea."

"Well, that's pretty cool," I said with a solemn nod. "So... you're a sailor?"

"Guess so," he replied, then tilted his chin toward a red moped parked up the street. "Though today, I'm just some doofus on a scooter."

I chuckled at his self-deprecation and glanced at my neon green watch. "I should probably head back. My mom's gonna start wondering where I am."

"Maybe I'll see you around, Veronica," he said as he pushed off toward the road.

As I walked home, the azaleas along the street fluttered in the breeze—bright pink, white, and red blooms painting the street corners like large confetti. I kept thinking about how I'd gone looking for Dorian... and found someone else entirely. Someone unexpected. Someone interesting.

Two strangers. Two days. And maybe, a connection between them I hadn't yet seen.

Chapter Four

By Tuesday evening, my brain still hadn't made sense of anything Dorian said. Time travel? Council of Chaos? A shadowy group hunting me like I'm in some bad sci-fi B movie.

It all sounded like a rejected *Twilight Zone* episode—something Rod Serling might pitch before lighting another cigarette and tossing the script in the trash.

And yet... I felt it, *felt* something. Those vibrations. The pauses. That flicker of silence no one else seemed to notice. But maybe I was just freaking out. I mean, could it be what Dorian told me, that I'm sensitive to some kind of quirk?

Claire pulled up to my place around 4 pm in her mom's boxy blue Buick Skylark, chewing bubble gum like she was mad at it.

"You've been weird all week, Six," she said, yanking open the passenger door. "Let's go burn some quarters."

SHE DROVE us across the bridge to the Ponce de Leon Mall. Inside the arcade, it was all synth music, fluorescent carpet, and the beeping chaos of *Galaga*, *Ms. Pac-Man*, and *Donkey Kong*.

Claire headed straight for pinball. I wandered toward *Dig Dug*, but something stopped me cold.

I could've sworn I saw Dorian at the far end of the arcade—hood up, watching me between blinking machines.

I blinked again, and he was gone.

"You okay?" Claire asked, after her last ball fell through.

"Yeah," I said too quickly. "It was nothing."

"See, you are acting weird. Weirdo," she chided.

I rolled my eyes, trying to be casual. "I'm fine, Claire."

We moved toward the food court, where the local radio station played over cheap, tiny speakers. I caught the tail end of a DJ's voice:

"...AND in national news, Coca-Cola has announced a reformulation of its classic drink. That's right—New Coke is real, folks. Taste tests coming soon. Please call in and let me know what you think. I've got some Billy Idol after the break!"

CLAIRE STOPPED mid-slurp of her Icee. "They're changing Coke? Why? It's *Coke*. It's already perfect."

"I don't know. A cola war thing?" I muttered, "It will probably be gross. Coke doesn't need to change."

While at the arcade, I tried to lose myself in *Ms. Pac-Man*, but the maze felt too familiar. Round and round, avoiding things that wanted to destroy me, grabbing fruit like that would make any difference.

When I looked up again, I *swore* I saw Bram this time—leaning near the change machine, arms crossed, watching. He even smiled when I noticed.

But when I blinked, it wasn't him. Just some older teenager with dark hair and *a Def Leppard* shirt. Nothing mysterious about that.

My heart wouldn't stop hammering. What if this was all in my head?

What if it wasn't time travel at all—just grief warping the edges of reality? Dad had been gone eight years. Maybe my mind had built this strange story to fill the silence he left behind.

Claire nudged me. "You sure you're okay?"

I nodded, forcing a small smile. "Just tired."

But all the sounds and lights—the shrill blips of arcade games, the flicker of neon, the synth-heavy music echoing off the walls—blurred together in a way that made it hard to breathe. And then there were the people I kept thinking I saw—Dorian in the shadows, Bram by the change machine—but when I looked again, they were gone. Just strangers. Or maybe nothing at all. Everything was too much.

WE LEFT the arcade and walked the narrow aisles of the Camelot music store. We fumbled through cassette tapes while *Tears for Fears* played overhead. Claire held up the cassette *Purple Rain* in its bulky plastic frame. "You still haven't listened to this? It's totally awesome from beginning to end."

"Can I borrow your copy? Or can you make me one?" I asked, knowing that I couldn't afford to buy my own.

Then, by the entrance, a figure passed by, hood up.

Was it Dorian? Or Bram?

Neither.

Claire followed my gaze, then gave me a look. "Six, it's like you're seeing ghosts or searching for someone. Something's wrong."

I smiled weakly, trying to play it off. But the truth was—I couldn't tell what was real anymore. Three times in over two hours. Three times, I thought I saw someone who wasn't there.

Something about this week had split my world open. And now, at the mall, everywhere I turned, I was catching echoes of someone who wasn't really there.

THAT NIGHT, back in my room, I sat on the edge of my bed with an old mixtape in my Walkman, staring at the space where my charts used to be. The bare wall felt colder than I remembered.

What if Dorian was lying?

What if I'm just a girl who missed her dad and wanted to believe something—*anything to* explain why he disappeared without a trace?

I pressed play, and the familiar synths from *A Flock of Seagulls* filled my ears, belting out their hit song, *I Ran (So far away)*.

AND I WANTED TO RUN.

Chapter Five

Friday morning, I found myself in my usual frantic dash from Earth Science to Geometry, which is on opposite sides of the school, naturally. As the bell rang, I lingered a moment after class to bring up something to Mr. Harrison.

"Have you ever heard of the analemma?" I asked.

I wasn't even sure why I asked, but something about the word had lodged itself in my brain like splintered light. But he looked intrigued and launched into an enthusiastic explanation about the sun's shifting position through the seasons. I was glad he didn't ask about Mom—he usually did when we were one-on-one.

Back in the hall, swallowed by the tide of students, I weaved through the noise and elbows, not wanting to be late for Geometry. Not with Mrs. Hanson watching like a hawk from her perch at the front of the room.

I SLIPPED through the door just as the bell rang—only to collide hard with someone at the threshold.

Laughter broke out as I staggered back, mortified.

Then I saw who I'd run into.

"Dorian?" I blinked. "What are you doing here?"

He gave me a grin that made my stomach flip. "Six—whoa, hey. I hoped I'd bump into you today, but I didn't mean it to be so literal."

"Veronica! Stop flirting and take your seat," Mrs. Hanson called, her voice echoing off the walls.

More laughter. Whistles. My face flushed red hot as I scurried to my seat.

"Class, this is Dorian Novus," she announced. Pick a seat, Dorian—it'll be your assigned one."

Dorian scanned the room and chose the empty desk next to mine. He caught my eye and gave a slight nod, like he was asking permission.

I stared a beat too long. His blue eyes held these silver flecks that shimmered in the Florida light. It was unfair.

"How?" I softly uttered in confusion, mouth agape.

"A priest. Umm, Father Cullen. I showed up at the rectory earlier this week, said I didn't have family. Told him that I wanted to finish high school," he whispered.

"That worked?" I whispered, confounded.

Dorian gave me a half-grin, "I'm here. He made some calls."

"Veronica!" Mrs. Hanson's voice snapped me back. "Focus. Or I'll have to separate you two."

"Yes, ma'am," I muttered as snickers rolled through the room.

I spent the rest of class sneaking glances, trying to figure out how the boy who talked about time travel was now in my school.

WHEN THE BELL RANG, I cut him off before he could say a word.

"Dorian—what is going on?" I asked, louder than I meant to. Heads turned as we entered the hallway.

Jenny Unsner paused between us, blinking at the tension. "Hi, I'm Jenny," she said to Dorian, her voice sweet enough to coat a Popsicle.

"You two know each other?" she added, already fishing.

"Not really, but—" I began.

"We spent two weeks as camp counselors last summer," Dorian cut in smoothly, tossing her a smile. "Good times."

"I'm Jenny," she repeated, like he hadn't heard her the first time —or like I wasn't even there.

"You already said that," I muttered with a smirk.

Jenny's eyes swept over me like a laser before she offered a tight smile. "Nice meeting you, Dorian."

Then, with a sharp flick of her ponytail, she disappeared into the Spanish classroom.

"Adiós," Dorian said, clearly amused, then glanced down at his schedule. "Looks like I've got lunch next."

"Me too," I replied, working hard to keep my voice casual. "Come on—I'll show you the cafeteria."

THE CAFETERIA BUZZED with the noisy clatter of trays and the smell of rotten milk. I led Dorian past the crowd to one of the shaded picnic tables under a wide Live Oak. The breeze stirred the leaves above us, casting shifting shadows across the table. I felt exposed— like everyone was watching, waiting to see what this mysterious new guy meant to me. My lunch sat untouched on the tray.

"I don't even know where to start," I said, gripping the edge of the table. "You show up out of nowhere, drop all this stuff about my dad—and now you're just... enrolled here? Like that's normal?"

Dorian looked up at the branches overhead, his eyes darting. "For now," he said, voice low. "We need to stick close. When the next wave arrives... Everything could get... stranger."

I squinted at him. "Stranger than a time traveler crashing my geometry class?"

He leaned in, glancing around nervously. "Don't say 'time traveler' out loud. Ever. Not around people."

His tone was heavy enough to kill any comeback. I just nodded.

We sat there, not talking, the silence getting deep. I took a slow bite of my apple. The crunch felt way too loud in the silence between us.

"Speaking of strange," I said, watching him unfold his schedule, "I met someone Saturday. In my neighborhood."

"Do you know where typing class is?" he asked, not paying attention or looking up.

"Dorian. *Focus.* He was...Sort of strange with a big tattoo on his arm."

That got his attention.

"What kind of tattoo?" he asked, locking eyes with me.

"He called it an analemma. Said his name was Bram."

Dorian's face went pale. "Wait—Bram? With a black analemma tattoo?"

I nodded slowly.

He dropped his gaze and muttered something under his breath—something I couldn't quite catch—then looked up again. "That's...worse than I thought. What did he say to you?"

"Not much," I said. "Seemed smart. Kind of charming, honestly. Talked about lighthouses. Said he was staying on a sailboat with his parents."

"The *Ampoletta*?" Dorian asked, eyes narrowing fast.

"Yeah. Why?"

Dorian exhaled hard. "Because if that boat's here, things are about to get bad. Bram and his 'family'—they're part of the Council of Chaos. And 'family' is generous. It's more like a cult. Dangerous people. I mean, Manson had a 'family'."

My stomach dropped. "Disastrous how?"

"First of all, this puts *you* in danger. Did Bram ask you to meet him somewhere? Was anyone else nearby?"

"No. I mean, people were going in and out of Navigator's Grill. He didn't ask me to go anywhere."

"Good," Dorian said, though his tone stayed tense. "Still. You need to stay away from him and anyone with noticeable markings or tattoos."

"Okay," I whispered, barely convincing myself.

I didn't even hear the bell ring, but the courtyard burst into motion—backpacks slung, trays scraped, voices rising.

As I stood to leave, Dorian reached out and grabbed my arm.

"Six. Listen to me. You and your mom could be in actual danger. Don't talk to strangers. Don't go near the marina. Seriously. Not right now."

I nodded, tears stinging my eyes. All of the warnings, the secrets, just everything, weighed on me so hard I could barely breathe. But what else could I do? I had to try to hold it together.

Chapter Six

I stepped out of the apartment wearing rolled denim shorts that hugged my waist, paired with a simple, crisp white t-shirt. Over it, I had layered a tan knit pullover vest, its texture soft and stylish. Around my neck hung the weighty compass, a large pendant, swinging gently as I moved, its tarnished metallic surface glinting in the light.

Claire, in her cut-offs and blue MTV t-shirt, jingled the keys like a dare, her smile flashing in the amber streetlight.

"You're driving tonight," she said, tossing them to me.

I fumbled the heavy ring, the metal clinking against my palm. "Claire, no way. If I wreck your mom's car, she would kill us both. My mom hasn't found time for us to go and get my permit."

With a shrug, Claire headed toward the curb, where the Buick sat. It looked like a boat on wheels — faded blue, red velvety interior, boxy, heavy enough to survive a Soviet nuke.

Claire looked over her shoulder, rolling her eyes. "It's a tank, Six. A Skylark from like, 1977. You could drive it into a wall at the fort and create a drive-thru."

I hesitated. I'd driven before. A few cautious laps around our neighborhood with Mom, but the thought of steering this hulk anywhere near a crowd made my stomach twist. Still, Claire was already sliding into the passenger seat, flipping the visor down to check her lip gloss, like it was no big deal.

Climbing behind the wheel, I adjusted the seat and turned the key. The engine coughed once, then settled into a low, uneven growl. The whole car shuddered like it hated me personally.

"Perfect," Claire said, kicking her feet up on the dashboard. "Let's roll."

We wound out of the neighborhood, onto A1A heading south, the thick night air pouring through the open windows. Somewhere in the distance, the ocean heaved against the shoreline. The radio buzzed with static until Claire finally tuned it to a local station — *Duran Duran* crooning *Save a Prayer* — low and dreamy in the background. *Save a prayer for me now*, as I'm the one driving.

WHEN WE COASTED past the last stoplight in town, Claire leaned over and pointed. "Pull into the gas station. I need a Coke before we deal with humanity."

I eased the Skylark into the cracked parking lot of the old Texaco, the lights buzzing like tired bees overhead. The station was nearly empty except for a rusted pickup at the far pump.

Inside, the cold air hit us like a wall. The unmistakable theme song to *Miami Vice* blared from a small television behind the counter. Cooler shelves rattled faintly as we opened the glass doors, pulling out two plastic bottles slick with condensation.

At the counter, we each fished a dollar from our pockets. Claire then twisted off her cap. A tiny hiss escaped as she checked under the green cap.

She gasped dramatically, waving the cap in my face. "One Free Coke! I'm officially a winner."

I chuckled, the sound startlingly loud in the quiet station. Claire struck a pose like she'd just conquered the world.

"You're looking at a lucky lady now," she said, handing the cap to the cashier. "This will cover her Coke," she added, nodding my way.

"Aww gee thanks, winner," I said as I opened my bottle, looking under it and reading out loud, "*Try Again.*"

"Someone has to be a total loser," she teased, taking a long swig, before burping out loud.

BACK OUTSIDE, the air was heavier, charged with the scent of salt and stickiness. Claire playfully pulled on the Buick's hood ornament as she walked to the passenger side. I slid back behind the wheel, the bottle sweating between my knees.

"Onward," she declared, raising her Coke like a toast to the humid night.

We left the last of the town lights behind, the sandy trail to Fish Island opening ahead of us like a dim, jagged wound through the woods. The shimmer of flames and the thudding bass of a distant truck stereo leaked into the sky.

WHEN WE ROLLED into the clearing, the chaos unfolded: kids hanging out around the bonfire, trucks parked like lazy beasts, someone doing donuts in the loose sand while others cheered.

Claire tapped the dashboard. "Aww, my chauffeur, you made it."

I killed the engine and sat there a second, hands tight on the wheel. My heart still hadn't slowed.

"You coming?" Claire asked, already halfway out the heavy groaning door.

I took a breath and followed.

The party was a riot of heat, noise, and muted, colorful shadows. Dirt bikes revved somewhere beyond the trees. Music — *Van Halen* this time — thumped from an open truck bed. Laughter and shouting tangled together in the humid air.

A guy in a sleeveless *Motley Crue* t-shirt caught sight of us and hollered something unintelligible over the music. Claire waved him off with a grin.

I stuck close to her, trying not to flinch every time someone bumped into me. Everything felt too intense: the sparks crackled like firecrackers from the flames, the sharp tang of gasoline and sweat, the neon streaks of shirts caught in the flickering light, like colorful phantoms in the night.

Claire steered us toward a battered cooler half-sunken in the sand.

"Drink up, wallflower," she said, tossing me a can of ice-cold beer. "It will help you be more social."

I cracked the top and took a sip. The beer was bubbly, but it had a biting bitterness that always left me wondering how people could drink this all the time.

Someone shouted in the shadows from the edge of the woods, "Hey! Those belong to Moose!"

Claire slammed the cooler shut and popped open her can. "It's cool, Skitter! Moosey and I are buds!" she called out, rolling her eyes like it was no big deal.

A few yards away, Moose revved his dirt bike, egging his friends into another round of reckless races through the trees. The sharp bite of exhaust mixed with smoke in the air, and the high-pitched whine of engines sliced straight through my nerves. Laughter and whoops bounced off through the woods. Not my scene. Not even close. I just stood there, weirdly stiff, like my body was bracing for an earthquake. This wasn't my place. Not in this noise. Not in this kind of wild.

Claire poked me with her elbow. "Come on, Six. You allergic to fun or something?"

"Maybe," I said, and tried to smile, but it probably looked totally uncomfortable. The truth was, my stomach had already twisted itself into knots—and not from the noise or the people. It was something else. Something I couldn't name.

Being here felt wrong somehow. Like I was stepping off a path I didn't even realize I'd been following. Like I was betraying... something. Or someone.

I sort of drifted toward the fire, letting the crowd thin out behind me as I edged closer to the trees, kind of at the edge of everything. That's when I saw him.

Dorian.

He was leaning against a tree, just outside the firelight, arms folded, just watching.

The fire caught the faint outline of his shirt, the glint of his hair — and then he stepped back, disappearing into the deeper darkness, melting into the trees.

I blinked, but he was already gone.

My heart climbed into my throat.

A HAND TAPPED MY SHOULDER, and I jumped, spinning around so fast I almost lost my balance. Bram was standing there, half in the light, eyes bright like he'd just thought of something funny. His hoodie looked extra gray in the glow, the fabric bunching around his arms and casting his face mostly in shadow.

"All this noise... You don't really fit in here, do you?" His voice was soft and a little slow, every word careful, but there was something sharp in it too.

I folded my arms, trying to look casual, except that my heart was pounding so hard I was sure he could hear it. "What are you even doing here?" I tried to sound bored, but my voice cracked, which was so embarrassing.

Bram grinned, just a little, "Making sure you behave."

"Meaning?" I raised my eyebrows and stared at him, not blinking, not giving in.

His eyes sparked, sort of teasing, but there was something else there too, quieter and harder to see.

The smile faded for a second. He looked past me at the woods, where the trees began, and everything went dark and quiet. When he looked back, he spoke so low I almost missed it.

"It's not safe here tonight. You're starting to draw the wrong kind of attention."

I swallowed hard, the bitter trace of beer still clinging to my throat. "You mean... from people like Dorian?"

His name just sort of hung there between us, like smoke that refused to clear. Bram didn't answer right away. He only watched me, the firelight catching in his eyes, making them seem older, heavier. I could feel him measuring me—deciding how much truth I could bear.

At last, he spoke. "Dorian's just the beginning," he said, the words low, deliberate. "It's already begun. And you're not ready."

The words hit. My breath snagged in my throat. "Ready for what?"

But before he could answer, a burst of loud laughter exploded nearby. A group of kids came stumbling into our circle, all energy and beer breath and noise, cutting right through the space between us.

Bram stepped in closer, his hand brushing mine—just barely, but it was enough to send a pulse of heat up my arm. I didn't move.

"Look," he said, leaning in close, his voice low and steady near my ear. "Let me get you out of here. I'll take you to the lighthouse— it's quiet. Safe."

I pulled back just slightly, enough to give him a look. "No," I said, almost automatically. It came out sharper than I expected.

But it wasn't because I didn't want to go.

It was because I *did*.

And that scared me more.

I looked past him toward the fire—toward Claire laughing in the distance, kids howling over music and revving engines and whatever game they were playing now. I should've felt safe, normal. But I didn't.

It all felt like a strange scene that I wasn't supposed to be in.

Bram just stood there, calm and still, waiting. The night seemed off as if it had the potential of becoming something else entirely.

I exhaled before biting my lip. "I don't know," I said, my gaze skimming past him into the darkness above. "I barely know you."

He shrugged, voice steady. "I know. But you can feel it, can't you? Something's wrong tonight."

I didn't answer. I didn't have to.

Because the truth was, I felt it in my bones.

I tipped back the last of my beer—warm, bitter—and tossed the can into the fire with a hollow clunk. Then I glanced toward the trees.

And there he was.

Dorian.

Or maybe just my mind playing tricks on me. Either way, the silhouette at the edge of the woods didn't move. I just watched.

"Six?" Bram's voice pulled me back. I turned to find him holding out his hand.

I hesitated—just for breath—and then I reached out.

The instant our palms touched, a peace that I hadn't even known seemed to settle over me.

"Stay close to me tonight," he told me. "Trust me."

I nodded. Gently. But it wasn't about trusting him so much.

It was about trusting myself.

CLAIRE APPEARED, rosy and pink-cheeked, beer in her hand. Her eyes flicked from me to Bram, and then back to me.

"You okay, Veronica?" she asked, intense eyes taking in the situation before her.

"I'm fine," I said, but even I didn't sound convincing.

Then, more firmly: "I'm leaving with Bram."

Claire froze, one foot half-planted like she couldn't decide whether to step forward or stop me. Her expression flickered from concern to confusion, maybe even betrayal.

I felt the sting of it, sharp and sudden.

But I couldn't take it back.

"Oh, umm, yeah... Claire, this is Bram. Bram, my best friend Claire," I said, instantly regretting how stiff I sounded. They did that awkward handshake thing, quick and sort of clammy, and Claire's mouth twisted into a smirk like she was already planning to make fun of me.

She pointed at Bram, then at me. "Be good to her, okay? I know people in the Minorican mafia," she said, half-joking, half...not. Her finger wagged. "Don't do anything I wouldn't do." I wanted to disappear. My cheeks burned.

Then her voice dropped, softer. "Call me later?" All the teasing was gone, just Claire being Claire, becoming kind of mushy after she'd had a few.

"I will," I promised, not even sure what I meant, but I said it anyway. The night felt heavy and secretive, like we were huddled close around something nobody else could see, and the firelight made us all look different.

BRAM GUIDED me gently toward a narrow path that cut away from the party, his hand warm and steady at the small of my back. Something was calming about him—comforting, sure—but also something I couldn't quite read like he knew more than he was letting on.

As we moved farther from the haze of smoke and laughter, I glanced back one last time. Someone was standing on the hood of a car now, yelling as it bounced recklessly down the rutted dirt road. The fire lit everything up in chaotic flashes—beer cans flying, arms flailing, people cheering like it was all just one big joke.

BUT PAST ALL THAT, just at the edge of the hammock, stood Dorian.

Completely still.

His figure was sharp against the trees, untouched by the firelight or the noise. Just watching and not moving, not joining. Eyes locked on us as we slipped into the dark.

And in that moment, I couldn't tell if he was warning me...

Or waiting.

Chapter Seven

Bram's moped zipped through the night like a mosquito in the dark. We rode over the still street of A1A, with humid salt air mixing with the scent of oily asphalt. The wind stung my eyes, and I held on to him tighter, taking in the traces of Stetson cologne, letting him guide us wherever we were going. My mind spinning along with the wheels beneath us—just who was this mysterious boy? How did he know anything about my life? What dangers had I attracted to myself?

He slowed as the charred ruins of the lightkeeper's house appeared. We ditched the moped at the edge of the old sandy service road and slipped through a gap in the fence.

Moonlight totally lit up the path, casting strange shadows on the old, busted brick walkway as we got closer to the tower. The air was condensed and heavy, not just with fog, but something else I couldn't quite name. Nerves? Dread? Or maybe that feeling when you know something huge is about to happen.

"So... why here? And why now?" I asked, kind of breathless, jogging a little to keep up.

Bram slowed down and turned around to look at me. In the moonlight, his face looked different. Sharper. Sort of haunted, honestly. But that streak of silver in his hair made him look less scary, more... I don't know, normal?

"This place," he said, and his voice was all low and serious, "it's not just a lighthouse. It's a gateway. And you're ready."

"A gateway?" I repeated, my heart doing this weird stutter. "To where?"

He stared straight at me. Didn't blink. "To endless possibilities, Six. To your father."

Before I could even process that, he turned and headed for the stairs.

I was trying to find words to say when his boots thundered against the stone, and he bent down and produced a key from under a brick. He then inserted it into the lock of the heavy wooden door. Then, a sort of groan, only in horror movies, was heard as it creaked open.

How on earth did you find that key?" I asked, half whispering, half accusing.

"I saw the lamplighter a few days ago. The guy who checks on the light," he smiled. "He hadn't realized that I had seen him hide a spare key under a loose brick after the tour."

He led me inside.

The air shifted immediately. Damp and cool, solid with that earthy mix of salt and decay. The tiled floor beneath us was stained and squishy in places—like something had been rotting underfoot for way too long.

"Careful," Bram called back, voice echoing. "Watch your step. The bat and bird crap is horrible down here. It's better the higher up you go."

"Wonderful," I muttered, picking my way across tiles so slick I almost slid. Suddenly, I was grateful I'd grabbed my black Chucks before leaving the house. If I'd worn sandals? I'd be face-planted in the guano by now.

Ahead: more stone steps, each one slimy with mud and algae. Every step was like a dare. "Are you sure this is safe?" I yelled, pinwheeling my arms a little. "Because it smells like something died in here."

"The iron steps are better," Bram said, and reached back with his hand.

I took it, no hesitation. His grip was solid, and I felt less likely to slip as we started climbing. Moonlight leaked through a low window, turning the black railing silver. The metal was cool and smooth, spiraling up into darkness.

We stopped at a landing to catch our breath. His hand was still in mine—steady, warm. I didn't pull away.

My compass with the coin inside pressed against my chest, pulsing faintly. A low, vibrating hum that I could feel more than hear. Each step we climbed seemed to make it stronger.

We reached a wider landing. Tall windows let in a silvery moonlight, but the glass was so caked with dust and webs that the light broke up into these shifting, patchy patterns all over the floor. The ceiling above us curved in a smooth, white iron, which made everything feel kind of echoey. I couldn't even tell if the pounding in my ears was my own heartbeat, the coin, or maybe both.

Bram glanced over at me, and his face sort of softened. "You okay?"

"I... I think so," I said, but my voice came out all breathless, and I realized I was gripping the compass so tight my knuckles felt numb. The vibrations were getting stronger. Like, really insistent.

"It's the token, isn't it?" Bram asked.

I nodded. "Yeah. But how do you know—?"

"I felt it," he said, and his eyes went a little wide. "When we were by the fire earlier. I could feel it just by being near you."

He let go of my hand. "Take it out of the pendant. Carefully."

So I opened the lid and let the coin drop into my palm. The vibration didn't stop, but it changed—it became softer and steadier, as if it were finally focused.

Bram's eyes locked onto the coin. He leaned forward, eyes wide, not even trying to hide his fascination. "May I see it, please?"

I hesitated, curling my fingers around the token. Something about the way he looked at it made it feel... priceless and me, vulnerable.

But I nodded, and slowly opened my hand, setting the coin in his. He picked it up gently, holding it between his thumb and finger. Looking at the markings as if they were part of some secret code.

"A Token Continuum," he whispered. "I've heard about them, but I've never seen one. They're almost mythical."

"So it's... important?" I asked.

"Important?" he repeated. "It's the most powerful relic in time travel."

There are only a handful left in existence. With this, you don't need to wait for the window of a gravitational wave. You can go wherever, whenever you want. And come back without anyone knowing you were gone."

I swallowed hard. "I think my dad left it for me," I said. "I found it inside the compass a few days ago. It was inside an old school box from my early grade school days."

He regarded me again, something inscrutable flashing across his features.

Finally, he gently handed the token back to me. "Protect it with your life," he said. No warmth at all. Flat. "I mean it. People would kill for this, Six. No hesitation." The words just landed. Heavy. I could feel it pressing on my chest, hard. I almost couldn't breathe. "Why is it vibrating so much more now?" I said, barely above a whisper.

"It's likely because we are very close to a portal, Veronica," Bram replied, his words echoing and eyes drifting upward to the ceiling as if he could see beyond. "It's just above us."

Chapter Eight

Adry oak leaf drifted down and caught on his shoulder. Unflinching, he let it fall. Dorian watched from the shadow of a twisted live oak as Six and her friends stood at the center of the clearing near the fire, their voices echoing in the distance. The moonlight pooled around all of them, leaving silver on their hair and shoulders, with the occasional whine of distant mini-bikes and drunken hollers. He'd been shadowing her as he always did, as silent as the tide slipping ashore. He knew Six would be here because of Claire's big, obnoxious mouth.

Dorian had intended to lure her into the hammock. He could tell she had seen him, but so far, she hadn't taken the bait. She'd stayed in the open, safe among friends. Secure, with the Token Continuum swinging from her neck. Then Dorian felt a sudden chill sweep through his body, as if an icy wind had blown through him. He was momentarily stunned the instant he saw *him* come into view.

The medallion pulsed faintly against her chest; he could feel it, and he knew that Bram could feel it too. A heartbeat out of time, a secret she carried that should have been his. She has no idea what she possessed—the power it had for anyone who held it. Dorian had been there, had shown her the rising edge of her traveler destiny. If she had stepped forward to meet him under this oak, away from all the others, it would have been all he needed—but she hadn't followed.

Instead, Bram had stepped forward, closer to Six. He'd whispered something that made her giggle, making her eyes light up in a way Dorian had never seen—never seen from her. And that laugh had cut him deeper than any blade could.

Dorian gritted his teeth.

Bram. The one person he had warned her about, to stay clear of, was now charming his way to her, to the token.

Bram. With his good looks, his sincerity, and his surprising presence.

Bram had wedged himself between Dorian and everything he had worked for.

Veronica took a sip of her beer, smiling at Bram, as she introduced him to Claire. Dorian felt the black ice of rage blossom in his gut. The thought came fast, without hesitation. He could kill her. A quick strike, the token in his hand, endless corridors of time opening before him. He'd wash away Bram's smirk with his own hands, and then nothing would stand in his path. Not Bram, not the Collective, not even the Council of Chaos if they dared to stand against him.

Was she leaving with him? To the boat, the Ampoletta? Dorian's blood began to boil as he watched them walk away. His knuckles whitened around the hilt of his dagger, a cold fury coiling through him like a viper. Every footstep they took together felt like a betrayal, as if the world itself was shifting beneath him. The moonlight glinted on the brass chain of the compass containing the token at her throat. He could strangle her with it. It would be Bram's steal or exploit if he wanted it to be. Something dark unfurled in his chest at Claire's teasing voice: "Take care of her, Bram. Don't do anything I wouldn't do!"

She laughed again, soft, musical, and cruel as the coin's pulse began to grow more distant from Dorian. He exhaled, unclenched his jaw, and let the knife drop back into its sheath.

NOT YET.

HE WATCHED Veronica slide onto the moped, wrapping her arms around his waist for something to hold on to as he pedaled to start the silly little scooter. It sent a flare of hatred through him. That embrace, that touch, was not meant for Bram. It was for him. It should have been for him.

He tested the weight of his blade at his side; it felt light, balanced, and eager. But tonight was not the night. The woods hushed above him, the wind shifted, and a chill ran down Dorian's spine. Something here, in the tree line, stirred and shifted. Time tugged at him, daring him to pull. History pressed close, begging to be rewritten.

He stepped back, resheathing his weapon. If he acted now, confronting Bram and killing him, he risked ripping open something neither Council nor Collective could repair. Dorian needed patience. He needed a moment when she was alone, when the token was there for the taking—a moment when Bram was not with her.

As Bram got moving steadily, Dorian could still see Veronica in the distance. She turned and threw a final glance at the boy in the bushes, seemingly defiant. Practically mocking him. In that look, he reached for the dagger; if they were closer, he would have charged at them, blinded by rage. In that look from her, Dorian saw what he had to become: colder, more focused, and a merciless killer.

As they drove away, the shadow of trees seemed to swallow him, making him suddenly feel small and empty. He clenched his jaw. He would wait. He would hunt. And when she finally stepped where he needed her, when Bram's lack of presence and comfort left her vulnerable, he would strike.

Because the Token Continuum belonged to the one who would fight for it, not the one who giggled in moonlit clearings.

And Dorian intended to take it.

Chapter Nine

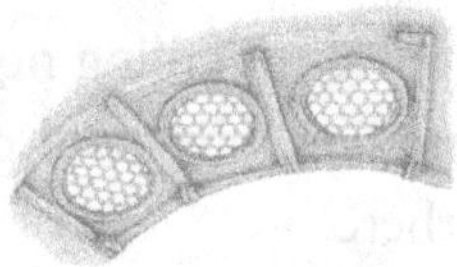

Bram led me up eighteen tight steps, his hand brushing the railing like he'd done it a hundred times. Each footfall rang out in the narrow stairwell, amplifying the hush around us, giving way to a narrow corridor that felt closer to the inside of an old iron steamer than a lighthouse. The walls, curved and close, shimmered faintly with age.

Above us, dim rings of light glowed from the ceiling—iron circles filled with fogged glass prisms, arranged in a honeycomb pattern. Their glow wasn't harsh or artificial. It was soft. Calming. Like moonglow trapped in a bottle.

As we continued upward in a slow spiral, I ran my hand along the cool, riveted wall. We passed a heavy metal door on the left—locked, with its brass handle—its hulking presence unspoken but impossible to ignore.

We didn't stop.

A few more steps brought us to a chamber bathed in the white light and the patina of time. At its center stood a heavy iron pedestal, painted a deep forest green. Inside, a quiet electric motor hummed like a distant hive, surrounded by polished brass gears that ticked with purpose.

Above the gears, bronze wheels turned in slow, deliberate circles, their motion transmitted through iron struts that reached up toward the great lens of brass and glass above us—an enormous, elegant behemoth shining out to sea.

I felt it then—that we were at the edge of someplace sacred, at the heart of something ancient. And maybe, something still alive.

"Just ten more steps," Bram said, his voice low and steady as he guided me upward. There was no railing now—just the narrow grey treads and open air on one side. His hand pressed gently against my back, not pushing, just... there.

I GRIPPED the token tightly in my palm. It buzzed faintly, as if it recognized our location. Beside me, the great apparatus turned—its prisms catching fractured slivers of radiance, rotating similar to a slow, rhythmic crystal capsule. The movement was hypnotic, almost mystical, and for a moment, I forgot to be afraid.

Each prism beside me shimmered with a clean, white glow, like frozen sunlight captured in glass. On the windows to my left, our dark reflections hovered—two shadows suspended in a slow orbit.

When the beam swept past, it sliced through the air in silence, casting our silhouettes outward—shadows flung miles across the coast.

As we curved around the deck, the clear crystals beneath our feet had once been overhead, part of the ceiling just a level below. In the distance, the rooftops of downtown St. Augustine shimmered. The great lens rotated steadily, casting its luminous signature across the city, a brilliant beacon in slow motion.

I spotted the bayfront, the Lions Bridge, the old fort, even the crumbling shrimp boats near the harbor—tiny pieces of home, seemed so distant and dreamlike from up here. Everything looked so small. So still. So emotionally moving. And I felt it again—that ache behind my ribs and my eyes watering. Almost everyone I knew was out there, and that made me want to find my father more than ever. Because wherever he was, he wasn't here.

I didn't say anything, but I felt Bram's eyes on me.

When I turned, he wasn't looking at the lens or the view—he was watching *me*. His expression had eased, the usual quick remarks gone quiet. He gave me a slight, knowing nod, understanding something I hadn't said out loud.

I looked away before the moment stretched too long. But his silence stayed with me.

After a long, lingering stillness, Bram finally whispered, "Everything's so beautiful from up here."

His eyes met mine for a beat longer than usual before drifting toward the massive lens. He nodded toward a narrow crawlspace along the bottom of it—an opening, leading into the heart of the lighthouse.

"There," he said softly. "That's the path inside," glancing back at me. "Is the token calm?"

I looked down at my hand, the coin still warm against my skin. "Yeah. Just a faint hum now. Not at all like before."

"Good," he said. "Then come with me. The Token Continuum will take us from here—if you're ready."

He crouched, disappearing into the low opening as if it were a natural movement.

I hesitated at the threshold, my voice catching. "But... where? Where are we going?"

From inside, Bram looked up at me and extended his hand. The glow from the fragments of crystals lit his face in a faint white and gold light.

"Think about a man named Lucian," he said gently. "Tell the token you want to see him."

"Who?"

"Lucian Aevum," he said. "You should meet him. And he should meet you. He's a Temporal Master. One of the last."

His hand stayed outstretched, waiting. I stared at it, unsure, until I finally reached down and let him pull me inside.

The space was tighter than I expected. I tumbled forward awkwardly, landing half-kneeling, half-folded into and on top of him. His arms caught me before I could fall too far, and suddenly we were tangled, embraced together in the hush of the rotating inner lens chamber. Close. Too close. Not close enough.

His breath was hot on my ear, sending a shiver through me.

"Lucian Aevum," he whispered. "Say it. Tell the token."

The name danced on the edge of my lips as my throat tightened. I closed my eyes, the weight of everything—my father, the truth, Bram, this new world crashing against me like a tide.

"Lucian Aevum," I whispered, closing my eyes tightly. "Take us to Lucian Aevum."

SUDDENLY, it felt as if the entire apparatus lurched free from reality.

A deep, gut-wrenching drop tugged at my stomach, and instinct took over—Bram and I clutched each other tighter, our bodies clinging close as the world tilted under us. The solid iron floor shifted beneath me, as if it had come unmoored from everything. Just floating or falling and shifting through something we weren't supposed to understand.

Above us, the hundreds of prisms began to tremble, humming at first, then singing in harmony.

Each one emitted a different note—some high and crystalline, others low and mournful. The tones layered together into a wild, impossible harmony. It wasn't music. It was something older, stranger, perhaps the sound of stars rearranging themselves.

My breath caught in my throat. Light fractured all around us— shafts of color rippling through the transparent mechanism with an intense, almost liquid spectrum. The air thickened, shimmered, turned electric.

The iron beneath us pulsed like a heartbeat.

And then more movement.

Not the sensation of spinning or rising, but *slipping*, as if the lighthouse itself was gliding sideways through folded space. The lens blurred. The prisms above us stretched and bent like reflections on water, distorting into ribbons of white, gold, and violet.

Bram's grip tightened. I could feel his pulse racing against mine. He leaned close, his forehead brushing mine.

"Almost there," he whispered roughly into my ear, barely audible over the storm of sound and light.

And then—just as suddenly as it began—it all stopped.

Without sound. Without further motion.

Silence so tight that it rang in my ears.

WE WERE STILL KNEELING, still holding on to each other, but everything around us had changed.

We stayed frozen. The air was heavy with something I couldn't name—a strange pulse, almost electric, but still at the same time. My breath came shallow and fast. My heart hammered so loud, it was all I could hear, thudding like it wanted out. Every sound was too much: the floor creaked, wind whispered around the windows, and Bram's breathing was steady and weirdly calm next to me. It felt like the world had pressed pause, like even seasons were waiting. The two of us are just stuck in this moment.

Bram didn't move. His arms were loose around me, not tight, but there, warm and strong. It was like he didn't know if he should let go, and I didn't know if I wanted him to. For a few seconds, neither of us said anything.

I could feel the heat of him, right there, and even though I thought about pulling away, I didn't.

Something was grounding about him, about this strange, unexpected place. My pulse was erratic, but with him holding me, the chaos in my head seemed to quiet down, even just for a moment.

Finally, Bram shifted just slightly, and I could feel the faintest grin tug at his lips. "We can get up, whenever you're ready," he said, his voice subdued, teasing, but warm. The way he said it sounded as if he was giving me the choice—because he seemed okay with us being so close together.

I jerked away from him. Not just a little, it was a sharp, almost violent motion, so fast it startled me. My heart did this weird lurch thing. I hadn't meant to pull away like that, but I just needed space. Clarity. The air felt suddenly cold between us, as if there was an empty spot where his hand had been, and for some reason, the gap was kind of a relief.

Not that I wanted to keep him away. It was confusing. I wanted him close, but also—I wanted to be in control. Of the situation. Of myself. I still had the token, but it wasn't humming anymore. I tucked it back into the compass around my neck and snapped the lid shut, hard. Then I wiped my hands on my shorts, like maybe I could get rid of the weird leftover feeling, but it didn't really work.

Above us, the lens had transformed—taller, older, its metal frame etched with unfamiliar marks. Cool, dry air curled around me now, stripped of humidity.

At the exit of the capsule, a mysterious black vapor swirled and drifted across the cold, iron floor, slowly dissipating into the surrounding air. As it faded, it revealed a year seared into the hot metal, the numbers 1888 standing out starkly against the darkened surface. The iron still emitted a faint, smoky heat, the edges of the numerals glowing faintly, evidence of the recent scorching.

"So here we are. Ninety-seven years in the past," Bram said in a slow, shaky breath while moving over the engraving.

We crawled out of the lens and stood just outside its broad, louvred frame filled with transparent prisms. The dim horizon stretched pale and unfamiliar. Mist curled against the panes as I caught sight of cliffs and large rocks in the distance, along with a vast, wild sea stretching out below. It was nothing at all like the south-eastern coast of the United States.

This was definitely not *my* ocean.

NOT FLORIDA.

I TURNED TO HIM, every word feeling too small for what had just happened. "Where are we?"

He nodded toward the horizon, his voice quieter now, almost reverent. "This is the Cordouan Lighthouse. Western France. And that..." He paused with his gaze following across the vast stretch of water before us. "That is still the Atlantic Ocean."

I followed his eyes, the endless sea sprawling out beneath the fading radiance of the tower. The sound of the waves was louder than any waves I'd ever heard before, crashing against the rocks like an ancient siren song. And for a moment, it felt as if time itself had stretched thin, as if we'd crossed into something beyond the ordinary.

And I realized, from the song of the rough sea, in this overwhelming moment, that the world I thought I knew was gone.

Chapter Ten

Bram and I descended the worn stone steps. The cool texture of limestone beneath our feet was a sharp contrast to the smooth, cold cast iron we'd climbed earlier. The walls around us were thick and cracked, the rock rough and ancient, like the lighthouse had been standing here long before us, guarding the surrounding sea in silence.

The air grew colder, carrying the damp scent of salt, and the faint echo of our footsteps whispered of those who had passed here before—bits of muted moonlight filtered through long, narrow openings, while the wind outside sounded furious. I ran my fingers along the jagged edges, feeling the history of each block beneath my touch.

He kept walking next to me, not saying a word, but it was as if his silence grew heavier the farther we went. I swear he could feel how big this was, how weird and important it felt. The stairs got steeper, tighter, and every step down made it seem less like we were inside a lighthouse and more like we were dropping into some ancient, secret place—a place that maybe didn't even want to be found.

We stopped at this little door, and he squeezed my hand—which, honestly, kind of snapped me out of the weird trance I was in.

"I can't wait for you to see this. Ready?" He was grinning, and it made me want to laugh, even though my heart was pounding.

I nodded. He reached for the iron latch. It made this haunted-house creak, and then he pulled the door open and led me inside.

I just stopped. Cold.

THE PLACE WAS HUGE. More massive than I thought it would be. Four torches on the walls, flickering and throwing shadows all over the place.

The whole room seemed to be breathing. Up above, the ceiling just went on and on—a perfect dome, so smooth it looked fake. Seriously, shouldn't this be in a museum? Or a castle? Not a lighthouse. I just stared. Honestly? It was maybe the coolest thing I'd ever seen.

"What is this place?" I said, my mouth hanging open, eyes tracking the shadows that moved across the dome.

It reminded me of the dome at the Presbyterian Church back home, mixed with the grandeur of Flagler College—both built in the 1880s.

"A chapel, once built for royalty," Bram said, his voice echoing in the stillness. "Built for King Henry III of France, who never even set foot here."

I could feel his eyes on me, but I couldn't stop staring at the crazy-detailed carvings over the arched doorways. It was almost too much—the kind of pretty that makes your brain short-circuit for a second.

"It's even more beautiful in the daylight," he said, quiet, but still totally staring. My face went hot—I could tell I was blushing, and the silence between us just kept growing, stretching out until I honestly couldn't tell if it was the room or him making my heart skip beats.

He reached for my hand again, his grip warm and solid, and we kept going, deeper into the halls where it was even darker. I could barely see, but there were shapes: old, fancy chairs, velvet curtains smashed against the walls, and the air felt like it was full of old secrets, dust, and maybe even a phantom or two.

BRAM OPENED ANOTHER DOOR, this one led outside, where the rush of wind hit us like a wall. The scent of salt and ocean spray stung my face as the storm seemed to swallow us whole. The world felt raw, a gale howling around us like a living thing. Waves crashed relentlessly against a far wall, or was that a building?

Across a narrow walkway, a long, squat building loomed in the distance, its rough, rocky walls blending into the storm. Three red doors stood out against the darkness. The storm made everything feel distant, but the doors beckoned—a refuge from the surrounding tempest.

He moved forward, pulling me closer to shield me from the harsh ocean spray, a steady anchor while the storm raged ferociously all around us.

We made it across the rocks, slipping all over the place, and somehow got to the middle door. He didn't even wait. He grabbed the giant iron lion head knocker and slammed it down. The noise echoed everywhere, like a dare, right in the middle of all that wind.

Everything stopped for a second. The storm was still howling, but it was as if time had just... froze. Bram squeezed my hand even harder, then knocked again.

THE DOOR SWUNG OPEN.

We darted inside and, instantly, the stormy world outside vanished. Warm air hit my face. It actually felt good. There was this giant fireplace, and its crackling flames pulled me in closer, like a magnet. It was perfect.

I looked around, the small windows framing the stormy ocean, its waves rolling beneath the glow of the tower.

SUDDENLY, a low voice boomed from near the door.

"Bram!"

I jumped. Then, proceeding into the dim light, I saw him—an elderly man with an air of quiet authority. His dark robes flowed around him, worn with age but still carrying the dignity of someone who had lived long and seen much. His eyes were sharp, clear, even behind his wire-rimmed glasses, which gleamed softly in the grey storm.

His beard was long and gray, matching the mess of his hair, both falling in bulky waves down past his shoulders. He looked like he'd just wandered out of some wizardly storybook. He gripped a tall staff of gnarled dark wood.

The whole staff was covered in these crazy-intricate vine patterns, curling all over like they were alive. And right smack in the middle was an hourglass. It was large and kind of fragile-looking, the sand inside drifting along, super slow.

Lucian looked at Bram and gave him this gentle, familiar smile, like he'd totally been waiting for us to show up.

"Bram. Welcome, my dear boy," he said, voice warm and sort of old-fashioned.

He glanced at me, but then he really looked, like he was reading a secret message written across my face. I almost wondered if he could see my whole life, just from the way I stood there. He took his time. Didn't rush. Finally, he smiled. It was tiny, careful, like he was letting me in on a joke.

"I'm Lucian Aevum," he said, steady. "And judging by your manner of dress, you must be Veronica Ingram. Six, right?"

"How did you know?" I asked. My voice came out way softer than I meant it to.

Lucian's grin got even wider, and his eyes went all sparkly and amused. "I've seen your birth record in the archives, my dear."

He just left it at that, hanging in the air. Heavy. Sort of awkward. It almost felt like he knew me, even though I was positive I'd never seen him before in my life.

"Six, you must have a million questions," he said, stepping back and giving me space.

I just stood there.

You don't have to worry. Everything will be explained in due course. Come closer to the fire. Let me prepare a steaming drink for each of you to help chase away the chill," Lucian said invitingly.

As we shuffled closer to the fire, I noticed something weird about a large glass tank in the corner. The water within was almost black, and then it began to churn. I squinted, noticing that there was this huge white eye with a sharp, flaming orange iris. Larger than a dinner plate. Just floating there, staring straight at us. I pointed it out to Bram. It was surprising, and I was almost totally freaked out.

Bram smiled and walked over to the tank. "Relax. It's just a baby."

"What kind of baby is that, exactly?" My voice came out scared, like I couldn't tell if I should laugh or bolt.

"Baby kraken," Bram said, like it was no big deal. "Kind of like a squid, but these guys get way bigger." He reached over the rim, and right away a plump tentacle slid out of the water.

The skin was all dark, glossy, and slick as it slithered, wrapping around the analemma tattoo on his forearm.

Lucian came back in, holding two mugs of hot chocolate and this ancient, dull, scratchy quilt that looked like it had been made by someone's great-grandma a long time ago.

He nodded at the tank. "So you've met Wilber. Or maybe Orville. I can never tell the difference between those two." He handed me a mug and tossed the quilt over my shoulders like it was nothing.

Bram just stared, one eyebrow up. "There are two of them in there?"

Lucian nodded again. "Two males. Not a lot of krakens left, unfortunately."

I pulled the quilt tight and took a sip. The hot chocolate was heavy and sweet, and I felt warmer right away.

The creature released its grip on Bram, its tentacle slowly retreating into the water, leaving a few wet drops on the floor.

LUCIAN TURNED his attention to me, his eyes shimmering from the fireplace. "I suppose both Bram and Dorian have told you a great deal of wondrous things that are seemingly unbelievable. No?"

I nodded, feeling a mix of awe and uncertainty. "Yes, sir. Time travel, from lighthouse to lighthouse, with a special token. If I weren't standing here, experiencing it all myself, I would never believe it."

I hesitated, the weight of everything sinking in—the strange new world, the dangers, the uncertainty of it all. I couldn't shake the fear that had clung to me ever since Dorian—and then Bram—dragged me into this impossible reality.

I took a slow breath, gathering the words that had been swirling around in my head. I pushed past the doubt that tugged at me and said, "But no one's been able to tell me anything about my father's whereabouts or what has happened to him."

My voice came out stronger than I expected. The uncertainty was in my tone, but there was something else—a resolve, a new sense that maybe I had the power to find out the truth.

His voice altered, an edge of sadness along it, like a shadow on the words. "No one knows what became of Jacob. He disappeared a very long time ago," he said, each word deliberate and cautious.

"In the enigmatic world of travelers, one must sometimes become a change agent, going quietly under cover. This undercover life may go on for years, wrapped in a haze that persistently refuses to clear. This haze may cloud over everything: not only where you are, but what you want and what you do." His voice softened, weighed down with unseen reality.

Lucian leaned forward slightly, his eyes intent but thoughtful, glinting with the fullness of his ideas. "You've heard of the Chronos Collective, then?" he asked. "They're devoted to maintaining peace, maintaining balance, and growing harmony along the timeline. All they're interested in is guiding history so it remains solid and orderly for everyone."

He froze, and his expression darkened as his tale went in another direction. "Then there is the Council of Chaos," he continued, his voice tinged with fascination. "They thrive on turmoil, fueling strife and warfare with the idea that out of destruction come new possibilities. According to them, without their intervention, humanity would not be forced to advance, to break rules or create."

I frowned, attempting to grasp the complexity of it all. "Well... they both want the same things, so neither is necessarily wrong?" I tried, hoping for greater comprehension.

He nodded, his voice falling almost to a whisper. "Just that. Peace is what the Chronos Collective is all about, but too much peace can lead to stagnation. If nothing changes, nothing grows. Yet, the Council of Chaos celebrates conflict and sometimes delights in outright chaos; however, not all destruction is negative. Great things often come of conflict." Neither side is entirely virtuous or malevolent—they both have vital roles to play.

He left his words hanging in the room, heavy and deep. "History is a balancing act, Veronica. At times, the world requires both sides to move it forward."

I nodded at what he said.

Lucian's eyes sparkled as though he shared a secret. "You're from 1985, so let's take the Cold War. Despite the possibility of war or annihilation, great strides are being made. Technology. Communications. Science. Both sides strive to outperform one another.

It's conflict, yes, but in that conflict on the verge of chaos, humans push themselves to go beyond what was once thought possible. The Soviets send the first man into space, and then the Americans put a man on the moon. Satellites, computers, even things that seem normal now—none of them would be where they are without the urgency that competition and conflict can bring."

I blinked as the thought registered. "So conflict can lead towards advancement?"

"Exactly," said Lucian. "Sometimes, but not necessarily always, where conflict or chaos occurs, it's then that the greatest breakthroughs come. It doesn't always come easy, and it doesn't come cheap either, but it's that pressure, through friction, that creates inevitable change."

My eyes could tell them both that doubt muddled my mind. "Which side is my father on? The Chronos Collective or the Council of Chaos?"

Lucian paused, his voice dropping. "I don't know anymore," he said quietly, as though the very question had grown older than him. "Occasionally, it occurs even with the best of us, though it isn't common. When the distinction between right and wrong becomes obscure, we all tend to lose count."

I stared at him, perplexed. "What do you mean?"

"I've seen it occur. Travelers pick sides and then flip back and forth, and sometimes without knowing it. It's the nature of this ongoing conflict—all of it isn't as black and white as it appears." Lucian settled back into his chair, his voice falling into a softer register. "Myself, as an example. I left the Chronos Collective years ago. I didn't want them to tie up the timelines in all these rules." Everything got way too restrictive, as if the rules were choking the life out of it. For an instant, something crossed his face—an unusual, tormented look, as if the words were nowhere close to what he really meant. He looked at me, but it was as if he saw through me, stuck in some recollection that he couldn't break free from. "There are things I learned later. Things I wish I could undo," he said."When you're caught up in something bigger than you, it's not so simple anymore. Right and wrong just sort of... blur together. You have to step back and see the whole thing."

I was just going to ask, but he interrupted me, gentler this time:

"I didn't go rogue so that things could go awry. I just felt time ought to run its natural course. No more interfering from either side."

He shrugged, like it didn't matter, but it clearly did. "Whatever your dad has done, you've still got that Continuum Token. That's a huge deal. With it, you'll be a formidable traveler, if you can guard it well," Lucian said, his tone steady. "With the token, you don't have to wait for gravitational waves; you can travel anywhere, to any time. Without the token, you'd have to choose between the Collective and the Council. Both sides will try to recruit you, and they will try to influence your decisions. With the token, you could choose neither and forge your own path, but without much knowledge, that would be rather reckless and dangerous. So choose wisely, and not because one boy makes your heart race or the other makes you feel safe."

His gaze softened, the warmth in his voice never faltering.

I felt a tightness in my chest as Lucian's words sank in.

Not because one boy makes your heart race or the other makes you feel safe.

My breath caught, and I quickly looked away. Feeling my face warming. Lucian's words struck too close to the conflict inside me. I had felt it, the pull between Bram's comforting presence and Dorian's mysterious intensity. The choice wasn't just about the factions anymore. For me, it was about choosing who to believe.

And now, the weight of everything seemed heavier than ever.

Chapter Eleven

The morning sun, streaming through the pollen-splotched window, cast muted lines of pale gold on the dusty floor. I awoke from a full-body spasm and found myself all tangled up in the sheets. The air in the room was heavy and stale—the sort of staleness that resulted from old furniture and shut windows. A scent I'd become accustomed to over the years.

For an instant, I could not recall where I had been. Then the memories came flooding back, engulfing me in a wave I could not escape. The night before lingered in memory: the cool stone steps we walked on, the tempest outside. But it was the St. Augustine Lighthouse that felt more familiar on return, its brick and iron seemed to feel like home.

What remained with me, however, was the feeling of Bram's touch—the awkward intimacy of it, the way we had been close in the cramped quarters of the lighthouse lenses. His breath so close to mine. How at times he gripped my hand—it was an intimacy I hadn't anticipated. Even when the turbulence of time travel subsided, that intimacy remained, heavy and unresolved.

Then his contact had not appeared important, but now it overwhelmed me. All of it felt like sparks that I could not extinguish. When he touched me in close quarters, or every time his hand grasped mine, the world outside stopped, and nothing else mattered. The lighthouse back in France felt so distant now, like a dream that I could not reach. But his touch remained, something I could not forget.

I finally sat upright, attempting to process it all. The journey had been all so strange, so incomprehensible in reality, and now it all felt suspended between sleep and wakefulness. My cramped room was still, far too quiet, other than the whine of the ceiling fan in the family room.

It took the sharp ring of the phone to break the silence and jar me back into the present. I could hear my mom's voice far away in the kitchen through the closed door.

"Hold on, let me see if she's up."

"Six, the phone is for you, it's Claire!!"

I winced and stood up, my bare feet planting on the rough carpet as I lurched out of bed. I still wore the same clothes from last night.

My mom had left the receiver lying on top of the telephone and retreated into her bedroom without another comment.

"Hey." I was groggy and not really awake yet.

"Well, well, look who woke up!" Claire's voice broke through the fog in my head, her sarcastic accent cutting through it. "You said you'd call last night, you little floozie."

"Sorry, I got in so late I didn't want to wake everyone up," I said, half embarrassed.

"How late?" Claire asked, her voice acidic with curiosity.

"I don't really rem—"

"You don't remember?" she interrupted, her voice shrill with suspicion. "Were you drunk?"

"No. I... it was late, that's all," I stammered, words tumbling over each other.

"Okay, all right. Well, what's your memory?"

I gazed. "What? What're you talking about?"

"Oh, Six," she said with a hint of sarcasm entering her voice. "You know full well what I am talking about. That guy was capital F, i-n-e, fine."

"Nothing happened. It was, it was… magical."

"Magical," I said to myself, the term an effort to describe something that could not be explained. It wasn't magic like Claire would think, of fireworks and grand romanticism. It was the sort of magic that made all of it real. More real than anything I'd ever experienced. The cold of the stone on the ground I stood on, the beating of the token within me—it felt as though the world had come to a halt for a second, and I knew what it felt like to be something other than me. Something much greater than myself.

The token! It was missing from around my neck. A wave of silent panic started to wash over me.

"Ooh…Magical?!" Claire stung me with laughter and an expression of exhilaration at my description.

"What? Did he pull a rabbit out of a hat? Or something, maybe a little more personal?" she mocked, her voice thick with spite.

"What? Ew… No! Nothing happened. We just went out to his boat, and I met more of his friends," I lied, hoping she wouldn't press any further.

"Well, does this Magic Man have any single friends?" she asked hopefully.

"Maybe, probably. I don't know. I'll try and find out."

"Oh, so you're going to see him again? On this boat? As your best and most desperate friend, Six, take me with you," she begged, her tone playful but insistent.

Just then, I heard the sound of my mom walking down the hallway, flipping through a *Women's Day* magazine. My heart skipped a beat.

I looked nervously towards the door, a rush of guilt washing over me. Claire's voice still echoed in my mind, so full of hope and questions, and here I was lying to her, and I was keeping it all about last night to myself.

"Hey, we'll talk later, all right?" I said quickly, my voice rushed and slightly harsh.

There was silence on the other end of the phone for a moment, and I thought for one second Claire would call me on it. Then she sighed in resignation.

"Fine. Six, whatever, I'm dying to hear every detail."

"Alright, I'll tell you. Bye," I said hastily.

AND BEFORE I could answer back, she slammed the phone down, hanging up. My heart thrashed within me. I rushed back into my room with an air of frenzy, glancing over every surface of it. There it lay on the upper plank of my improvised shelf of cinder blocks and boards, the compass sitting quietly in the low light. Once I picked it up, I could feel a gentle throb. I opened the compass with a shaking hand to convince myself that the token remained securely inside.

Staring fixedly at the Token Continuum, its complex pattern whirling in my hand, was like a ticket into a world I hardly knew. Shining and black and gold, I felt its weight, like the obligation I'd been handed unbidden. Bram could have taken it from me at any time. But he hadn't. Bram only ever advised me, never urged me on, never badgered me. That self-control, that caution, was more than loyalty. And then it struck me that I knew it for the first time: I wasn't alone in all of this.

The weight of that truth settled in. Bram wasn't just someone caught up in this mess of time and power—he was someone I could trust. Because he had proven his loyalty without hesitation. With him and the Collective by my side, the path ahead suddenly felt clearer. I didn't have to face it alone. I could trust him, and in this new world, where everything felt uncertain, trust was the one thing I could hold on to.

Chapter Twelve

I didn't see him at first.

I was juggling my books, trying to close my locker before the bell rang, when the hallway noise shifted—voices quieted just enough to notice something was off. Then I saw him.

Dorian.

He was stalking down the hall toward me, fast and furious, his boots striking the floor hard enough to echo. His eyes locked on mine, and for a split second, I couldn't move.

Veronica!" he shouted—hard, indignant. The kind of shout that makes everyone stop dead in their tracks. Talk ceased. Heads turned.

I stiffened, my hands clenching around the cover of my history textbook.

"You left?" he shouted once more, voice grating and cutting. "With him!"

My stomach fell.

"Dorian, not here," I huffed, looking around. There was already a cluster of kids staring, their eyes darting back and forth between us like we were a scene in an after-school special.

He didn't care.

"I waited for you out there."

His voice cracked, and something in his expression twisted—part betrayal, part disbelief.

"I... I thought you weren't coming. You never showed..."

"You knew I was there. I know you saw me. You looked my way several times."

His hand clamped around my wrist—tight. Too tight. Pain flared, just for a second. And then he let go, like he realized it too. Like something in him pulled back at the last second.

"Dorian," I said quickly, trying to keep my voice even, like staying calm might stop this from spiraling. "I didn't choose him. He found me. He said it was important—"

"You believed him instead of me?"

His voice rose a level, harsh and edgy. I automatically retreated.

"Besides all that I've said? Besides, I've warned you about him?"

His words cut more deeply than I expected. Louder now than anyone needed to know. Students stood motionless in the hallway, pretending not to hear, yet they could still hear the sounds. Someone snickered quietly behind me. A lone locker door slammed shut down the hall.

And suddenly I felt it—that horrible, burning kind of spotlight feeling, like I was standing on a stage in front of everyone with nowhere to hide.

"I'm sorry," I said, my voice catching. "I didn't mean for it to happen that way. Maybe you should have stepped out and joined all of us."

He stared at me, breathing hard, fists clenched at his sides. And for a second, I didn't know what he was going to do.

I didn't know him—not this version of him. Not this hurt, furious boy shaking in the middle of a high school hallway.

"I trusted you," he whispered.

Then he turned and walked away, pushing past a group of under-classmen who scattered in his wake.

The bell rang. No one moved.

I swallowed hard, forcing my feet to walk toward class. But my hands were still shaking.

Whatever this was between us, it had just cracked wide open.

Whatever this was, it made Bram feel even closer.

LATER AT LUNCH in the cafeteria, I picked at my slice of pepperoni pizza, chewing even though I wasn't hungry.

Dorian sat across from me with one leg jumping up and down under the table. He hadn't eaten anything.

"I didn't plan to leave with Bram," I said. "It wasn't some secret mission."

"No?" Dorian's eyes narrowed. "Because as far as I could tell, it seemed as though you couldn't resist taking off with him."

"It wasn't like that," I answered with a sigh, trying to keep my voice level.

"Then what was it like, Veronica?"

His voice faltered, softer. "You vanished this weekend. You come back different. I can tell."

I looked around. Our conversation was dulled by cafeteria noise. We'd settled into a corner table, away from the worst of it.

Claire was sitting with some drama kids, casting worried looks every few minutes. I gave her a quick wave so she wouldn't come over.

"I know you're not carrying the token. Not now. But it was with you Friday," he quipped, voice sharp. "And I want to know where it is."

There was a long pause. I said nothing. How could he know about the token? It was as if he had read my mind at that moment.

"Travelers can be, well... sensitive, when it comes to something so powerful. I could feel it on you. I knew you were special, but not *that* special. If I could sense it, then I'm certain Bram definitely felt it. Why do you think he charmed you away from the others, from me?" he asked, his voice sly and prickly.

Dorian stared at the table between us for a long moment.

"Well? Where is it?" he asked directly.

I wasn't ready to answer him.

So I changed the subject.

"He showed me lighthouses," I explained. "Not just ours. One in France, too. It felt as if we moved through a dream—real and terrifying. The air was different. The walls hummed."

Dorian's eyes narrowed.

"You traveled?" Dorian's words were so soft that they sounded like they hurt him to utter.

"With him?"

I nodded. "Yeah."

He searched my eyes, wanting more.

"And... I met someone there," I went on, taking a little breath. "A man named Lucian Aevum. He... he's more or less like a guide. Or maybe a guardian? I'm not quite sure yet."

Dorian stiffened.

"Lucian's alive?" he breathed.

I nodded again, more slowly. "You know him?"

Something flickered across his face—recognition, shock, maybe even guilt. Like I'd spoken a name he'd spent years trying not to think about.

"Everyone knew him," he said finally, his voice quieter now. "Lucian was... he was more than a mentor. People from both sides— the Guild and the Council- listened to him. Respected him."

He stopped, as whatever came next was more difficult to speak.

"But then he began questioning all of it. Stopped taking charge and began... wondering. Ideas, theories, questions no one wished to pose."

Dorian leaned in a little, his voice more intense now.

"He thought time couldn't just be a straight line. He said it was more like fabric—woven, stretchy. Interconnected. But also fragile. Thin in some spots. Torn. Coming apart already."

He looked straight at me.

"These places of the fraying," he said, "those are where history beckoned to be comprehended, not rewritten, but mended."

"And they exiled him for that?"

"Not exactly."

Dorian's tone darkened. "They erased him. Quietly. Travelers were warned to forget his name. Some didn't. Some followed him anyway."

He didn't have to say it.

My father had been one of them. I could feel it.

"You think my dad was following Lucian?"

"I know he wasn't with the Council. And he wasn't Guild. That only leaves the third way—Lucian's way."

I swallowed hard.

The idea settled over me like dust.

My father hadn't gone rogue.

He'd chosen something.

"So now Bram's pulling you into that same path," Dorian said. "And you don't even realize how close you are to walking down the wrong one."

"I know more than you think," I replied. "And Lucian... he didn't seem dangerous. He seemed wise—someone who still believes time can heal."

Dorian shook his head. "That's exactly what makes him dangerous."

He stared at me—then past me.

"So let me ask you," he said, voice low. "Where's the Token?"

My hand curled around the edge of the table.

"Safe."

"I'd like a real answer, Veronica."

I met his eyes. "That *is* the real answer."

Dorian stared at me like he was trying to feel my pulse through the table.

"I'm going to ask you this once more," he said, his voice almost a whisper. "Where's the Token?"

I hesitated. Just long enough for the silence to stretch.

"It's with Bram," I lied.

The words came out smoother than I expected—but I felt them land like a stone between us.

Dorian recoiled, just slightly. Like I'd slapped him.

"With Bram?" His voice sharpened. "You gave it to him?"

I didn't answer.

"Are you serious right now?" he barked. "You let him carry it?"

People at nearby tables turned. I kept my voice calm. Cold.

"I trust him."

Dorian shook his head because he couldn't make those words compute.

"You don't even know what he's tied to. What side he's on."

"And you think you do?"

He leaned in, jaw tight. Eyes searching mine for something—maybe a way to walk this back.

But there wasn't one.

"You should've told me," he said finally, voice brittle. "You should've trusted me."

"I don't know what to do. Who to trust?" I whispered, confused.

He stood quickly, jaw clenched.

"Just remember—once a thread starts to unravel, you don't always get to stop it."

And then he was gone, swallowed by the cafeteria crowd—

while I sat there feeling that every part of me was coming undone.

Not only that—

A lie was out in the world now, unraveling something between us.

Chapter Thirteen

The TV news was playing when I walked into the kitchen; the anchor's voice was calm and practiced—unshaken, as if this was just another tragedy to tick off the morning list.

"...NO word yet on the identity of the deceased. Authorities report the vessel, The Ampoletta, registered out of Greece, was found burning in the St. Augustine Marina shortly after 4 a.m. Nearby boaters say flames reached twenty feet high before the harbor master and fire units extinguished the blaze. The famous research vessel, the Calypso, anchored nearby, was unharmed. The Coast Guard says the blaze is under investigation."

I FROZE IN THE DOORWAY, one hand gripping the edge of the frame.

The Ampoletta.

My heart stopped—then stuttered violently back to life.

That's Bram's boat. He *lives* aboard the Ampoletta. He told me that himself, as if it were nothing, as if it were normal to sleep on a boat full of secrets.

Mom stood at the counter in her robe, stirring cream into her coffee, half-watching the screen.

"God," she murmured. "That's terrible, I hope it wasn't someone local."

She turned toward me, eyes tired, still half in her sleepy world. "Didn't you say you walked up to *The Calypso* last week to have a closer look?"

I couldn't answer, I just nodded. Still staring at the screen, which showed the smoldering hull, as colorful streaks shimmered across the water, slicks from oil or gasoline. Then a cut to *The Calypso*, floating beside it, pristine. Untouched.

One boat destroyed—one left whole.

One person is dead.

"No," I whispered.

My hands were shaking.

"I... I need to go," I said, my voice thin.

Mom blinked at me, confused. "Go where? What about school?"

But I was already backing toward the door.

What if Bram was on that boat?

If he was gone?

No. He couldn't be.

"I'll be back," I said quickly.

"Veronica?"

I DIDN'T ANSWER.

By the time I hit the bottom of the rotting stairs outside, my breath was short and tight in my chest. I crouched underneath the stairway and yanked off the blue tarp covering my old Huffy, a beat-up, ten-speed, bought at a police auction years ago. Spider-webs clung to the curved handlebars. A surprised tiny long-tailed lizard bolted from a pedal and crawled up a wooded post. The chain, streaked with rust, and the back tire looked half-flat. I didn't care.

I kicked off anyway, the pedals groaning beneath my feet as I rode out through the narrow lighthouse neighborhood streets, wind whipping past, sand crackling beneath my wheels.

I was already halfway down Palmetto Avenue before I realized what I was wearing.

Sweatpants. My Garfield tee with the hole at the shoulder. Electric blue plush slippers slapped against the pedals every time I pushed down—no real shoes. No backpack. Just me, shaking, biking like my world was on fire.

Because maybe it was. I didn't care.

The news report kept looping in my head—the image of the *Ampoletta*, scorched and charred, drifting beside the still-perfect *Calypso* like some cruel joke. One boat burned. One person dead.

I gripped the handlebars tighter. My fingers were numb, not from cold, but from the pressure building in my chest. Like if I didn't get to the marina fast enough, the truth would harden into something I couldn't handle.

He told me he lived on that boat.

The wind stung my face as I pedaled faster, every bump in the sidewalk along A1A rattling up through the rusted frame of my old Huffy. My legs burned. My eyes burned. My thoughts spiraled—had I said enough? Had he known how much I trusted him?

I couldn't finish the thought.

I just kept riding, slippers soaked from a puddle I didn't see, heart pounding like maybe, if I got there fast enough, none of it would be real.

By the time I hit the incline on the Bridge of Lions, my legs were cramping. Every push of the pedals sent a burning ache up my thighs. My lungs felt raw.

Halfway up the bridge, the wind hit harder. The kind of wind that tastes like salt and iron and everything heavy. I stood on the pedals, forcing the old Huffy to climb. One slipper was soaked, my breath coming out in uneven gasps. But looking over the rail, I finally saw the marina, and forgot how much my body hurt.

There it was.

The *Ampoletta*.

Or what was left of it.

Its hull was black, wreckage warped in on itself, broken like a crusted-over scab floating in the water. It bobbed sluggishly against the floating dock, behind yellow tape and shadowed by a white tent standing between the miniature golf course and the seawall. Investigators moved around like slow ghosts, scribbling on clipboards. Further back, cameras lined the railings. People stood behind ropes, talking in low voices, trying to get a better view of the wreck.

A sick wave rose in my stomach.

This was real. This wasn't a bad dream or some twisted warning. The boat Bram lived on—the one he told me felt like *home*—was a scorched ruin floating in the morning light.

My legs gave a little under me, and I coasted the rest of the way down the decline on the other side of the bridge until too many people crowded the walkway. My heart was racing faster than the bike ever could. I didn't even feel the tears until one slipped past my cheek and caught in the corner of my mouth.

I walked my bike through the crowd gathered at the base of the bridge, weaving past news vans, bystanders, and cameras. One of the marble lions loomed to my left, its stone expression calm and unbothered, like it had seen it all.

I kept glancing at the tent, then out across the bay front. My breath stuttered. I turned, fast, scanning the sidewalks, the marina building, the benches by the water. Nothing.

My throat squeezed up tight like someone was pressing on my chest. Like I couldn't get enough air. And then—

Across the street, by the wax museum, there he was.

IN THE SHADOW of the pillar where the bronze statue of Ponce de León stood, Bram sat with his arms looped over his knees, his head down, looking pale, lost, and alive.

My heart jolted so hard it hurt.

Tears spilled over without warning, hot and sudden. My knees nearly gave out with the force of it, all the panic, the desperate what-ifs crashing against the reality of him, sitting there, real and whole.

Dropping the bike with a sharp clatter, I kicked off my stupid, soggy slippers, not caring where they landed. The rough dry grass, then the warming asphalt of the street beneath my bare feet, barely registered as I ran—my only focus was him.

"Bram!" His name tore from my lungs. Bram looked up, then stood and moved towards me.

With each stride, an overwhelming wave of emotion swept over me—relief, fear, something softer that twisted inside me, something I couldn't name. The closer I got, the more the ground beneath me seemed to tilt, but I couldn't stop.

I crashed through the hedge and almost faceplanted into the statue, my hand smacking the cold stone pedestal. But then—I felt it —his arm. I latched on, totally breathless, and suddenly everything snapped back into place.

"Bram..." My voice sounded like I'd swallowed gravel, barely a squeak, but somehow it said everything I couldn't. His face went all soft, eyebrows up, and for a second, he looked surprised—but then he just got it. No speeches. No big dramatic moment. He just stepped forward.

Next thing I knew, his arms were around me, squeezing tight, and I was hit with this tidal wave of relief. All the panic, the buzzing in my head, the feeling like I was about to fly apart—it just stopped. For once, I could actually breathe.

I felt his warmth surround me, and I buried my face against his chest, breathing in the scent of him, of his clothing caustic and smoky, grounding myself in the simple comfort of his presence. We stood there for a long moment, my heart still racing but slowing, the world fading around us. We didn't have to say anything.

Pulling away, I wiped the tears from my face, my hands trembling. I looked up into Bram's eyes, filled with something soft, almost sad. "I was so worried, Bram," I choked out, my heart racing with relief.

"I'm okay, Six. We're okay," he said, and his voice was calm, but I could see the way his eyes kept flicking over my face, as if he was checking to make sure I was really there. Like he wasn't really sure what he was saying was true.

"I choose you, alright?" I blurted, and my cheeks went hot. "I want you to know that. I trust you with everything... this journey, the Chronos Collective, but mostly you. I choose you." Saying it out loud made my heart thump in a strange, heavy way, but it was true— even if I still couldn't figure out why I deserved it.

Bram just looked at me for a second, not saying anything. His eyes didn't leave mine, and his brow scrunched up a little, like he was trying to solve a puzzle he'd never seen before. Then, suddenly, he reached for me and pulled me in, and his lips were on mine.

It wasn't gentle, but it wasn't rough either. It was something else —a kind of kiss that felt tangled up and real, like it was the only thing that mattered. I could still taste a salty edge from where I'd cried, but it mixed with the warm, sweet feeling of him. My heart was pounding, and for a few seconds, the entire universe shrank down to just us —the way we breathed, the way our mouths fit together, the way our hands clung like we'd never let go with our bodies pressing together.

Then, just as quickly as it started, he pulled back—softly with a quiet kind of understanding.

He leaned in and kissed my forehead.

It was just a quick press of lips, warm and soft, really gentle, almost like he was afraid I might break. His hand stayed on my cheek. The heat from it kind of stuck around. For a second, I felt like I was actually here, like I was real, like maybe he was saying I was safe. Not alone. Maybe that was all I'd wanted, the whole time.

THEN, out of nowhere, something moved. A flicker, shadows shifting behind the stone pedestal. We both froze. The moment snapped, just like that.

We edged apart, but the space between us still sizzled with an electricity in the air.

The first one around the corner was a woman. Tall and gaunt and almost otherworldly in her movement, as though she'd just stepped off the cover of a magazine. Black hair, sleek and polished, cascaded in waves around her face. She appeared as though she'd rehearsed this a thousand times in the mirror. Something about her prevented you from being able to look anywhere else, as though she was constructed of moonlight and secrets.

She was older than Bram, and that only made her more intimidating. Her eyes were black and piercing. When she looked at me, it felt like she might look through me. Like she searched every part of me, every imperfection, and every idea I'd ever thought of.

"Well, well, Bram. Who's this?" she said, her voice silky and slightly derisive. Teasing, but weighted, as though she tested me and already knew what I'd say.

Bram rolled his eyes. "Come on. You know exactly who this is. She's why we're here," he said, voice tight.

Her gaze remained fixed on me, measuring and savoring. It caused me to shift my weight onto one foot. I yearned to move back, to increase the distance between us, but I didn't. I remained fixed where I was, attempting to calm my breathing, trying not to notice that she seemed to be stripping me bare with her eyes, undressing me with her gaze.

Her eyes glinted as she advanced, her presence not to be ignored. "Ah, and so this must be our client, Veronica," she said with a sly grin spreading at her mouth. "I'm Sirianna. The pleasure is all mine, dear," she said in a silky voice, far too intimate.

I felt a flush of unease as she leaned in, her gaze as keen as a knife. She wasn't merely looking into my eyes. She was analyzing me, measuring me. My heart raced, but I couldn't help feeling as though she had already figured me out.

I extended my hand to shake hers. As soon as we touched fingers, I felt a cold feeling run along my arm. She didn't release my hand right away.

The air between us felt heavy and charged, as though I stood on the threshold of something I didn't know anything about. Putting more effort into understanding it only confused me more. What game was she playing?

There were two other men behind her. They were big, bearded, and burly, their sharp features softened only by their long coats and the understated European-style fashion they wore. Henchmen, I thought, standing in silence, their posture stiff and their expressions unreadable. They made no move to engage, merely observing from behind their apparent leader with a cold, detached air.

AND THEN, hidden away behind them, until she walked around to the front, was a small, spritely-looking woman whose eyes sparkled when she saw me.

"Oh, you must be Veronica," she said excitedly, reaching for my hand. "I'm Lyrica... running on caffeine, bad decisions, and midnight confessions."

"Nice to, uh, meet you," I replied, my confusion probably showing more than I wanted.

She gave a little shrug, like that explained everything. "Yes, I've been told I live in future songs. Don't hold it against me."

I tilted my head, still trying to figure her out. "Future songs, huh? It must be nice to know that your life has a soundtrack. All I've got is Casey Kasem's American Top 40."

That made her grin wider, like she was waiting for someone to try and keep up. "What can I say? I was born in *Midnights* and raised by *Wildest Dreams*."

Before I could even start to untangle that one, Sirianna leaned in beside me, her voice low and dry. "We don't understand it all either. Don't encourage her."

I looked at all of them, and my heart became heavy with the weight of the moment. "Did someone die in the fire? I'm so sorry," I asked, my voice low and mournful, not sure what to expect.

Bram's gaze shifted to the ground for a moment, as if the question brought him back to something painful. Something that he had been trying to avoid.

"Meridian Locke," he said, so quiet I almost didn't catch it. "Meri was a great traveler. He lived for the adventure, for the discovery." Bram's eyes kind of glazed over, like he was replaying some old movie in his head. "He was in on the hunt for the lost treasures of the Aztecs, finding stuff that had been missing for centuries. The things he found... they were wild."

The way Bram said it, you could tell Meridian had meant a lot to him. Like, a lot. "But it wasn't just the treasure hunts. Meridian thought time travel could actually fix things. He believed you could go back and make history better. Right the wrongs."

Bram's mouth tightened, and for a second, he looked like he wanted to be anywhere else. "In the end, that's what got him in trouble. He tried to stop the Great Fires of both Rome and London. He thought that he could prevent them, save hundreds of lives. But... you can't play with time like that, not without consequences. It was his mistake—and he paid the price for it. He didn't just disappear, like so many do. The fire took him. Meridian's fate is always fire, but he will return in time."

The silence hung in the air, heavy with the weight of Meridian's absence, but it only left me with more questions.

"So umm...everyone has a... a way to die?" I asked, glancing at each of them.

Sirianna's gaze softened, and she spoke as though it were the most natural thing in the world. "Yes, dear, we all have our fatal fate, so to speak. For me, it's usually being strangled or hung by a noose, my throat crushed."

Bram added with a slight discomfort, "I fall, usually from high places. Understandably, then, I'm terrified of heights. Some of us drown, others are pierced, stabbed, or shot."

I stared at him, incredulous. "How do you know all this?"

Bram's eyes darkened as he explained, "After living so many lives, you start remembering things—especially something as traumatic as all the ways that you die."

Sirianna's gaze shifted between Bram and me, still hand in hand. She smirked, her eyes sharp.

"So, since you two are... together, let's cut to the chase. Where's the Token Continuum? It's obviously not with you, Veronica. We'd all feel it if it were."

My stomach did this weird flip. "It's safe at home. When I heard about the Ampoletta, I got here as fast as I could," I said, trying to sound steady. It sort of worked, but not really.

Sirianna threw back her head before smiling, like she knew something I didn't. "It's not safe at all unless it's with you, darling."

Bram interrupted, his voice now considerably more fervent. "She's right. Nobody's safe." He scanned across the bay front with narrowed eyes. "This fire? No accident. Dorian, or perhaps someone else from the Council."

That hit me hard; my chest constricted.

"What is it, Six?" Bram's eyes were on me now, sharp and focused.

I shook my head, and my eyes stung. "I didn't mean for this to happen," I managed, but my voice sounded all wrong. "Dorian kept asking me where the Token was, and I finally... I lied. I said it was with... with you." The words came out in pieces, and I could barely breathe.

Sirianna looked at us, still smirking. "Bram, it seems your little project wants to risk all our necks," she said, rolling her eyes.

Bram tensed forward, his fists curled. "She's not a project, Siri!"

He almost shouted it. "She has no idea what we're all facing." His words cut through all of it.

The way that he defended me? That should have helped a bit, but only made things worse.

Sirianna stepped closer, not breaking eye contact with Bram. Her smile was thin and mean.

"She doesn't know because you've kept her in the dark, keeping her insulated from the danger we're facing. And now look where we are." She paused, letting the tension hang in the air. "All of this... It's on you, too."

Bram's face turned red with anger, his fists clenched at his sides. He opened his mouth, "All of this... is about protecting Veron..." but before he could say anything more, I spoke.

"Stop," I said, my voice barely a whisper, the weight of it pressing down on me. "This is all my fault." The words spilled out of me, bitter and heavy. "The fire, the chaos, Meridian's death... everything. It's all because of me. I lied! And I've made everything worse."

"We need the token," Sirianna cut in, her voice sharp, with this weird edge, like she was already bored with the whole conversation. "Seriously, I'm dying to get out of this ancient backwater. The air here? It's like breathing disappointment."

Bram looked at me. His eyes did this thing, I don't even know what it was. But before he could say anything, I wiped my face, trying not to ugly-cry. I looked up. My voice was shaky, but I meant it: "I'll fix it. Whatever it takes. Even if it costs me everything."

Chapter Fourteen

I waited across the street, behind a tangle of bottle-brush and a sagging wooden fence, watching as Veronica's mom backed out of the driveway. She didn't even look up. Just checked her mirror, adjusted her sunglasses, and disappeared down the street, her sedan rattling and coughing, seeming as if it was tired of going anywhere. I waited until the car turned right onto A1A and vanished.

Then I crossed the street and climbed the rotting wood stairs.

The front door was old wood—cheap and stubborn, but unlocked. That made it too easy. I couldn't appreciate how natural it felt, how I barely hesitated before slipping inside.

Was this a trap?

I wasn't here for her.

I was here for *it*.

The Token.

Inside, the apartment was cooler than I expected, morning light filtering through slanted blinds and sheer curtains that did nothing to hide the dust. The place was small, lived-in. I didn't have to go far. Her room was past the kitchen at the end of a short hallway, past a faded lighthouse painting and a small bathroom with towels on the floor.

I walked softly.

Her door was open. She wasn't here. School maybe. Or at the marina—with *him*.

My jaw clenched.

Did she know about the fire?

When I reached the Ampoletta last night and realized the Token wasn't there and that she had lied to me, I had to send a message. I wanted to let them all know and feel the heat of my warning.

Her room was a mess, morning sunlight pouring in and catching on every scattered item, as if it were accusing her of being a slob. The bed was unmade, sheets twisted as if she'd wrestled sleep—clothes draped over a desk chair, sketchbooks and half-used notebooks spilling onto the floor. A makeup bag had exploded across a milk crate she used as a nightstand—lip gloss, bobby pins, a broken eyeliner pencil.

The room smelled like her: citrus shampoo, old paper, and a trace of damp mildew that clung to everything in this building.

And underneath it all, I felt it.

The Token.

That low hum. Faint. Almost shy. As if the air had a heartbeat.

I hadn't felt it on the Ampoletta.

Not even a flicker.

But now, it was here.

I followed the tug. Past her closet, past the small shelf stacked with dog-eared paperbacks and VHS tapes labeled in fading Sharpie, the pull was stronger near the bed. Beneath the window, a lazy pile of animals: a Care Bear, several My Little Ponies, and a stuffed lion with matted fur that had seen better days.

The hum sharpened.

I crouched down, fingers barely grazing the lion's mane. And just like that—it stopped. Gone. The air went flat. My heart was pounding in my ears, loud and weird. It had cloaked itself. Hidden. Because it knew. It knew I wasn't her.

My hand simply floated there, fixed on the lion's head. I didn't budge. I simply waited.

"Don't," I breathed. "Don't close me out."

NOTHING.

NO PULSE. No warmth. Just scorching, agonizing silence.

I started tearing the lion open, slowly and carefully, searching the seams and digging through the stuffing.

Nothing. No coin. No compass. No sign that anything had ever lived here besides a girl who scribbled in notebooks and left half-drunk sodas in her room.

I backed away slowly, scanning the room again. It was here. I *knew* it. But it had gone quiet, and still, the second it sensed me.

Because it had chosen her.

A sour taste crept up my throat. I crept back, fixing what I could. I straightened a few books and ensured that items were back in their proper place. One last glance—her messy bed, her life, her yellow-tinged window.

I was going to leave quietly.

But something in me snapped.

She didn't even understand what she had. She let the Token swing from her neck like a charm. And it had chosen *her*. Not me. Not the one who had studied it. Bled for it. Tortured her father for it.

I spun and ripped a stack of VHS tapes off the shelf. Plastic cases clattered to the floor. Books followed—paperbacks, journals, spiral notebooks. A stack of photos fluttered like scattered birds. I knocked over the milk crate nightstand. A hairbrush, makeup, and a radio cassette player landed with a thud, all lying on the carpet in an ugly burst.

The lion, surrounded by its stuffing, slouched against the mess. Silent. Empty.

"You don't deserve it," I muttered.

The room looked as if a storm had passed through. My chest heaved, and my lungs pulled in sharp gulps of dust and disappointment. I scanned the floor again, hoping the Token had revealed itself in the chaos.

Nothing.

Still silent.

Still mocking me.

Leaving her room in shambles, I turned toward the hallway.

Hearing the rattle of steps outside, bumping against the building. Someone was climbing the stairs.

Then—

CLICK.

THE FRONT DOOR CREAKED OPEN. Slow. Deliberate.

Footsteps. Pausing. Listening.

My heart thudded so hard it hurt. I clutched the dagger's handle under my shirt, not letting go. Ready. Ready to do it, if I had to.

A shadow slid across the floorboards.

"Hello?" A guy's voice. Kind of calm, but not totally. "Uh... exterminator? Here about the roach problem?"

I didn't answer. Not yet.

He got closer. Then this big man in saggy green coveralls showed up, dragging a wheeled canister that hissed chemicals. He stopped. Blinked at me, surprised.

"Oh—sorry," he said quickly, lifting a hand. "Mrs. Ingram said she'd leave the door unlocked. Said nobody'd be home."

I loosened my grip on the blade.

"It's fine," I said smoothly, stepping fully into his line of sight. "My mom said you'd be by. I was just leaving."

He nodded, still wary, but he bought it. I passed him and slipped out into the humid morning.

Behind me, the room remained—a ruin of paper and plastic and memory.

Would she think it was the exterminator?

Let her.

Let her wonder who—or what—had rifled through her secrets while the sun was shining.

Let her worry—

when the light is gone,

when she's alone,

when no one will hear her scream.

Chapter Fifteen

My bare feet hit each rickety step as I climbed to the front door. A yellow flyer clung to the doorknob—"Exterminator Visit" with some cartoon bug printed upside-down as if it was dead. Mom had warned me about this. The door swung open with its signature creak, but the house greeted me with unnatural silence and a sharp chemical tang that caught in my throat.

The living room felt like a stranger's as I crossed it, the morning's disaster replaying in my head: flames consuming the boat, debris scattered across dark water, someone dead because of me. My legs still trembled from pedaling so hard to reach Bram at the marina.

I FROZE at my bedroom doorway.

HALF-OPEN, it revealed chaos. My stomach clenched at the sight—books with spines cracked and pages jutting at odd angles. My milk crate nightstand lay on its side, makeup tubes rolling beneath the bed, my radio facedown on the carpet. The carefully stacked notebooks and cassette tapes had been ransacked. My childhood lion stared with cotton innards spilling from a jagged tear.

I navigated my way through the wreckage, looking at all the casualties. My clothes, which I'd left in semi-organized piles, now draped over every chair and drawer like limp rags. The blankets on my bed, rumpled in a way I'd never leave them, as if someone had patiently sat there, patiently tearing things apart with care.

A violation was what this was. My safe place, totally trashed. I could feel panic rising, prickly and hot, but then something tugged at me—a weird, familiar pull, like a thread yanking at my insides.

My eyes went to the shelf. The VHS case was still there, jammed between a couple of old, dusty tapes. I didn't even think. I just lunged for it, nearly tripping over a pile of blue jeans. My hands shook as I grabbed the case. Right away, I felt it, a faint buzz, steady as a heartbeat under my fingers—the Token. Even the air felt different now.

I popped open the case, barely breathing. The Token remained tucked inside the compass. Relief shot through me so fast I almost laughed, but the Token's pull didn't let go. It buzzed in my palm, alive. Heavy. I couldn't pretend anymore. This was real, and it was just getting started.

Whoever had been searching had come dangerously close to finding it. Was this the work of the Council of Chaos? Someone from the Chronos Collective?

I held the Token tighter, the pulse inside it growing sharper. Then I slid it into the compass and pulled the chain over my head, the weight settling at my chest.

Then it hit me: this wasn't just about time travel. It was about me, my life, and all the things I cared about, tangled up in something way bigger than I could even begin to figure out. The worst part? Besides Bram, I didn't have a clue as to who I could trust anymore.

I grabbed a couple of books off the floor and shoved them back onto the shelf. Then I heard footsteps on the stairs outside. My heart jumped as I pressed myself against the half-open door.

The door creaked, and I held still. Hoping that whoever had done this wasn't returning.

"Six? Six? Are you here?" My mom's voice echoed down the hall, louder than I expected.

RELIEF CRASHED OVER ME. I stepped into the hallway near the bathroom, trying to look normal. "I'm here, Mom."

She appeared in the kitchen doorway, eyes flicking over me, pausing on my messy hair and the wrinkled clothes I'd slept in. She looked totally thrown off, caught somewhere between worried and confused. Then her gaze shifted again, like she could sense something off in the room.

"Is someone here... with you?" Her voice was low and suspicious, like she was expecting someone to jump out from behind the fridge.

I shook my head almost too fast. "No, it's just me. I just got back from the marina." I tried to sound normal, but my voice came out shaky and weird.

She stood in the hall, staring, trying to figure out if I was lying. Her face got even more stressed, her brow wrinkled. "What was that about, Six? You can't just go running off like that without telling me. I didn't know what to do, and I had to leave for work."

Oof. That stung more than I thought it would. The way she said it—all frustrated and scared, but still trying to keep it together. My chest tightened up. She wasn't used to me sneaking out or disappearing, especially not now, and all I could feel was this huge wave of guilt.

"I'm sorry, Mom," I mumbled, her worry pressing down on me. "I just... I didn't know what else to do."

I know one of the guys aboard the boat that burned. I had to make sure he was safe. Thankfully, he was."

My mom took a few steps toward me, and for a moment, I thought she was going to pull me into a hug. But instead, she paused, her eyes shifting over my shoulder, moving past me toward my room.

"A guy? Is there a guy here right now, Six? We've talked about having boys over—"

"What? No, Mom." I cut her off, hands up, heart thumping. "He's not here. I swear."

She didn't look convinced. Her eyes slid past me, searching the hallway, and then she just marched straight into my room, like she needed proof.

She stopped in the doorway and made a face. "What on earth...what happened here, Six? This room is a disaster."

"I know," I muttered. "One of the cinder blocks slipped off the shelf, and this whole side of the room crashed. Sort of like that game, you know...Mousetrap." I shrugged, hoping she'd just let it go.

She stepped into the bathroom, peering around as if she expected to find something else. Her brow pinched, with her worry clearly growing. "Six, I got a strange call at the museum from the exterminator. He said he sprayed the place, but he didn't mean to disturb my son. I told him he must be mistaken. I have a daughter, not a son. He swore there was a boy here."

I just stood there, stuck, frozen, my heart banging around like it was trying to get out. A boy? Why would the exterminator say that? Had Dorian actually been here?

"That makes no sense, Mom," I said, but my voice sounded wobbly and thin. "There's no boy. Seriously. I've just been here. Alone."

She turned to look at me, her eyes scrunched up and kind of suspicious. She hesitated, and for a second it felt like the whole room shrank. "Then why would he say that?" she said, softer this time, like she was trying to figure out a puzzle. "And why does it feel so... weird in here?"

I wanted to say something that would make her feel better. Anything. But my mouth wouldn't work. There was no way to explain it. No way to make it seem like everything wasn't about to fall apart.

She grabbed her purse, heading for the door. "I need to get back to work. But we'll talk about this later tonight," she said, her voice firm yet tired. "And since you're not at school today, you can clean up that mess of yours," she added with a sigh.

She opened her mouth like she was about to say something else, but she didn't. The screen door clapped shut behind her, and just like that, I was alone again.

I just stood there, blinking, Mom's words still bouncing around the room. Everything felt heavier, as if the rooms were closing in or the air had become soup. The place was a total disaster. So was my life. The fire, the death, the guilt—they weren't some far-off nightmare anymore. It was all right here, breathing down my neck, making everything feel wrong.

I glanced out the window. Mom's car was already rolling away with storm clouds spinning across the sky. Then thunder gave off a low grumble, shaking the entire apartment, and gusts hurled heavy magnolia leaves against the windows. The sky looked exactly the way I felt: dark, scattered, and restless.

I COULDN'T STAY HERE. Not in this silence. Between the mess in my room and the mess in my head, I couldn't stay here. The lighthouse was calling. I could almost feel it, tugging at me. Bram and the others—I'd told them I'd meet up, and I had to face whatever this was.

But as I reached for my raincoat, doubt crashed in. What if I couldn't fix anything? What if the lighthouse just made everything worse? I didn't even know who to trust now—but sitting here, waiting, doing nothing? That was worse. If I hadn't gone, if I hadn't moved, what would have happened?

I shook my head, trying to clear out the panic. I had to decide, because I couldn't just keep hiding. I grabbed the raincoat and went for the door, heart pounding in my ears.

Lightning split the sky—a jagged white flash that lit up the apartment, just for a second, sharp and blinding, like a warning or a sign.

The thunder came right after, low and heavy, like the storm itself was answering me.

I couldn't stop now—not when everything felt so uncertain.

The lighthouse was the only place left where I might find answers. And I was going to face whatever was waiting for me, even if it meant stepping into the storm.

Chapter Sixteen

The sky got wicked dark as I pedaled down the narrow, rain-slick streets toward the lighthouse. The wind was going wild, whipping through the trees, and thunder kept rumbling in the background, dramatic as if it was trying to warn me. My breath came out in these short, panicky bursts. Every time I pushed the pedals, it was like I was forcing myself closer to whatever was waiting, to the answers I'd been practically dying to find.

The battered beacon towered in the distance, the black and white spirals cutting through the gray sky. I could feel the pull of it in my chest, the weight of everything that had led me here—everything I couldn't understand, but knew was coming for me, for all of us.

As I reached the foot of the lighthouse steps, the squall roared through the trees, as if to stop me.

My legs were already killing me from the bike ride. I needed to be here. This was the only place where things might actually make sense.

I shoved open the heavy door, hinges groaning more than the distant thunder.

The inside was way darker than I expected, but there was a low hum of voices, so I knew I wasn't the first to arrive.

Bram was the first to see me, standing in a doorway to a side room, his face creased with worry. When his eyes met mine, something in his expression softened, like he was both relieved and confused to see me standing there, soaked from the rain.

"Six," Bram said quietly, stepping forward. He looked different somehow—more serious than I remembered, but also more present. Like for once, the weight of the world wasn't between us.

Then, of course, interrupting the moment, Lyrica appeared wearing a vacant sort of grin.

She twirled into the hall as if she owned the storm itself, splashing through puddles from leaky hall windows. Then she stopped, leaning back against the brick with her arms folded, smirk already loaded.

"Well, if it isn't the anti-hero herself," she said, voice all sing-song and sharp at the same time, like a lyric that's supposed to sound sweet but doesn't. "Nice of you to join us in this cruel summer."

I attempted to speak, but my mouth just couldn't. The words got stuck in my throat and fused like snapped guitar strings. I nodded instead.

Lyrica shrugged and tipped her head back. "Don't look so surprised, Six. You knew I'd be trouble the moment I walked in."

The storm outside intensified, shaking the tower's windows.

AND THEN I saw her again. Sirianna.

She was just within the doorway, eyes sparkling with something I couldn't quite identify. She was polished, every hair in order, but she had an edge that made my skin crawl. She was lovely in an unfair way, with dark hair surrounding her face, and she stared at me with the same cold, calculating gaze as she had at first.

"Well, well," she said, silky smooth, voice honeyed but acidic below. "The prodigal daughter comes home."

I winced but didn't say anything. Couldn't let her get to me. Not now. Not with everything else happening.

"We need to talk, Six," Bram said. He sounded urgent. I nodded and stepped farther into the hall. I let the door slam shut behind me. The storm outside got louder, with a long, low rumble that made the walls shiver. For a second, it felt like the whole tower might just collapse. The air buzzed. Tense. Heavy. Waiting.

"We're not safe here. Not anymore," Bram said, his voice all gravel and on edge. He glanced at Sirianna, then at me. "Not with what's coming."

"Not with him coming," Sirianna said. Barely a whisper, but it sliced right through the room.

My heart thudded. I took a step closer and finally asked the question I'd been avoiding. "Who?"

Sirianna smiled—a slow, cold smile, the kind that never reaches your eyes. "Dorian."

The name hit me like a slap. But there was no time to process it.

"The Token isn't safe anymore, Six," said Bram. His tone remained firm, but below it lay panic. "Dorian and the Council know about it. They will come for it. And we don't have a lot of time."

His words hit me like a heavyweight in my heart. The raging thunderstorm outside didn't hold a candle to what I was experiencing within. But there was nowhere for uncertainty, nowhere for doubts. All I had left was the lighthouse—the only spot where I could begin to make any sort of sense of it all.

I straightened, meeting Bram's eyes, trying to sound braver than I felt. "Then we fight."

Sirianna's laugh rang out, sharp and bright, echoing off the brick walls.

"Fight?" she repeated, mocking, like I was a little kid. "Dear child…"

She stepped closer,

"You are *nowhere* near ready for any such conflict."

Moving even closer, the air around her seemed to grow colder as she closed the distance between us. Her dark eyes glinted with something almost predatory, a smirk playing at the corners of her lips.

"Bram, where does she get this... aggression?" She said it with a little eye roll, barely glancing at him before zeroing in on me, all squinty and mean. "You told me she was a timid girl." Like it was a disease or something, the way she said it. My fists curled up so tight my knuckles hurt, and I could feel my whole body stiffen. But I didn't budge. No way was I giving her the satisfaction.

I made myself stand up straighter, even though my whole insides felt like they were about to melt. "I'm not timid anymore," I said. My voice came out calm, but there was this edge in it I didn't even know I had.

Sirianna's face curled up into a grin, but it was all an act. "We'll see about that, won't we?" She spoke slow and icy cold, like she was challenging me. The way she glared, it felt like she was deciding on just where she could poke me and make me jump. I didn't budge. I just stared back at her, and it seemed like time went on and on and on. My chest got tight and I grabbed for the chain around my neck, but it was too late—it didn't feel right, not now. She flicked her eyes at Bram for half a second, like she was making some calculation, then looked back at me with this icy, smug look.

"How cute," she said, practically purring, but every word was dipped in sarcasm. "You think you can protect it, don't you?"

Before I could react, one of her henchmen—tall, broad-shouldered, and looming—shifted his weight closer, blocking my escape. I swallowed hard, trying not to show the panic rising in my throat. I could feel my pulse thudding in my ears, like a countdown to disaster.

Sirianna reached forward, her fingers brushing the edges of my raincoat as if she had all the time in the world. Then in one fluid motion, she tugged at it, pulling it open, sending a shiver down my spine. The rain-chilled air kissed my skin, and I felt the sharp pull of fear clench my gut.

Her fingers shot out, and before I could even step back, she yanked the compass off the chain with surprising strength. I gasped, the weight of the token gone from my chest in an instant. The chain links of the compass had dug into the back of my neck. The token—a weighty part of me—was gone.

I barely registered what had happened until I looked down and saw her pull it from the compass, turning it between her fingers with an almost affectionate reverence. She dropped the compass to the floor. The token's gold color seemed to shimmer under her touch, as if they recognized something dark in her.

"You think this is yours?" Sirianna's voice cut through the silence, low and mocking. "So many have died for this; most recently, Meridian, and your father has most likely been tortured for this," she said softly, her voice tinged with something almost reverent, her gaze briefly meeting Bram's. She nodded to him, and a flicker of something unspoken passed between them.

My stomach churned at the mention of Meridian's name and then my father, but I couldn't look away as she slipped the token into the pocket of her cloak.

I tried to move, to stop her, but one of her bearded henchmen stepped up, blocking me with his massive frame. Just the way he stood there was enough to make my skin crawl; the quiet threat of it pressed in, heavy, and suddenly my arms and legs felt like they were full of sand. Like my body already knew I'd lost.

Bram opened his mouth, but before he could say anything, the noise outside got even louder, with the storm pounding at the walls. I glanced at him, hoping for something, anything, a word, a sign that he'd do something—but he just stood there, eyes narrowed. He knew it too: that there was no way out.

The rage outside hit its peak as Sirianna stepped back, moving with this strange, sharp grace.

"We're done here," she said, and there was no arguing with the way she said it.

Bram's jaw clenched. He looked at me, then quickly away, like he'd caught me crying or something. I didn't want him to see how shaky I felt, so I stared at the floor, arms wrapped tight around myself. The token was gone, just gone. One of the only things I cared about, an object that made me feel real and solid in the world, was taken, and all I had left was this wild, sick feeling in my stomach, like I was about to drop off the edge of something huge.

For a second, nobody said anything. Bram's eyes bounced between me and her, like he was waiting for someone to fix it. Finally, he looked right at me, steady, like he was trying to anchor both of us. "Six, they need the token. It's the only way to transport everyone—to another time, another lighthouse."

Thunder roared, making the whole tower tremble. Deafening, as if the sky was yelling at us. The sound bounced around the hall for seconds.

Then Lyrica whirled around, her pixie voice more assertive than the storm. "The token," she said, throwing her arms wide as though she stood on stage. "Another boy thinking that something shiny will mend what's been broken."

She looked at me then, her sharp smile.

"Let me guess, Six. You're still hoping this is your love story, but what if the prince has already left the building?" Lightning flashed outside, splattering her face in a silvery glow. She just rolled her eyes and started backing toward the stairs. "But fine," she said, kind of bored, "we're only borrowing the little magic coin, so just shake it off."

I just stared at her, not sure if I was supposed to be mad or what. "What are you even talking about?" My voice sounded all shaky. "Do you ever stop with the riddles and just say something normal for once?"

She tilted her head, eyes burning through me like a hook in the bridge of a song.

"Normal is overrated. I was forged by reputation, lost in evermore, wearing a crown of folklore."

Bram cut in then, voice low and steady but sharp. "Enough, Lyrica, none of this is helping."

Lyrica gave him a slow, deliberate bow, the sound of the downpour falling around her like applause.

"Sorry, Bram. This is me trying," she quipped.

Sirianna's gaze lingered on me and Lyrica for a moment longer, her eyes calculating before she turned sharply, striding toward the stone steps. Her henchmen and Lyrica followed as they ascended the remaining steps of granite.

Bram and I exchanged a brief, loaded glance before following her. The weight of the token was still fresh in my mind, its absence pressing down on me. And as we ascended the steps, the tempest seemed to sound more fierce, inside the bottom of the hollow tower.

Sirianna paused at the base of the black iron steps, her eyes flicking between Bram and me with a cool, assessing gaze. "Wait here," she said, her voice low but sharp, carrying an unmistakable edge. "You'll have to trust me, though I'm sure you don't have much choice. Once we're within the lens and we begin to cross over to the Pharos, the token will come back to you."

She just dropped that on me like it was nothing, but the words hit me like a brick. I felt them hit and then sink low under my ribs. I looked at Bram, hoping he'd have some sort of soothing look or insider grin, but all I got from him was this little nod. Not exactly confidence-building. My stomach knotted up further.

Up ahead, Sirianna and her goons started climbing the steps. Their boots echoed off the iron, bouncing around the tower. I couldn't stop staring at them as they got farther away, leaving me and Bram in this weird, echoey silence. Just us, the wind, and my nerves jumping everywhere.

I swallowed. "What is... the Pharos?" It came out in a small voice as if I feared the walls might hear.

His face relaxed. He got up and pulled me into his arms, his hand wrapped securely around mine, his touch hot and solid. "The Pharos of Alexandria," he said confidentially. "The tallest lighthouse in the world back in ancient times. Doesn't exist anymore. For the Collective, it's sort of a haven. We go there to reorganize, or hide out, plan, sort things out."

I tried to take it in, but it slid away like trying to remember a dream. The wind outside kept pounding at the tower, rocking the walls as if it wanted to come inside.

Bram brought me back to the stone steps. We sat side by side on them, listening to the storm.

The thin hallway lay before us as the darkness gathered behind, consuming the space we'd abandoned. The tension between us felt weighted down by unspoken words. I needed to question him further—about the Council, about the token, about what was being done with us—but I couldn't, so I sat there under the protection of the storm.

As it raged outside, an odd feeling pulled at my chest. It began as a whisper, a gentle thread tugging at me from somewhere deep within. The tension built, turning cold and tight, until I felt something inside me begin to rip away.

The emptiness spread through my body like ice, leaving me numb.

I could barely breathe. The question sat in my chest like a brick. I tried to ignore it. I really did. But I couldn't, not after what Sirianna said. I pressed my lips together, but they were quivering, and finally the words just blurted out, all tangled. "Is it true... what she said, about my father?"

I wasn't sure I wanted the answer, but I couldn't pretend I didn't care. Not anymore.

Bram reached for me. His hand was warm on my cheek, which was unusual because I felt cold all over, as if my insides had turned to ice. His fingers brushed away a tear—I hadn't even noticed I was crying. He looked at me, and I couldn't tell if it was regret or just regular old pity, but either way, it didn't help.

"I don't know, Veronica," he said, and his voice was soft, but it sort of wobbled. "It's very possible."

Those seven words just sat there, like a spider in the middle of the room. My stomach twisted. I could tell Bram didn't want to say it, didn't want to believe it, but I could feel it in my bones: this wasn't just some random maybe. It was real, and it hurt.

I squeezed Bram's hand, probably too tight, but it didn't make me feel any less alone. The token wasn't just leaving—I could feel it slipping away, not just from my hand, but from somewhere deeper, too.

A pull, a shift.

Bram's grip tightened around my hand as he must have felt it too, his eyes scanning my face as if to check for the same panic he saw in my eyes.

"The token will come back, Six," he said, but his voice was soft, like he wasn't quite sure, "We'll get it back."

But I could already feel it - this weird, magnetic pull. It felt like the token and I were being pulled increasingly far apart with each step that Sirianna took. Something ancient and macabre awakened in the air of the tower, all at once colder and thinner. Thunder slapped the sky and rain blasted at the bricks, as if it was telling us we didn't belong. The gusts grew almost shrill, and somewhere beneath it all, beneath the storm and the pressure in my chest, I thought I heard a whisper.

Not in my ears.

In my bones.

Chapter Seventeen

Asudden jolt rocked the entire lighthouse, as if the earth itself had cracked open beneath it. Then a deafening roar thundered through the tower, like lightning had struck its heart. Rings of electric blue light, wreathed in swirling fog, spiraled down the interior like ghostly smoke rings. One by one, they sank into the marble tiles and vanished into the brick walls. Then, with a scream of light, a brilliant blue beam shot down the center of the tower like a rocket from another world. The Token Continuum plunged into the center circular pit—only to rebound and land neatly into my outstretched hand. My ears still ringing from the thunderous crash, I heard Bram next to me let out a yelp, before colliding into me with a joyful embrace.

We both held on to each other tightly and looked down at the Token Continuum together, pulsating in my palm, until we heard the door of the lighthouse open from down the hall.

"I KNEW IT," a voice boomed out, all gruff and bossy, like he'd been waiting to bust someone. "You kids shouldn't be in here! I know exactly what you two are up to!"

The shadow got closer, and then you could see him—a guy, old, maybe sixty or something, with denim pants that were stone-washed, as in actually washed with stones. Leather boots so worn they looked like artifacts, and this stained, faded white button-down that might have been new in the 1930s. Suspenders stretched over his shoulders, hauling his pants way up. And the cap on his head? Heavy, old, tilted just right to make him look even more like he was in charge.

A cloud of pipe tobacco smoke followed him up the narrow stone steps, a trail thick and pungent, filling the air with a scent as old as the lighthouse itself. Smoke twisted through the damp air of the tower, curling as if it had spent years trying to escape.

"This ain't no juice joint now," he said with a voice that cracked like a whip, the gravel in his tone unmistakable. "This here is government property, and you two are trespassers."

He reached the top of the steps with surprising ease for a man his age, his boots clomping against the stone as he made his way to the lighthouse rotunda. He stopped in front of us, planting his feet firmly as he assessed the situation with a look of both confusion and annoyance.

His eyes scanned me from head to toe, pausing at my bare legs, and his focus lingered on the yellow raincoat I wore. His gaze softened only for a moment before his mouth twisted into a scowl.

"Listen here, lil' flapper, with those gams," he said, his voice dripping with condescension. "I'm the big cheese here. And both of you need to git, there are no tours now."

He shook his head, his eyes narrowing in disbelief as he sized us up, clearly unimpressed by our presence. I could tell he was more annoyed by our intrusion than anything else, with the slow, deliberate pace of someone who had spent decades telling people when tours began.

Bram and I shuffled to the far side of the tower, away from him, but I couldn't help but notice the glint of his newsboy-style cap as he neared. It bore the brass lighthouse insignia, a symbol of authority; it all seemed oddly old-fashioned, as if he had wandered out of a time long past.

Bram's eyebrows shot up, like he couldn't quite believe what he was seeing. "What year is it?" he asked, and I could tell he already sort of knew, but wanted to hear it anyway.

The old man's eyes went wide, as though the question itself was offensive. "Lord, have mercy on these two saps! 1922! Don't you know anything?" He all but growled it, each word laced with annoyance.

I looked at Bram, and my heart skipped. 1922? This couldn't be. This didn't make any sense. Had we somehow just departed from my current time?

"We're sorry, sir," Bram said after a beat, his tone now more respectful, trying to make amends. "So, when can we visit the lighthouse?"

The man grumbled, clearly tired of his job, his patience worn thin. "After lunchtime, so 1 p.m. The hours are posted on the door," he said, his tone sputtering with irritation. "I'm so tired of chasing trespassing tourists around."

Bram and I exchanged a glance, a mix of disbelief and confusion clouding our faces.

We left the lighthouse as the man turned to descend the stone steps, following us and muttering under his breath.

THE SUN BROKE through the clouds. Everything around us still shimmered, like the storm had left a wet shine all over. It was supposed to be back to normal, but everything felt odd and charged. Did we fall into some other time zone? A place that was not actually ours? That notion just hung around, heavy and frigid. Even the air seemed stretched out, warped, as if it was trying to remember how to be regular again.

Everything looked the same, but I sensed it all was completely different. I turned, my gaze snapping to the house.

The keeper's house stood there, exactly as it had when I first walked into the lighthouse. Charred patches still marked the building. In other areas, new raw lumber had been nailed into place, the raw wood stark against the remnants of blackened beams, all signs of the ongoing restoration.

We stood at the brick gate, the air heavy with tension, and watched the keeper. He climbed the stairs up to the porch.

He reached the door. Turned the knob like he'd done it a thousand times before. My stomach twisted. He pushed the door open and went inside, gone in a blink, like he'd slipped into another world.

Bram just stood there, next to me, not moving, staring at the empty spot where the keeper had vanished. His face was pale, lips pressed tight. Then, all at once, he turned to me, eyes wide, like he'd finally figured something out.

"Six, I think we're back to 1985. He believes he's in 1922, but he's actually in 1985!"

His voice was all freaked out, like shock and disbelief and something else, too—a little bit scared. I'd never seen him like that. You could tell, just by looking at his eyes, he knew something was seriously wrong.

"This... this is bad. This shouldn't be happening." He just stood there, and the words sort of hung there, heavy and weird and impossible.

My heart was pounding. The lighthouse, the keeper, the place that was supposed to be normal, had just turned into some kind of nightmare.

We were no longer part of the story we had thought we understood. Time was a tangle, or a rip, or a wrinkle, or something that Bram seemed to know nothing about.

We hadn't traveled through time; the keeper had somehow *fallen* into it, stuck in a time that didn't belong to him anymore, in a place where nothing was certain.

Chapter Eighteen

The best way to describe downtown St. Augustine after Bram and I left the lighthouse, walking over a mile back to the downtown area: Total chaos.

AS WE WERE CROSSING the Bridge of Lions, there was an electricity in the air that suggested that things were off. Way, way off.

Bram and I stand in the shade of an oversized palmetto, looking out over the Plaza de la Constitución, which looks surreal. Several groups crowd the square—townspeople, tourists, and others who don't belong at all. We watch conquistadors on sweating horses, their armor dulled and dented. Victorian women in lace gloves and parasols clutch their pearls next to a group of Black men and women in shackles. Just yards away, another group of African soldiers in regal, faded uniforms stands frozen, their expressions stoic and searching. A half-dozen Native Americans—each dressed differently, as if pulled from separate tribes and centuries—linger near the statue of Ponce de León. Redcoats argue with Spanish soldiers. A boy in a Duran Duran t-shirt takes a photo with a Kodak camera, as if it's all just one big street performance.

But no one's acting.

Everyone is disoriented, animated, and dazed, except maybe the horses.

I watch, keeping both hands around the Token Continuum. "Please tell me you're seeing all of this, too," I whisper to Bram.

"See it? Not only that, I smell it. I hear it. I could probably taste it if I kept my mouth open," he whispers back. "The air smells of body odor, gunpowder, citrus, and strangely, like fried shrimp, with a touch of horse manure."

The wind shifts. He's not wrong.

We edge into the disorder, careful not to make eye contact with anyone. "Bram, what the hell is going on?" I ask, trying to keep up as he weaves through the crowd like he's done this a hundred times before. "Did we break time? Is this our fault?"

All around us, people are talking in a mess of languages—Spanish, English, something that might be French, Italian, and maybe even strong Irish. Everyone's confused, but they're all acting like they belong. The conquistadors are arguing with French sailors. A Victorian woman with a parasol is side-eyeing a guy in a neon tracksuit.

Bram finally backs away, shaking his head. "We need to get to the marina," he mutters, as if that'll somehow make everything better.

We start walking in that direction, but it's hard to move fast when you're dodging a military jeep packed with Coast Guardsmen. They're hanging out the sides of the jeep wildly like it's their personal parade float, whistling at every lady they pass. One of them starts serenading a group of Victorian women with a song that makes me cringe.

Then, the strange belch of an antique horn shatters the air. We both turn in time to watch a very old Model T honk its way toward the statue of Ponce de Leon. The honk is so loud and ridiculous, it actually spooks the group of Indians standing nearby. They jump back, screaming war chants like maybe they're about to charge. They don't have any weapons, but I can't help but notice that some of them are in leg irons, which is not reassuring.

We continue, trying to ignore the chaos, but it all feels so bizarre; the entire history of St. Augustine has decided to meet in this square and hang out for a while.

We finally reach Bram's moped, but then we are stopped by a group of men sporting wide, curly mustaches, all dressed in old-fashioned one-piece bathing suits. They look as if they've just stepped off the set of a black-and-white silent film. One of them, squinting at the sun, asks, "Hey, you two—where's Capo's bathhouse? We're looking for a proper soak."

I glance at Bram, unsure whether to answer them or run, but before I can say anything, he's already fiddling with the moped, trying to get it started. He mutters under his breath as he pedals, and then, with a sudden burst of motion, it roars to life.

"Hop on," he yells, already straddling the moped. "There's no way I'm traveling through this circus on foot. You think I'm hanging with these guys?" He gestures toward the bathing-suit-clad men, who are still waiting expectantly for an answer about the bathhouse.

I roll my eyes, but grab onto his shoulders at first, then wrap my arms around him. At this point, getting on a moped is probably the sanest option in the middle of all this madness.

BRAM SWERVES US ONTO A1A, the moped sputtering as it picks up speed. The breeze hits my face in salty gusts, carrying the briny tang of the Matanzas River mixed with something earthier.

As we ride past the Castillo de San Marcos, I catch sight of cows —actual cows—eating grass on a hill near the seawall as if it's just another day. Their blank stares follow us as we zip past, their hooves kicking up clumps of turf. Just beyond them, a cluster of women in bonnets and hoop skirts is shrieking at a line of grim-looking Union soldiers. The soldiers stand still, rifles shouldered, looking confused and offended.

Further up the road, a wagon train of horse-drawn carts rattles by in the opposite direction.

These carts have wooden wheels that clickety-clack and produce an ear-piercingly awful, squeaky sound whenever they encounter a bump, and they are piled high with oranges. It really does smell good for half a second, nice and citrusy and sweet, but then, whoa: something totally worse, like horse droppings, the smell just smacks you in the face. No kidding—it's so pungent, my eyes water. It's not some lame history fair. This is the real thing, and yeah, it smells way too real.

By the time we actually get down to the base of the Great Cross, things are in complete chaos. Priests are running back and forth, waving their arms and yelling, but confusion is everywhere. Some wear scratchy brown robes, while others have silk cloaks and puffy shirts, carrying various religious symbols for rituals. They're all bellowing orders at individuals, but no one knows what to do.

They shout in multiple languages, gesturing wildly as they try to corral a crowd that includes bewildered tourists, curious locals, and a handful of Indigenous people in ceremonial dress. No one seems to know who's in charge.

BRAM SLOWS as we maneuver through the crowd. I lean forward and point. "There... those guys."

A group of Black men in worn-out, faded militia uniforms is marching single-file along the shoulder of the road, steady and proud. Their boots hit the pavement with a rhythm that cuts through the noise. Bram calls out, "Where are you coming from?"

One of the men glances our way. "Fort Mose," he says, his voice rough but steady as he points north. His eyes linger on the moped with a frown, as if it might be dangerous, or sacred, or both.

Others glance at us too, their expressions unreadable, but their pace never slows, as we leave them behind in a haze of dust and history.

We pass a group of pirates arguing with a Spanish officer in a ruffled uniform. The officer is holding an actual cutlass and swearing, screaming something about the garrison's missing payroll.

BRAM CRUISES into an area called Lincolnville, where, at the corner of Central Avenue, we notice a group of black children marching down Bridge Street, holding hand-painted signs. Behind them, walking steadily, is Martin Luther King Jr., arms swinging in time with their steps. His presence is magnetic, calm, and strong.

In a single file line, the children chant, with their voices rising: "We want justice! We want freedom!"

People on the sidewalk watch, some clapping, others sneering. The time-bending weirdness continues, but this moment feels solid, grounded, and important.

King notices us. His gaze lands on the moped, then shifts to the Token Continuum clutched in my hand.

"Travelers from every dimension will see us," he says simply, his voice rich and steady. Not a question. A statement.

I nod, awestruck, almost speechless.

"Remember this," he says, slowing as the children move ahead. "Time doesn't just pass—it leaves footprints. Where you walk matters."

I want to say something profound. I really do. But all I manage is, "Yes, sir."

King smiles gently. "Then travel with purpose."

The march continues, disappearing around the corner.

Bram exhales. "Well, I did not expect that."

We both stand straddling the moped, stunned into silence, when a voice calls from the corner.

"Hey there, kids. You look like you've seen a ghost."

A woman in a stylish but simple 1930s dress steps forward, her eyes sharp and curious. She has a notebook in one hand and a cigarette holder in the other. Marjorie Kinnan Rawlings?

"Wait... you're—" I start.

"Yes," she interrupts, with a dry chuckle. "Marjorie. Don't worry, I'm aware."

From the opposite side, another woman walks across, her stride purposeful, her smile quiet and knowing.

"And I see that someone has brought us here together again," says Zora Neale Hurston. Looking so stylish, regal, and confident in her feathery, wide-brimmed hat.

She meets my gaze, and I feel a strange shiver run down my spine.

"Time is messy, honey," she says. "People think it's a straight line, but it's more like a rugged old quilt. Threads, scraps, memories... all stitched together by a hand we'll never see."

Marjorie nodded, slow and serious. "That's right, Zora. And it was once our time to write about all of it."

"Yeah," Zora said. "This moment won't last. You're at a crossroads, child. Best choose your path. You'd best choose your path."

Outside, the air was different now. The chanting had faded out, and in its place, a wild jumble of voices from different centuries started up again. The Token vibrated in my hands, getting warmer, almost hot.

"Thank you, ladies," I said, and nodded as they walked off together.

I turned to Bram. "We have to figure this mess out."

He nods, jaw tight. "There's one more place I want to check. It's between the lions."

"The bridge again?" I ask impatiently.

"Not exactly," he says as we move together on the moped, Bram pedaling it to life. I glance over my shoulder one last time. Zora is waving—Marjorie's scribbling in her notebook. I wave to them both.

THE WORLD BEGINS to blur again, timelines bleeding together. And I think about how my dad would probably enjoy all this. In the city he loves so much. I also realize this isn't just about finding my dad anymore. This is bigger.

Way bigger.

We travel past the Plaza again, where things are only getting louder and more chaotic for everyone, especially the refugees from every era of St. Augustine. A group of wretched souls steps into the street, causing Bram to slow his moped. Their clothes hang in tatters, their faces gaunt from sickness and hunger. Their words carry tones of the Mediterranean, mixtures of Spanish, Greek, and Italian accents, softened by years of hardship and brutality. They explain to anyone listening that they have walked all the way from a failed indigo colony in New Smyrna to the south. Now, they plead for a meeting with British Governor Tonyn.

Meanwhile, several police cars from various eras are now present, but the police seem just as confused as everyone else. Bram turns and looks at me with a wide grin as we zip past the movie theater. On the marquee is a movie I've never heard of: *Back to the Future.*

WE TURN DOWN KING STREET, the wide avenue stretching out in front of the old Ponce de Leon Hotel, which is now *Flagler College.* Bram pulls the moped up to the wide sidewalk outside the main entrance. I hop off, staring at the magnificent courtyard past the tall iron portcullis that stands between two carved lion heads with manes of shadow and terra cotta. Beyond the gate lies the court-yard, featuring more intricate carved stonework and tiled twin towers that gleam in the sun. The air is peaceful here, with the relaxing sound of the frog fountain, and the grand building itself seems to be holding its breath.

We walk past the heavy wooden doors and step into the grand rotunda. And there, standing beneath the magnificent dome, is the college's namesake, Henry Flagler himself, wealthy oil baron, railroad tycoon, and Florida developer. No mistaking him, dark suit, impeccable mustache, and that kind of self-satisfied poise that says, I built an empire, I built so much of this town, this hotel, and you're standing in the heart of it.

He turns toward us, his eyes curious. "You're not guests, are you? No one dressed the way you are can be coming in here for tea."

Bram clears his throat. "No, sir, we're just passing through. Sort of a... historical malfunction."

Henry raises a single brow, amused but not entirely surprised, before he strolls off towards a parlor.

But I'm surprised, and not just by Henry Flagler's poise. The octagonal dome overhead, made of dark wood and featuring painted plaster frescoes, shimmers in a bright, golden glow. Below the rotunda, standing gracefully on the broad stairs in front of us, are eight stunning figures; muses, or goddesses, maybe both, each draped in very sheer, flowing fabric that clings like mist to their statuesque forms. Their outfits are unmistakably Greek, and their presence is otherworldly.

I freeze, barely breathing, watching the group closely, there's *Fire*, *Air*, *Water*, and *Earth*, each emanating a distinct energy: *Fire's* wild red curls and fierce eyes; *Air's* silver-white robes floating as if in a breeze; *Water's* dark blue skin shimmering with droplets; and *Earth*, dark complected, cloaked in green, solid and maternal.

Above them, on the upper step, are their counterparts. *Discovery*, draped in blue with windblown hair, clutching a globe; *Adventure*, wild-eyed and armored, holding a sword; *Conquest*, tall, wearing scarlet, with a breastplate of chain mail; and *Civilization*, poised and regal, clad in white, holding the book of knowledge in one arm.

They sing—not like a choir, but like wind across ancient stones, a melodic weave of tones and echoes in a language I can't begin to understand. It wraps around the rotunda as a living thing, brushing against my skin, nestling in my chest.

Bram, of course, notices them too. His eyes widen in awe, and maybe a little bit of something else. The goddesses are luminous, some bare-chested, wearing sheer gowns, their bodies carved from myth, their beauty both inviting and unearthly. He's staring a little too long, jaw slack, eyebrows raised.

"Bram, maybe we should… uh… move on," I whisper, trying—and failing—not to sound irritated. Heat floods my cheeks.

But he doesn't budge. He holds up a hand, not rudely, but reverently. "Shhhhhh."

I let out a sigh, but then I catch the way his expression changes. It isn't just that look boys get when they see something alluring—it's more complicated. He tilts his head, squinting a little, like he's trying to see something, although not much is hidden.

"They're not just making noise," he says, and his voice sounds sort of dreamy, like he's half here and half somewhere else. "It's… an invocation. A song of time."

I blink at him. "What does that even mean?"

He shuts his eyes, like he's listening for something. "Each one sings a verse. It's like their own domain. *Fire* sings of transformation and destruction, how all things must burn to become new. *Air* chants of breath, of thought and freedom—of voices rising in rebellion. *Water* mourns and celebrates the endless flow—tears and oceans, loss and rebirth. Earth hums of memory, of roots that dig deep into the past and refuse to let go."

He gestures upward. "And then come the others. Discovery sings of the courage to question. Adventure is the thrill of stepping into the unknown. Conquest's voice is heavy, full of ambition and sorrow. And Civilization, her verse is about structure. The stories we build, the monuments we raise, the price of order."

As the song crescendos, I feel it through my bones.

Bram opens his eyes, glassy with awe. "It's a warning, I think. That all of this... What we're finding, the chaos outside... It's a ripple in the fabric of time. And all these muses seem to be stitching it together, or trying to."

I glance back at the women—no, the forces.

Their mouths move together, totally synced up, eyes glued to something way past where we're standing. For the first time since all this started, I get this chill—and it's not fear, not even close. It's, like, awe or wonder.

"Six, give me the Token," Bram says. His voice is sharp, really urgent, and he doesn't even blink. He's just staring at the goddesses.

I don't argue. The way he says it, it cuts right through all the music and strangeness. I shove the Token at him. He takes it and instantly, he's backing away from the stairs, still locked in on the muses, like he's forgotten anything else exists.

The singing shifts. It is unified and much louder. The air around us pulses with ancient power, a storm of voices summoning something I don't understand. Their harmony is too perfect, too inhuman —my skin prickles.

Then I see her—*Conquest*, eyes like blue steel on fire. She turns her gaze straight to Bram. Flashes a smile that says it all.

Forget mythic reverence. *Conquest.* Of course, she would be the flirtatious little temptress.

"Are you serious right now?" I hiss, but Bram doesn't respond. His focus is absolute.

The chant reaches a fever pitch, and then—

SILENCE. No fade, no echo. Just an instant, absolute stop.

IN THAT BREATHLESS MOMENT, Bram hurls the Token downward with all his strength, slamming it into the very heart of the rotunda. It hits the marble tiles with a thunderous sound, a sharp *crack* that splits the stillness. For half a second, nothing happens.

Then it bounces—impossibly high—spinning like a coin in slow motion.

It seems to quietly detonate.

Light. Blinding, searing, holy light bursts outward from the Token, a radiant explosion of energy that surges through the room as a living force. A force hurls me backward, driving the air from my lungs as I slam into the cold marble, grunting on impact.

Bram is on the ground too, a few feet away, one hand up, trying to shield him from whatever this is. But it's not fire or wind—it's purer than that. It's as if a star is swallowing us.

White light floods my vision, blinding me completely. No shadows. No edges. Just pure, featureless brilliance stretching in every direction.

And then—

Silence.

I'M NOT sure how long I've been lying there. Seconds? Hours? Time feels shattered; the Token's explosion didn't just blind us, but shattered the very idea of now.

Then I feel it, a hum in my chest, a whisper brushing inside me. The Token, lying in the middle of the floor, is calling.

I push myself up on shaking arms, my vision swimming with afterimages and rings of light. Bram's somewhere in the glow, and I squint until the world begins to settle. I crawl to the center of the floor and pick up the Token as a voice cuts through, casual, almost bored.

"What exactly are you two doing on the floor?"

A college security guard stands in the archway as if he's walked into a routine scene. As if the last few minutes—the chanting, the sirens, the explosion of light—never even happened.

Bram doesn't miss a beat. "We were examining the mosaic. I think we noticed a flaw."

The guard raises an eyebrow, half amused, half suspicious.

"Yep, right here," Bram says, crouching beside the edge of one of many circular designs. He taps the spot. "There's a missing triangle tile. See? The whole pattern is perfect everywhere else, except for this one piece."

"Huh," the guard mutters, leaning in. "You don't say."

We leave him squinting at the floor like it might reveal something, and step back out into the sunlit courtyard. Downtown St. Augustine moves along again, like any ordinary afternoon.

But I know better.

Everything looks the same.

But nothing is.

Chapter Nineteen

We don't say much as we leave Flagler College behind, the echo of the goddesses' voices still trailing me like smoke. Bram walks beside me, pushing the moped down King Street past the wax museum. The sun's out now—bright, hot, indifferent. People pass us, still confused about what had transpired earlier.

We cross past the white marble lions at the foot of the bridge. Their frozen stares watch everything but tell no one.

The tent from last night's fire is gone. There is no police tape, no forensics, and no reporters. The remains of the Ampoletta still float near the marina dock, its blackened hull smudging the water like an old bruise.

But not one remnant exists from the past hour or so.

Not a single sword.

Not an iron shackle.

Not a headpiece, a feather, or a ripe orange.

Not even horse manure or its smell has been left behind.

The marquee on the movie theater now reads: *Desperately Seeking Susan.*

WE SETTLE on a concrete bench overlooking the bay at the seawall. I keep the Token tucked in my palm, warm and steady, like it knows we're getting close to something.

"Bram," I said finally, my voice low, because the quiet felt like it might shatter if I spoke too loudly. "What did they say? What were they singing?"

He just stared out across the water towards the lighthouse.

"Bram," I call out pleadingly.

"I'm not sure I wanted to hear it," he said finally, voice thin.

The answer sent a ripple of dread through me. "What does that mean? What did they say?"

A soft wind swept off the water, lifting my hair as Bram turned toward me. I could see his face now in the spill of sunlight, with shadows under his eyes and a strain around his mouth. He looked older than he had an hour ago, worn down in a way I'd never seen before. "It was... voices, layered over each other. Chanting like they'd been waiting for me to listen."

He paused, drawing a sharp breath.

"They said someone close to you is in danger. Someone who matters. Someone who might not survive what's coming if we don't act fast."

I felt the ground tilt under me. "You think they meant my dad?"

Bram hesitated—too long—and my stomach dropped. He was choosing his words carefully, and that scared me more than if he'd just said yes or no.

"I don't know. It was just, like, a vague warning," he said, his voice sort of drifting off, almost lost in the breeze. "They didn't give a name. But they were clear about one thing: this person's a target. Something bad will happen."

I watched him, the way his shoulders tensed up, and how he wouldn't meet my eyes. Suddenly, it hit me. Cold, sharp. "Bram... wait, you don't think it's you, do you?"

He blinked, almost like I'd surprised him, then turned away fast, staring at the stone lions instead of me.

"No," he said, and it was too fast, too practiced. Then, softer:

"I don't know." The thought of him being the one the muses had warned about punched a hole right through me. Bram was the one person I now trusted when everything else in my life was unraveling. The idea that I could lose him—that whoever was out there could take him from me—was too big to process.

"It could be you?" I whispered, voice breaking. "It could be you, Bram."

He dragged a hand through his hair, frustrated and raw. "Or your mom. Or your dad. Or anyone else the Council or the Collective could use to hurt you," he said. "Six, this isn't just the Council of Chaos anymore.

There's someone in the midst of all of this. Someone powerful who has the capability of keeping everyone on either end guessing. The muses claimed they've been shifting pieces around forever. Observing. Waiting to make their move."

THE BRIDGE MIRRORED across the bay, broken up and dispersed across the water, like pieces of glass. I looked at it and considered how quickly things could shatter, how delicate everything was, and how fragile everything felt.

"The muses said something else," Bram went on, his voice rough now. "They say you stand at the center of it—that only you can stop the Council and the Collective from tearing each other apart. That you're the one chosen to change everything."

The word just sat there, heavy as a rock. "Chosen," I said again, and it sounded so pathetic I hated myself for it. "I don't want that. I don't want any of this. I just want my father."

He nodded like he got it, stepped in closer, and his eyes caught mine. "Yeah, I know. But pretending you're not part of it? That's over. They spelled it out, and you have to choose Six. And whatever you pick, that's what decides who gains and who loses."

I shook my head hard. "I'm not some leader, Bram. I'm not a

weapon. I don't even know which way is up half the time. I don't know anything about all this. I just..." My voice cracked. "I just want the people I love to be safe. That's it. That's all I want."

He reached out then, fingers brushing mine, hesitant and brief but enough to make my breath catch. "I know," he said softly. "You have a lot to learn. But if we ignore this, if we keep hoping it'll go away... someone close to you is going to pay the price. And maybe all of us will."

I stared at him, at the tired lines around his mouth and the bruised look in his eyes, and something inside me twisted. If the muses had meant him, if he was the one they'd been warning me about, I didn't think I could handle it.

An idea occurred to me, "If we could use the token to reach Lucian, why not use it to reach my father?"

"It's not that simple," Bram answered. "I knew where Lucian was, and more importantly, I knew when Lucian was."

The wind gusted suddenly, carrying the brine of the bay. I thought of my mom at home, my dad lost somewhere in the unknown, and Bram standing here in front of me with his voice shaking. Which one did the muses mean?

"How do we stop it?" I asked finally. My voice came out thinner than I'd meant, threaded with fear.

Bram closed his eyes for a beat, as if steadying himself, and when he opened them, I saw the truth there: he didn't have a plan. He was just as lost as I was.

He reached up, hesitated, then brushed a loose strand of hair from my face. His touch lingered for the briefest moment, steadying me in a way words couldn't.

"We'll find the ones who are conspiring," he said softly. "But this time... we'll do it together. Before they ever get the chance to touch you."

The quiet certainty in his voice made my chest ache. I wanted to believe him.

I swallowed hard, blinking against the burn in my eyes.

"Bram..."

He gave me this weird, lopsided smile, like he was supposed to be the brave one, even though I knew he was just as freaked out. His fingers brushed mine—a tiny spark, gone almost before I felt it.

"I'm not letting them take anyone else from you," he whispered. "Not if I can help it."

I nodded, but the truth twisted inside me, sharp and cold: even if we found whoever was doing this, I didn't know if I was strong enough to do what the muses wanted. The idea of failing or losing Bram is way more than I could handle.

Chapter Twenty

Back home, I couldn't settle. My brain was a mess, everything from this morning still spinning, none of it making sense. It felt like trying to put a Rubik's Cube together in the dark, all mixed up, none of the same colors clicking into place.

Bram had dropped me off earlier, saying he'd check into a motel the Red Cross was setting up because of the fire.

It was home—the same walls, the same furniture, the same humming fridge in the kitchen. But nothing about it felt the same. Not even a tiny bit. Too normal. Aggressively normal. And that was terrible, because then everything seemed worse. After all, the house had plainly not received the notice about the complete and utter disintegration of the axis of the globe. As if it were still going about things as usual, and acting like nothing had ever transpired.

I wasn't acting. I was strangely tilted, as if the floor pitched at my feet and I was the only one who cared. The fire. The chaos at the marina. Men and women from, like, other centuries, packed together like it was any other Tuesday. And the sirens. Real sirens, singing sirens, moving through the smoke like some hallucination of a fever dream. My mind was still jumbled, ideas ricocheting off of each other so quickly I couldn't nail any of them down.

And Bram? He was strangely composed. As if the insanity brought him into focus, sharper, steadier, every step solidified as if he had practiced this before. And I was doing everything I could to avoid tripping over my own feet.

He looked like he belonged in the middle of all that. Me? I was just trying to breathe, trying not to lose it. Trying to figure out which reality I was supposed to believe in now.

BRAM HAD MENTIONED that he was going to check in on the morgue situation. The body of Meridian was still in limbo, his charred identity forensically unknown. The fire had burned every-thing—Passports, records, anything that might have connected the victim to the world. Bram had told the authorities that Meridian was a Greek citizen, a detail that would take time to verify.

He had this odd, weighty thing going on in his voice, but he attempted to make light of it with some dark humor: "Honestly, it was much simpler to retrieve and dispose of a body a century ago. No one actually investigated, no one was bothered." I made an effort to smile. But even with the morbid humor and insincere smiles, we seemed to be caught up in something totally unknown.

Now, as I stood alone in the apartment, the weight of everything settled in. This place felt normal and calm compared to the craziness outside. But then I looked at the mess still scattered on the floor in my room, and the unease crept back in.

Someone had been in here this morning, searching through my things, and it again hit me with a jolt. With everything else happen-ing, I had forgotten someone had searched my room. It was as if a month's worth of events had been crammed into the past six hours.

I had rebuilt the shelf with cinder blocks and 2x4 boards, trying to restore some order. I began placing the books and VHS tapes back where they belonged when the phone rang, a sharp and sudden sound. I jumped at the sound and then went into the kitchen to answer.

"Hello," I said, my voice steady, trying to keep it together.

"Where were you today, ho?" Claire's voice practically screamed through the phone. "I would've skipped with you if you'd given me a heads-up," she added.

"Claire, I swear, skipping wasn't the plan. Did you hear about the fire at the marina? It was Bram's boat. I had to go downtown to check on him," I said.

Her voice rose at the news, "Oh my god, Six! Is he okay? I heard someone died."

"Yeah, Bram's okay, but his friend didn't make it. So you can probably guess how he's doing," I said, my voice dropping.

She sighed into the reciever, "Whoa. Do they know what happened?"

I shrugged, glancing down the hall at the mess still scattered around my room. "Right now, it's suspicious, I think."

Claire's whole tone changed. "Wait. Were you downtown when the entire town went bananas?" She was practically bouncing.

I hesitated, pretending not to get it. "What do you mean?"

She started in as if it was juicy gossip, "Well, during band practice? We were on the field, and this group of armed men—like, full-on, dressed from the 1700s? They ran right across it. And there were a couple of Indians, too." Coach Miller was out there and was having none of it. One of the guys said they came from Georgia, for Oglethorpe, but Miller chased them off with his whistle. They all ran off into the woods, spooked by a whistle, can you imagine? Then the police came but couldn't find any trace of them."

She took a breath, then added, "People are saying weird stuff like that's been happening all over town."

"What time was this?" I asked, keeping my voice even, pretending I had no idea.

"I guess it was fourth period, so... around 11:00."

"I think I was taking a nap," I said with a small sigh.

"A nap? Of course you were," Claire snorted. "You totally missed it, Six. It was insane. Everyone's freaking out about what they saw. Mary-Louise in Home Ec was saying that it was probably professional reenactors or something, but I don't buy it. I mean, wouldn't the Cross and Sword cast have been there? I never heard anything."

I winced. "Wait a sec, you got the part in Cross and Sword?" I said, hoping to change the subject. "That's amazing!"

Claire paused for a second, then sighed. "I didn't tell you? Yeah, well, I'm Indian Squall Number 4. Not a speaking part, but I get an awesome sexy costume. I thought I did better at tryouts, though," she added, sounding deflated.

"Well, hey, it's something for summer. A paid gig, right? I bet most of the Drama Club is jealous," I reassured her.

"Yeah, I guess..." she said, voice dropping to barely a whisper.

Footsteps creaked on the stairs, then the front door banged open. My mom, wrestling two Winn-Dixie bags, paper crinkling and thumping against her knees.

I tried to sound cool and calm. "Hey, Claire? My mom just got home. Oh, was Dorian at school today?"

"Nope, he wasn't," Claire shot back, sing-song. "I figured you two maybe skipped together. You know. For... uh... private tutoring or whatever."

"What? Gross, no, Claire! I gotta go. Bye." I quickly hung up the phone, my cheeks flushed.

"HI, MOM," I said, greeting her as she set the grocery bags down on the table. "How was the museum?"

"Six, you won't believe it. I chased a dozen men dressed in vintage 1920s swimsuits around the museum," she said straight-faced.

I laughed out loud, probably for the first time all day, "Mom, you're not serious."

"Yes, seriously. They kept asking where the swimming pool was. Now the large indoor pool behind the museum hasn't had water in it in over fifty years. They said they arrived here to practice for the 1924 Olympic Swim team."

"Mom! Stop!" I said while laughing. "We're any of them cute?" I added to play along.

"What? No. Some... Well... They were hairy. Others had long, gross mustaches. It was all unbelievable. The really strange thing was that some of them came back into the museum, wrapped in towels, soaking wet, as if they had actually taken a dip in the pool. Their swimsuits... well, you know... some were too tight, or too loose, I don't even want to remember."

I was almost on the floor, crying with laughter as she described it in nearly too much detail.

"Weird things happened all over town. The cashier told me that some people passing themselves off as Indians came in and started eating the produce right off the shelves; the store manager had to chase them out. The natives loaded up and threw tomatoes at him."

I was laughing until my sides ached.

"Six, it was all bizarre today, everywhere. Did you see anything strange?" she asked in all seriousness.

"I started straightening up my room and fell asleep," I answered. "I guess I missed all the excitement."

<hr>

LATER THAT EVENING, on the local television news, plenty of local eyewitnesses had been interviewed about what broadcasters were calling "History Havoc in the Nation's Oldest City."

"A PIRATE FORCED *me to give him coins for him and his crew," said one frustrated local. "They took all my quarters, and I couldn't even pay the parking meter!"*

In an unusual turn of events, police were flooded with calls about citizens encountering people from various time periods, causing chaos downtown. Reports included everything from trespassing to unusual currency demands, but no arrests have been made.

Some speculate this bizarre scene could be part of a tourism stunt orchestrated by the local Chamber of Commerce, though officials have yet to comment. In other news...

Chapter Twenty-One

The television was still on when I drifted off. Somewhere, a local news anchor is trying to explain away the complete collapse into chaos that has happened in St. Augustine, voices stretched thin by commercials, time travel, weather, and sports.

I think about turning it off, but my eyelids feel heavy, and the quilt from the back of the couch is a soft trap I have no intention of escaping. The screen's flicker paints weird blue shapes on the ceiling, and I watch them move as sleep pulls at my brain, hard.

THEN I AM RUNNING, barefoot, but it doesn't hurt the way it does in real life. The ground is cold, smooth, like polished stone. Around me, a corridor stretches forever, curving gently so I can never quite see what's ahead as the air hums, thick with ozone and salt.

I know this place—not by sight, but by the peculiar way it makes my heart ache. I'm moving fast, faster, but every step lands soundlessly. I look down, and my feet are clean, but everything else about me is blurry, like I've lost my edges.

A man is walking just ahead. He's not running, just walking with intent, as if he's already been here a thousand times. His arms are long and folded behind his back, and his silhouette is tall. The further I chase, the harder it is to close the gap. He suddenly stops and turns around, as if he has heard my footsteps. The man wears a long, green coat with a furry cap featuring a red star, possibly a Soviet insignia.

"Where are we?" I ask the tired-looking soldier, but he seems to look right through me.

He turns and just keeps walking, his steps rhythmic and slow. The echo of his shoes against the stone grows louder, a steady rhythm, and then all at once the air splits with a metallic crash.

I BLINK. The scene shifts, snapping to a new location —a room lit by a single hanging light bulb that burns with a strange, cold yellow glow. The battleship-grey walls have deep streaks of brown from the rusted, corroded metal. My father hangs with his arms shackled on a wall, wrists ringed with polished iron bands. His dark hair is greasy and messy, but his face is as I remember: soft lines, tired eyes, the dark shadows from years of not sleeping enough.

He grins as soon as he sees me. "Six," he says, "I was starting to think you'd never catch up."

My brain scrambles for words. "Where are you? Are you—?" My voice cracks, and I'm crying, except in the dream it feels like tears of static.

He looks around, as if trying to map the place for my benefit. "Somewhere between here and the end of the world." His smile is crooked. "Don't worry, I think I'll see you soon."

He raises his wrists, and the chains clatter. I get a better look at the links now, and each of them has tiny numbers on them, moving and flashing, like ants going round and round in circles. Dates? Years? The headache I get just gazing at it.

"Who did this?" I demand, even though I already have an idea.

He rolls his shoulders, but they are stiff. "Everyone wants something," he says. "Power, secrets, time in a bottle. Someone's always scheming. Sometimes, Six, it's the people you trust the most who will close the doors."

A sliver of fear slices through me. "Can you get out?"

He shakes his head, but then makes a little show of the chains, as if they're not quite as tight as they look.

"There's always a way for powerful, clever girls. Sometimes you just have to look at it from a different angle."

I stepped closer, but the floor was getting sticky, as if honey had been poured all around, or the floor was melting into nothingness.

"Listen," he said, and it was one of those words that drops like a brick. "You have to be careful. You can't tell who's who. Some change shape, some change sides. Some are lost and don't even know it." His gaze sharpens. "But you... You have the token?"

I blink at him, nodding. "Yes."

He nods. "Don't let anyone take it from you, not even Bram." He sighs, his breath fogging the air. "His heart is in the right place, and he's smarter than he lets on, that one, but he could still be a pawn. Remember, Six: not every knight in shining armor is on your side."

He leans in as far as the chains allow. "Find the right lighthouse. Use the token wisely. Time's running out for all of us." He grins again, this time sadly. "You know how to find me, Six. You always have."

A loud crack, and the chamber begins to shake. My father jerks upright, startled for the first time.

"They're here," he whispers.

Several dark figures pour into the room, their faces hidden, their arms reaching out. I reach for my father, desperate, but my hands pass right through his, like smoke. His voice is still in my ears, whispering, "Hold onto the token, Six, and take care of your mother!" Then he's swallowed up, vanishing into black particles of ether.

THE SOUND of the television pulls me back, abrupt and jarring. I'm sitting bolt upright on the couch, heart racing, sweat damp on my skin. The Star-Spangled Banner seems to be blaring; the image on the screen is a flag waving across a blue sky, with Mount Rushmore in the background. And then static.

I rub my eyes, try to slow my breathing, but there's a raw feeling in my chest that isn't going away. Not now. Not until I can do what he told me to do.

THE NEXT MORNING is gray and wet, as if the clouds got too lazy to drift and decided to just spit rain intermittently for hours. I'm up before the sun, my brain on fire with half-melted fragments of my dad's dream-clues.

Is Mom the one in danger?

And the warning: *Trust no one—not even Bram.*

Which is highly inconvenient, since Bram is the only person I can talk to about this stuff without sounding certifiably insane.

I stood in the entryway, gazing at the rain cascading over the clogged gutters, and hoping Bram would just appear at my door, with that smirking, "Oh, hey, I was just in the neighborhood," and I knew he would have no qualms doing just that.

But the phone began ringing on the wall in the kitchen, piercing the morning silence.

"HELLO"

"It's time," said Bram. No greeting. Simply his tone, crisp and rapid.

I gazed at the coffeepot. "Time for what, exactly? There are a lot of things in my life that I could have time for," I say playfully.

He ignores that. "It's rising. The signature's spiking every hour. I can feel it—can't you?"

I frown, flex my free hand. "You mean that gravitational wave thing?" I admit I feel like a wave building and rolling in, except it's inside my bones.

"Not just the wave," Bram says, voice softening. "The pull. The beacon."

"The lighthouse," I say. "You think it's gonna happen today?"

"I'd bet my last silver dollar," he says. "Dorian's already moving. I saw him near the fort last night, walking along the bayfront towards the bridge."

That gets my full attention. "You want us to follow him, don't you?"

Silence, then: "If we don't, we lose him—and whatever he's scheming."

I close my eyes, picture the dream again. "You sure we're not walking into a trap?"

He's quiet. "You've had dreams again, haven't you?"

I hesitate. "They're getting worse. More detailed. My dad's clearly in them now. He's shackled, but he's still trying to help. He said to use the token. And not to trust anyone—even you."

Bram laughs, a sad, hollow sound. "Your dad always did have good instincts, a little overprotective perhaps." Then he's serious again. "But if we want to save him, we don't have a choice. Meet where we first met in a few hours, and bring the token."

"Wait, is my mom—" I begin to ask, but the line clicks. He's already gone.

Before I can even set the receiver back in its cradle, I hear her voice behind me.

"Is your mom *what*, dear?"

I nearly launch into the phone hanging on the wall. "Oh geez—Mom! You scared me," I say, my voice pitching higher than I'd like.

She's standing in the doorway in her robe, her hair a sleepy mess, rubbing one eye with the heel of her hand. "Six, who's calling *this* house at 6:30 in the morning?" Her tone's more tired than angry, but I know that could change.

"It was that boy," I say, trying to sound casual as my heart rate does jumping jacks. "The one whose boat caught on fire."

"That boy again," she says, fully stepping into the kitchen now, voice sharpening. "At this hour?" She gives me a look.

"Does this boy have a name?"

"His name's Bram," I say quickly. "He was just calling to let me know his flight time." The lie slips out smooth as butter.

"Flight?" She cocks her head. "Where's this *Bram* from?"

"Uh...some island in Greece." I fake a shrug. "He told me, but I don't remember exactly. One of the little ones."

She raises her eyebrows. "So this Bram, from a mysterious Greek island, calls my daughter at the crack of dawn? Sounds *very* serious." There's a smirk playing on her lips now as she makes a beeline for the coffee maker.

I roll my eyes. "He's just a friend, Mom."

"Uh-huh." The way she hums it tells me she's not buying a word of it. "And when is this *just a friend* leaving?"

"In a few days," I say, fiddling with the cord of the phone.

"Well then," she says, spinning toward me with her mug in hand, "plenty of time to invite this *international mystery boy* over for dinner and a movie. Give your lonely mother a little company."

"I don't think that's gonna work. He's... busy. Tying up loose ends. Paperwork and stuff. He's taking his—" I pause. "He's escorting his friend's body back. It's... not really the time."

Her smirk fades just a touch. "Oh." She exhales softly, then lifts the mug to her lips. "Still, it might be nice to have someone else at the table. Just once."

I soften, just a little. "I'll see what I can do," I say—which means no.

By 8:30, the morning rain eases, but muggy air presses against my skin, as if the sky's still weighing its next move." The pavement glistens, reflections ripple in shallow puddles, and palm fronds drip like melted wax. My sneakers splash quietly as I make my way to the pier, my heart hammering.

I spot him near the end, leaning on the wooden railing like he belongs there. Bram's in black jeans and a long-sleeved tee, his hair combed for once—not a strand out of place, like even *he* knew this day felt different. There's a stillness surrounding him.

He turns and grins, pretending to tip a hat—crooked, charming, dangerous. "Lovely weather, Miss."

I raise an eyebrow, but ignore his playfulness.

"What's the plan?" I ask, trying to ignore the thrum in my chest.

We walk together behind Navigator's, shoes crunching softly on the damp, sticky sand.

"We shadow Dorian at the lighthouse," Bram says, his voice low. "He'll have a window when the Continuum Coil contracts—"

"English, please."

He smirks. "When the wave hits, he gets a single shot to open a portal. We stay close and follow," he says, gesturing subtly to the compass pendant resting against my chest.

"And if he sees us?"

"We improvise," Bram says, and then—without warning—he reaches for my hand. His fingers find mine like they've done it a thousand times, like they *belong* there.

I glance at our hands, surprised at how steady his is, how mine feels like it might float away. But I nod anyway, jaw tight.

He stops walking.

"Wait." His voice is softer now. "You feel it too, right? It's building. Closer, stronger."

"The wave?" I ask.

His eyes search mine. "Not just the wave."

Then he steps in—close enough that I can feel the warmth of him cutting through the muggy air. My breath catches, and for a second, time does that weird thing it always does around him. It becomes still.

Before I can overthink it, he leans in and presses his lips to mine.

It's firm, but not rushed. His hands settle gently on my waist, anchoring me as my whole body goes weightless. My heart stumbles. I gasp, just slightly, and then my mouth opens—and so does his— and we fall into something neither of us has said out loud but both of us have been circling for days.

His kiss is heat and rain and adrenaline. We kiss, slow at first, then deeper, until our tongues find a rhythm—charged, instinctive— like my body knows something my mind never learned. My fingertips curl into his shirt, needing something solid to hold onto as the whole world tilts.

When we finally pull apart, I feel breathless because I forgot to breathe.

He keeps his forehead against mine, and I swear the silence between us hums.

"Well," he says, a little unsteady himself. "That was... not improvising."

I smile, dazed. "How much time do we have?"

"Not enough, Six. Not nearly enough," as he exhales.

Chapter Twenty-Two

We walk the rest of the way to the lighthouse in near silence, but it's not awkward. It's the kind of quiet that feels full instead of empty. Every inch between us hums, like the static in the air after lightning, like something else is about to happen. What's that song by Katrina and the Waves? *Walking on Sunshine*. That's exactly how it feels—even if the skies are still gray and the sidewalks are wet. Bram holds my hand like it's fragile, his fingers loose but warm. As if he's ready to let go if I pull away, but I'm praying I won't.

I don't.

The path to the lighthouse winds through soft sand, pocked with puddles and crushed seashells. The lightkeeper's house stands half-finished, its frame exposed in places like a rib cage, with plastic tarps flapping against it in the breeze, slapping a strange heartbeat in the silence. The gulls above us cry now and then, circling wide beneath a

155

sky that's turned that pale, moody gray-blue that only comes after a storm. It's the color of recovery or sorrow.

Bram stops, crouching by a cluster of purple flowers pushing up through the wet sand. He plucks a handful, shaking the droplets from their petals.

"Spiderwort," he says. "Weed or flower?"

"Is this a trick question?"

He smirks. "Both."

"Both?"

"Usually a weed," he admits. "They bloom in the morning and are gone by nightfall. People don't place value on things that vanish so soon."

"That's sad," I say softly.

"Maybe. Or maybe that's what makes them worth noticing at all," Bram says. He keeps the bouquet instead of handing it to me.

THEN WE SLIP inside through a gap in the plywood and step into the scent of wet lumber and sawdust—the room's dark, except for the soft glow slipping in through a large empty hole where a window will be. Electrical cords snake across the floor, and there's a tower of paint cans near the back wall. Bram leads me to a little alcove behind a pair of sawhorses and some sheets of plywood, crouching low so we're hidden but still have a clear view of the path.

"We'll have to wait," he murmurs, eyes scanning the entrance. "But he'll come. Probably go and get orders, now that things haven't gone the way he planned. He might lead us to your father."

My pulse ticks faster. I realize I'm trembling—not from cold, but from anticipation. Excitement. Dread. I've never done anything like this. Not even close.

Bram seems calm, but I notice the subtle way he keeps flexing his fingers, like he's trying to let the tension bleed out of them.

"Do you think he'll bring friends?" I ask.

He shrugs, his lips twisting into a kind of half-smile. "It's Dorian. He probably thinks he doesn't need friends."

I gaze at his face, the shadowing of it making his cheekbones appear cliff-like. His face is lines of angles, sharper than before.

There are raindrops still clinging to his hair, and they catch the light like glass. He carries the storm in his bones, wrapped in silence.

"So..." I say, nudging the quiet, "about earlier."

He glances at me, and for just a beat, he looks scared. Not scared of what's coming or what Dorian might do—but scared of me. Of what I might say.

"If you want to pretend it didn't happen," he says softly, "I'll understand."

His voice cracks on the last word like he already knows he wouldn't understand at all.

I shake my head, heart thudding in my chest. "No. I just... I didn't expect it. That's all."

"Me neither," he says, but we both know that's a lie. Probably the first one he's ever told me.

The air between us eases. I want to say something else, something real, but my throat closes up. So instead, I bump my knee into his, hard enough that it startles him. We both wince, then laugh—quiet and quick—and the tension breaks just enough to breathe again.

He keeps his hands and fingers busy, weaving the thick stalks of Spiderwort into a long, flowery chain.

We sit like that for a while, knees touching, shoulders nearly aligned. The construction materials creak and settle around us. Bram peeks over the plywood now and then, checking the lighthouse entrance, but most of the time, he's still, like he's waiting on more than just Dorian.

Finally, I looked over and Bram has completed a weaved ring of Spiderwort.

"For my queen," he says in a terrible attempt at a British accent.

I playfully placed it onto my damp hair and chuckled softly.

"I hope you're not allergic," he mentions playfully. "The crown will only last the rest of today."

We both smile widely, and I leave it on. Unsure how regal or ridiculous it looks.

"I told you on the phone that I had a dream last night," I say, voice barely above a whisper. "My dad was in it. It felt real. He told me to use the token… and not to trust anyone."

Bram turns to me slowly, his expression unreadable. His eyes flick to the compass around my neck, then back to mine. Something in him softens.

"You have incredible power, Six," he says. "You don't fully understand it yet. But it's there. With or without the token."

Then he reaches up gently, brushing a strand of wet hair from my cheek. His fingers linger. "Dorian is foolish for thinking he can take your power away," he says. "But he's not half the fool I am."

"You think you're a fool?" I ask, caught in the way his eyes hold mine. His palm stays resting on my cheek, warm and steady.

He exhales, slow and unsteady. "I'm the worst kind," he says, voice low and aching. "A fool in love."

My breath catches.

"I've tried not to be," he goes on, his thumb tracing the edge of my jaw. "Tried to stay focused, tried to remember the mission, the danger, the thousand things that could go wrong. But none of it matters when you're near me. Time bends around you, Veronica. Like it's just waiting for you to decide what comes next."

I swallow hard. My heart's in my throat, my lungs barely working.

And I know it's selfish," he says. "But if this ends badly—if I don't get another moment like this—I need you to know. I love you. Not because of the token. But because when I look at you… I see something worth staying in one time- this present time for."

I don't say anything.

I can't.

But I lean forward, close the space between us, and press my forehead to his.

Because I'm starting to feel the same.

And maybe, because of school, mom, and now Bram, I'll remain in one time, and in one place, this place.

OUR FOREHEADS SEPARATE when we hear the rattle of a chain at the fence surrounding the lighthouse. Both of us peer over the plywood in the shadows and watch as Dorian, in black jeans and a dark trench coat, climbs the stone steps to the lighthouse door, opening it with ease.

"Ready?" Bram asks.

I look at him, really look, and for a second, I see the confident boy from the pier where we first met. My heart fills with hope and possibility.

"Let's go," I say, pulling off my purple crown, and together we move.

We climb through the empty window frame, landing with soft thuds in a patch of weeds, sand, and ash. Sand sticks to my damp sneakers as we dart across the narrow strip of brush toward the gate.

Bram reaches it first, one hand gripping the rusted chain to keep it from clanking. I slip through the gap, heart pounding, breath shallow. He follows, quick and quiet.

Up close, the lighthouse doesn't look like a past postcard. It's not quaint or charming—it's a looming column of peeling paint and weathered brick with rusted iron—a forgotten relic.

We bolt to the granite steps and huddle beneath the small overhang at the base. Bram raises his hand like a traffic cop, signaling me to stop. His chest rises and falls fast. Mine does too.

"If he looks out any windows while he climbs," Bram pants, voice barely a whisper, "he won't see us if we stay back under here."

His breath is hot against my cheek, laced with adrenaline and sea salt.

We hold hands, both of us tense as coiled springs. The token against my chest begins to buzz again—soft at first, then stronger, like it's waking up. The vibration pulses through my ribs, spreading into my arms, my teeth. Bram stands frozen, eyes locked on the half-built lightkeeper's house in the distance, his whole body gone rigid.

THEN I SEE IT—HIS shoulders tighten, a flicker of pain in his eyes. He winces, jaw clenched, as if something invisible is grinding against him from the inside.

"Bram?" I whisper, inching closer. "Are you okay?"

He doesn't answer. He doesn't even blink. His grip on my hand tightened slightly, like a current is moving through him.

The token's hum turns into a thrum, and then—abruptly—it stops.

A strange silence follows.

Bram gasps and shudders, as if surfacing from deep water. He locks his wide eyes on the ground, awe, or maybe fear, flashing across his face.

I touch his arm. "Bram. What was that?"

He swallows hard. "That was... intense. You didn't feel that?"

"I did," I say slowly. "But I think it hits you harder. Like you're... more in tune with it, or the token absorbs the energy."

He nods once, still catching his breath. Three slow beats of silence pass before he whispers, "Let's move."

THE HINGES GIVE a soft groan as we push through the heavy wooden door. We take off across the hall. Every step feels louder than it should, with our shoes moving across grit, and the humidity against our breath.

We make for the black iron staircase, winding up the center like the skeletal remains of some ancient serpent. It rises into a darkness, only broken by slivers of twilight slicing through the windows. As we climb, my legs burn, but I don't stop. We can't afford to.

Near the top, Bram gives me a look, "You good?" I nod, trying not to pant like a wet Saint Bernard.

We climb the final spiral of steps just as the sun begins its slow descent across the small St. Augustine skyline, casting a molten glow across the horizon. At the last step, we both watch as the lens slowly turns, creating graceful swirls of fractured, chromatic light. I see Bram's reflected face, warped and gorgeous, as both of us gaze into the lens, marveling at the classic magnificence of the lighthouse's heart. We both stand still, heads tilted toward the glowing mechanism. It's low, mechanical purr hums beneath our feet, feeling ancient and alive.

We duck through the narrow opening into the glass capsule, careful not to bump our heads. The lightbulb above us on an iron tripod is dark for now. Crouching side by side in the cramped space, we press in close, shoulders brushing. My fingers tremble as I reach for the token, now calm, tucked inside the compass at my neck. I clutch it like a prayer. Bram gently tucks a strand of hair behind my ear, his breath brushing my cheek.

"You need to say—" he begins.

POP.

THE LIGHTBULB FLASHES on with a jolt, buzzing to life in an explosion of brilliance. We both jerk in surprise, nearly knocking foreheads together. A beat of silence—then we dissolve into laughter.

"Oh my God, I thought we triggered it," I say, wheezing.

Bram grins. "Clearly, you are a goddess. A Lighthouse goddess."

"Speak for yourself," I giggle. "I just jumped like a squirrel in traffic."

We laugh again, breathless and close, as the lens continues to rotate around us, casting our shadows in slow arcs along the curved glass. Outside, the last light of day fades.

He tries again, voice thin and fraying at the edges, like a thread pulled too tight.

"Tell it…" He swallows hard, the words trembling against my skin. "Tell it to take us to the location and time of the last traveler."

His breath is warm in my ear, but his hands are cold—ice meeting fire.

I look down at the token in my palm. It pulses faintly, as if it's waiting, like it already knows. My fingers tighten around it.

"Take us…" I whisper, voice cracking like the first note of a hymn, "to the location and time of the last traveler."

THEN LIGHTHOUSE GROANS softly around us, a sound like shifting bones. The massive lens above us tilts, ever so slightly, then begins to slide with surreal grace, the world outside warping into a watercolor of motion and light, color fractures and blurs.

Everything stutters.

Bram's arms wrap around me, and I cling to him as the floor beneath us hums with impossible energy. My bones feel like lightning —my skin stretched too thin, vibrating. The atmosphere loosens, bending and folding inward. My heart slams in my chest, and I can feel Bram's echoing the same wild rhythm.

There's no sky. No sea. Just light and breath and trembling.

And then—

In the moment before everything gives way, I press my lips close to his ear and say, steady and confident:

"Wherever we're going… I'm not letting go of you."

Chapter Twenty-Three

Pain blooms behind my eyes, a dull throb that pulses in time with my heartbeat. When I try to move, the world swims around me, lurching and tilting like the inside of a funhouse mirror. I blink hard, trying to ground myself. Cold, gritty stone bites through my jeans. My hand finds the floor—rough, damp, real.

Above, the ceiling curves into a soot-blackened dome, ancient and oppressive. Smoke has kissed every inch of it, century after century, turning it into a skyless void. A narrow spiral staircase hugs the wall, chipped and crumbling, spiraling down like a stone strand of DNA.

Bram shifts beside me. I feel him before I see him, his body heat retreating as he climbs out of the lens chamber and crosses to the window. The moment stretches, soundless but heavy, until his voice cuts through the stillness.

"We're back."

I DRAG MYSELF UPRIGHT, swaying, one palm braced on the wall. My knees protest, and my vision swims again before settling. "Back... where?" My throat is raw, like I've swallowed smoke and time itself.

He looked back at me. The moonlight hit his face, sharp and cold, and I could see how tense he was. "The Cordouan," he said, and his eyes were dead serious. "Lucian's lighthouse."

I knew that sound—the ocean, just hammering away at the rocks, over and over. I knew the smell too: salt, oil, smoke that had been there forever. And the way the lens buzzed all around us.

I made myself stand up, even though my knees felt like they might give out. The lens was weird here. Smaller, older. The light didn't blaze; it sort of flickered, quiet and strange, like a candle in a crypt. But it was still beautiful, in this dangerous way. It still whispered things, but only if you knew how to listen. The floor of the lens burns and smokes as if branded again: *1888*.

"So why here?" I asked, keeping my voice low. "Why would Dorian come to the Cordouan?"

Bram came closer, hand out. I didn't even think about it—I just took it. His hand was warm and steady, and for a second, it was the only thing that felt real.

"I don't know," he says. "Lucian was never part of Dorian's circle. If anything, they were... opposed. I don't see Dorian making this kind of trip for anything friendly."

I nod, throat tightening. We both know Dorian doesn't travel without a reason. And probably none of his reasons are ever good.

We start down the spiral staircase, one slow step at a time. Our footsteps echo, swallowed by the stone as we descend deeper. The air thickens with every turn—colder, damper, sharper somehow. It tastes metallic on my tongue.

I start to shiver. Not from the chill, but from something older. Something ancient and unseen.

Something feels wrong.

At the bottom, a heavy wooden door. Bram shoulders it open,

and the world becomes regal and luxurious again, as the torches burn against the walls in this chamber fit for a king. We hurry across to another large metal hatch on the other side, unsure how far ahead Dorian is.

"Maybe he missed the jump," he says, not sounding convinced.

"Or maybe he's just hiding," I counter. "It's what I'd do."

BRAM UNLATCHES the heavy iron door, and we step out into the howling dark.

The wind hits like a slap—wet and wild, heavy with salt and something stranger, deeper. The sea crashes just beyond the stone railing, each wave battering the rocks like a warning. Foam sprays across the balcony. The night is alive with noise—the roar of water, the howl of the wind, the cries of seabirds tossed like paper through the sky.

A screech cuts through the air, piercing and human enough to make my heart stop.

Bram scans the shifting shadows crawling along the curved balcony, his eyes locked ahead. The path wraps around the outer rim of the lighthouse, the railing no higher than my hips, slick with spray. I follow his gaze.

There, at the far end of the walkway, hunched against the low wall, is a figure. Motionless. Head bowed.

For a heartbeat, I forget how to breathe.

"Dad?" I whisper, the hope flaring so suddenly it hurts. But the shape is all wrong. Too slender. Older. Frail in a way my father never was.

Bram tenses beside me.

I take a hesitant step forward. "Lucian?" My voice catches in my throat, disbelieving.

The figure lifts his head slowly, as if waking from a long dream. Even in the dark, I see the unmistakable lines of his face—deeper now, his beard soaked and clinging to his cheeks, his eyes gleaming with a strange weariness. It's him.

He doesn't speak. Just offers a small, startled smile.

"What are you doing out here?" Bram asks, his tone low, guarded.

Lucian turns back to the wall and raises one arm. In his hand is something pale and slick, a whole raw chicken, glistening in the moonlight.

He lobs it into the churning dark beyond the railing.

We freeze.

A massive tentacle whips out of the blackness and snatches the meat mid-air with horrifying grace, then disappears beneath the waves in a slithering moment of impossible muscle and suction.

"Oh my god," I breathe. My legs threaten to fold.

He glances at us again, as if we're ghosts. "Didn't expect anyone else to find their way here tonight," he says. His voice is raspy, but steady. "Much less you two."

Bram moves in front of me, protective. "You're feeding it?"

He nods wearily. "Them. Keeping them calm. Or trying to. They're restless tonight."

He throws another hunk of meat into the void. Another tentacle rises, this one larger, tipped with glistening suckers the size of dinner plates. It grabs the offering, then curls slowly toward the tower like it's tasting the air.

Lucian doesn't flinch. "They usually don't come this close to the lighthouse. I released them weeks ago," he says, more to himself than us. "Not unless something's out of balance."

I grip Bram's arm tightly. "Lucian, what's happening?"

He finally turns to face us fully, and something in his expression chills me more than the wind.

"If Orville and Wilbur are going to the North Atlantic to nudge an iceberg into the unsinkable ship, they have to stop being so dependent on me," he says with a twinkle in his eye.

I realize what he is talking about, "Wait. You mean the..."

But I'm interrupted. Lucian changes the subject.

"You brought the Token here, didn't you?"

We don't answer. We don't have to.

He sighs, dragging a trembling hand through his soaked beard, water running down his face like tears he doesn't have time for. His eyes—gray and distant—fix on us with a kind of exhausted knowing.

"Why would you use the Token," he rasps, "when a wave struck earlier?"

"I carry it with me, always," I say.

Bram shifts beside me, his jaw tight. "We were following Dorian," he says. "He used the wave, and we followed."

The old man nods once, a solemn gesture like he already knew that would be the answer. His gaze slips past us, back toward the heaving ocean.

Then, without warning, he tilts his head back and lets out a sound—deep, raw, and unearthly. Not quite a scream, not quite a growl. It splits the air like a blade and echoes out over the sea, bouncing off the cliffs and circling back like a stormfront.

The water stills for a moment, and then there is a massive reply.

The deep answers with a chorus of roars, wet, guttural, massive, like the ocean speaks a terrible language we will never understand.

The tentacles, which two seconds ago were all wriggling and twitching, just kind of slithered back down into the black water. Like, one minute they're hungry and all over the place, and the next—they're gone. Splash, ripple, nothing. It's totally silent.

Lucian drops his head, and the sound he made is still rattling around somewhere in my bones. "Feeding time is over," he says, sort of under his breath. "For now."

HE PICKS up his hourglass staff, which is leaning against the damp wall, turns, and starts walking along the balcony, his boots clumping on the wet stone. No drama, no explanation. Just leaving us there with the echo.

We follow, not because he tells us to, but because there's nowhere else to go. He walks with a faint limp, his long coat dragging behind him like kelp, and his shoulders bowed beneath more than just the storm.

As we round the curve of the lighthouse, a soft orange glow appears ahead, muted and flickering, like a candle left in a forgotten window.

Lucian leads us through an arched doorway that stands along the outer wall. The wind lessens here, replaced by the groan of old wood and the scent of salt, oil, and something faintly herbal. We step through and into the old keeper's quarters, now Lucian's, which is roomier than before, now with the kraken tanks gone.

The space is warm in a weathered, monastic sort of way. The large stone fireplace is still glowing, and maps pinned across the walls—maps of oceans and currents, constellations, and strange symbols drawn in Lucian's hand. A wool blanket hangs to dry beside the fire as shadows dance against the curved walls of the room.

He shrugs off his coat and hangs it on a crooked peg, water pooling beneath it. He doesn't speak right away. Just moves to the small hearth and stokes the flame with a practiced hand. It flares back to life, casting his gaunt features in warm light.

He gestures for us to sit on a pair of creaky wooden stools. Then, quietly, almost like a man trying not to wake the past, he says:

"I haven't seen Dorian," he said, his voice deep and steady, like the ocean under moonlight. "Nor would I understand why he'd come here. I highly doubt this would be his destination."

He turned to face us fully, the flickering oil lamp catching in his silver beard, making him look more like an old prophet than a keeper of secrets.

"I asked the token to take us to the last place traveled," I said quietly, not sure if I was allowed to speak so freely to someone like *him*. My fingers curled around the edge of the compass, still warm against my chest.

Lucian's gaze didn't flinch. "Then Dorian must not have traveled," he said, matter-of-factly. "At least, not yet."

Then he moved to a narrow shelf stacked with mismatched tomes and scrolls. His fingers hovered before selecting a hefty, crimson-bound book—aged and fraying at the corners, its spine cracked from centuries of use. It seemed like it belonged in a cathedral, not in this forgotten lighthouse.

"I knew of you, Six," he said, softer now as he carried the book to the wide oak table. "The *Aeon Chronicles* mentioned your name long before your arrival.

When you left last time, I started digging around deeper into your lineage."

Lucian dropped the book on the table, and it landed with a thump. Everything rattled. Dust poofed up in the lamplight. He started flipping through these super-thin pages. The edges were all soft and worn because so many people had touched them.

"There used to be, like, twelve travelers," he said, voice all low and dramatic. "Now there are thousands. Travelers are mostly human, and humans... well," He looked up briefly, the lines in his face sharpening. "Their basic biological urges and desires have also shaped time."

He found the page and turned the book toward us. "Here," he said, his finger tracing faded ink.

Bram and I leaned in.

"Your father, Jacob, is well known to us," Lucian said quietly. "But what surprised me..." His finger stopped, resting on another name. "Was your mother. Marsha Ingram."

The air punched out of my lungs.

"My... mom?" My voice cracked. "She's a traveler?"

Lucian just kind of stared, like he was looking through me, not at me.

Bram leaned in, talking softly, like he was worried I might shatter. "No. Not yet. She doesn't know about any of this."

I shook my head, trying to catch up. "But you just said—"

"She's a carrier," Bram interrupted, even quieter now, like the words might hurt if he said them too loud. "She has the ability, but she's not able to use it. Sometimes it remains dormant for like, generations." He looked over at Lucian, who gave this tiny nod. "She could've passed it down to you without even knowing. She never felt it herself."

I backed away from the table, heart slamming so hard I could barely hear anything else.

My mom—the woman who burned casseroles from recipe clippings, who swore off microwaves, who hated ever leaving our small town—had unknowingly given me the key to the entire spectrum of time?

"She has no idea, does she?" I whispered.

Lucian looked down, almost shy. The firelight made his silver hair glow. He stepped back, towards a small table with a chessboard laid out on it. For a second, it felt like he was about to say something dramatic. "Not every player remembers the opening move, Six," he said. "But the one who lost does. Your mom played her part years ago —moved a piece that mattered. Now someone's been studying the board ever since, waiting to take her off it."

The words barely registered before the panic hit.

I DIDN'T THINK—I *moved*.

MY FEET HIT the floorboards hard as I launched myself toward the front door, heart pounding like it was trying to escape my chest. "My mom's in danger?" I shouted, spinning back toward Lucian. "Is that what you're saying?" I whispered, betraying the fear clawing up my throat.

No one answered. They didn't have to.

I flung the door open and the storm hit me like a slap—wind howling, rain needling my skin, the world outside already halfway to chaos. Bram was right behind me, his hand on my back, steadying but silent.

I turned to him, barely breathing. "We need to go... to get back," I said, my voice breaking on the words.

Then I glanced out into the wild, black night, stones slick with sea spray, with the aged lighthouse towering above us, like a warning.

"*We need to go home.*"

Chapter Twenty-Four

Let me just say that Bram and Six aren't exactly subtle. I saw their shadows flicker across the torn plastic tarp in the old house. Two amateurs playing spy in a game they barely understand. You'd think they'd realize by now that I can *feel* the token when it's near. Its pulse hums through my bones ever so lightly at a distance.

But I didn't call them out. Not yet. Let them think they were clever. Let them think they were close.

I slipped into the lighthouse, heart pounding—not with fear, but with something sharper. Almost joy. The thrill of being ten steps ahead. They'd follow my footprints, right into the trap, chasing shadows while I slipped through the cracks.

Halfway down the hall, I stopped at the twin windows, their glass staring out at opposite sides of the world.

I slid the right one up, the old frame groaned, and swung the faded grey shutters open just wide enough. Outside, the air smelled of wet stone and moss.

I climbed onto the pedestal beneath the window—the thick, black concrete base of the lighthouse, its surface cool beneath my hands. With one final glance inside, I lowered the window and drew the shutters closed, locking the light out.

Then I waited in anticipation of the wave.

Which hit wicked hard and fast. Slammed into my chest like a fist, knocked me off the pedestal, feet skidding, knees locked. I clenched my teeth, tried not to let the energy tear me apart.

Not long after, through the shutters inside the hall, I heard them. Footsteps, soft, scraping along the cracked tiles, their voices whispering.

They passed by the window where I had been, clueless, still chasing the story they thought they understood.

I smiled then—a sharp, thin smile. Victory tastes cold and bitter when it comes too easily.

But hurting Bram? Outsmarting him? That wasn't enough. Not tonight.

If I really wanted to break Six...

I'd have to strike where she lived.

So I turned from the lighthouse and walked into the twilight streets of the lighthouse neighborhood, where shadows stretch long and familiar.

IT WAS time to visit her mother.

THE UPSTAIRS APARTMENT on Magnolia Drive was quiet. Almost too quiet as a single lamp burned in the front window—soft yellow light spilling across the porch and out into the damp, still night. It was one of those warm Florida evenings where everything feels like it's waiting for the storm to break. Even the trees were tense.

I stood at the edge of the lawn, half-hidden behind the trunk of an old oak, and flicked the first pebble toward her bedroom window.

Tik.

A QUIET SOUND. Barely audible.
Waited five seconds. Another.

Tik.

I WASN'T TRYING to wake her.
I already knew she wasn't home.
The point was a romantic performance.
The third stone—larger this time. It hit the window frame and bounced off with a satisfying knock.

THAT DID IT.

THE FRONT DOOR creaked open behind the screen, and she stepped out—bathrobe, slippers, a magazine still in her hand. She blinked into the darkness, as if trying to remember what the outside world looked like.
"Hello?" she called, peering out.
I moved forward just enough for the porch light to catch my face. Tilted my chin upward like I was caught red-handed in a boyish, innocent sort of way.
Her eyes squinted behind her glasses. "Bram, is it?"
I gave her the smallest of smiles.
"You must be Marsha," I said. "Veronica's told me about you."
"Well, I wish I could say that it's mutual," she said, folding her arms across her chest. "She mentioned you once. I thought you were leaving the country, headed to Greece, right?"

"Plans changed," I quipped.

Her shoulders softened slightly. "Six is not home. She went out... somewhere nearby, I think. Probably over at the pier near Navigators."

I nodded like I believed her. Like I cared.

She stepped down one of the porch planks slowly, cautious like someone not used to late-night visitors or sudden movements. The wood moaned beneath her slippers. The wind picked up just a little and pulled at her robe.

"If you find her, tell her not to be out all night," she said, more maternal than stern.

She took another step. The wood sagged a bit under her weight.

Then her face shifted—confusion first, then wariness. "Bram, you seem a bit older, so..."

THAT WAS THE MOMENT.

CRACK.

THE ENTIRE STAIRCASE collapsed beneath her, rotten, moist wood giving way like paper. She pitched forward—not even a chance to scream. A rotted support beam below jutted up like something waiting. Her body hit it with a sickening *thunk*, the jagged end piercing her chest cleanly.

SHE CRUMPLED.

One last breath. No more.

For a long second, everything went still, like even time recoiled from what it had just done.

I stared at her from the sandy pavement. The wind fluttered the edge of her robe. The rain returned—soft at first, then steadier, washing water and blood along the grains of the wood.

There was no one nearby.

No neighbors watching.

No lights flickering on.

Just me.

And her.

And whatever would come next.

I walked away, knowing that Six would soon return. And when she did, the storm would truly begin.

Chapter Twenty-Five

The jolts, tilts, and blinding blurs of our transference were getting easier to endure, or maybe I was just too desperate to care. My mind wasn't on the in-between anymore. It was on my mom.

I could still feel the pulse of fear running cold through me. If Dorian had gone after her, if I was too late...

I'd tell her everything. I no longer cared about the rules. Time travelers, the token, the alliances, her husband, everything; I'd rip open the truth if that's what it took to save her life.

The instant Bram and I crawled out of the lens, we didn't pause. No wide-eyed wonder, no catching our breath. The world around us was still spinning, but we didn't wait for it to stop.

We hit the metal floor running. Our shoes rang out against the iron of the deck as we bolted for the spiral stairs, hearts racing faster than our feet could keep up.

Down we went, the steps twisting and warping in my vision as the remnants of the transfer still spun through my skull. I gripped the railing so hard my knuckles burned, but we couldn't slow down. Not now.

My legs ached, lungs screamed, but we kept going, Bram a silent shadow leading me, our feet nearly in sync. The lighthouse felt endless, the flights stretching longer with every turn, as if the tower itself didn't want to let us go.

Then—near the bottom—on the landing by the east window, we stopped dead.

Everything slammed to a halt.

Waiting for us was something we weren't ready for.

We stumbled onto the landing—and froze.

THERE WERE THREE OF THEM.

TWO GIRLS STOOD near the railing, their forms pale and dripping as if they'd just climbed out of the sea. The third, older girl sat slumped in the window well, her back against the solid brick wall, knees hugged to her chest. Moonlight spilled over her like thin silver skin, turning her soaked dress into a tangle of shadows and folds.

Their clothes looked like something torn from a faded history book—frilled collars, faded muslin skirts, stockings sagging at the knees. Something out of a century-long dead. *Little House on the Prairie*, maybe, but worn thin by salt and time.

The smallest girl, maybe eleven or twelve, had her hair tied up in dripping ribbons. She was crying softly, a fragile sound that barely filled the space. Tears mixed with rainwater, tracing ghostly lines down her dirt-smudged cheeks.

Then the girl in the window slowly turned to face us.

Her eyes met mine, empty, distant, far older than the girl wearing them.

"Eliza, stop being such a crybaby." She said it with zero emotion, as if someone were pressing play on a broken cassette tape. "Can't you see we have guests?"

Not warm. Not sweet. Just... worn out.

I swallowed, throat scratchy. "Who... who are you? Why are you here? Why are you?"—my voice went weird and shaky, "all wet?"

The girl just smiled, slow and empty, like the question was beneath her.

She tilted her head, light cutting across her face like a blade, and said in a voice that sank straight into my bones, "We're here to remind you... that worse tragedies have happened on this island."

She turned back to the window, staring into the black sky beyond. Her voice dropped to a whisper that still somehow filled the whole room.

"Go on. But you're too late."

The wind rattled a loose pane of glass in the window frame, and for a second, I couldn't tell if it was the night or the past breathing down my neck.

Bram moved quickly past the sobbing girl, Eliza, and as he brushed her thin shoulder, something strange happened. His shoulder passed through hers like a vapor in the air, and for a fleeting second, her form wavered, scattering into faint particles that floated around us like ash suspended in the air. It wasn't dust. It wasn't real.

These weren't just lost children from another time.

They were echoes of young lives drowned.

Ethereal, sorrowful phantoms—trapped in the place where their story had ended, still waiting for someone or something that would never come for them.

I FOLLOWED Bram down the last two flights of stairs, our footsteps pressing against the cool iron, until we burst out into the damp night air.

I drew in a shaky breath, the chill wrapping around my ribs. "Have you ever seen anything like *that* before?" I asked, still hearing the mournful voices in the back of my mind.

Bram let out a breathless laugh, wiping sweat from his brow. "Once in a while, but not often. And if you thought *that* was eerie..."

He paused, catching his breath. "Wait until you meet the ghost of Mary, Queen of Scots. There are worse ghosts in history, Six, much worse."

By the time we reached the corner of Lighthouse Avenue and Carver Street, the night had come alive with flashing lights—red and blue strobes ricocheting off every car window, mailbox, and puddle like some chaotic, broken kaleidoscope.

That's when it hit me.

THE SPRINT STOPPED. My legs buckled. And I broke.

I dropped to my knees right there on the damp pavement, the sobs tearing loose from my throat before I could stop them—loud, raw, and ugly. The kind of crying that doesn't care who's watching.

Bram was there in an instant, arms around me, grounding me. His warmth pressed against my shaking frame as I gasped for air between sobs. He didn't tell me to be quiet. He didn't tell me it was going to be okay, because maybe it wasn't. He just held me as if that was the only thing keeping me from falling apart completely.

"What happened? I *have* to see her..." I choked out, already pulling away from him, legs trembling, ready to bolt toward the chaos.

But Bram caught my hands and gently pulled me back. His voice was soft but steady. "Six... listen to me. If something's happened... You don't need to see her that way. Not like this."

I shook my head, tears blurring the lights into streaks of red and blue. "I *have* to..."

"You don't," he said firmly, his thumb brushing a tear from my cheek. "Let me go first. Just... Just give me a block's head start. I'll find out what happened. She could be fine... All this could be for someone else. If... if she's not fine. I'll let you know. I'll shield you from whatever you don't need to see."

He sounded torn, like he wanted to keep me safe but also had to hurry.

He put both his hands gently on my face, making me look at him. His voice got soft. "You've seen enough darkness for one night. Trust me with this."

I nodded, but I could feel my chest stuttering, breath coming in little gasps.

Bram squeezed my hands, once, then let go and jogged off down the street. His shadow pulsed through the red and blue lights.

I KEPT MOVING, pacing closer, cold and shaky and alone, watching the chaos throb at the end of the block like a storm you could see but not stop.

Then I stopped beneath a wide, gnarled live oak that stretched its limbs over the street like one of Lucian's Kraken tentacles. Its heavy branches curled against the night sky, casting jagged shadows across the road like claws waiting to close.

I crouched down to avoid a clump of wet Spanish moss dangling from a limb and pressed my back against the rough, solid trunk, the bark biting through my shirt. It didn't matter. I needed something *real* to hold me up, because my legs gave out beneath me, and I sank to the damp earth, gasping for breath I couldn't seem to catch.

The flashing lights, the darkened windows of the houses nearby, the blurred outlines of a world that suddenly felt too big and too cruel.

I pressed my fists against my ribs as if I could hold myself together.

PLEASE. *Please.* Let her be okay.

MY MIND WOULDN'T STOP SHOWING me the worst—images of her lying motionless on the floor, her eyes wide with fear, of Dorian's voice whispering some awful truth into her ear before he left her broken. I clenched my jaw, shaking my head hard enough to make myself dizzy, trying to chase the thoughts away.

She had to be fine. She *had* to be alive.

I felt so small crouched under the silent sprawl of the oak, the world spinning on without me while I waited for Bram.

Waiting in the shadows, praying that her time hadn't already run out.

Chapter Twenty-Six

The first thing I noticed was the warmth. Not the kind that skims your skin, but a heavy, steady heat, dry and deep, like it wanted to settle right into my bones.

When I opened my eyes, the ceiling soared far above me, lost in dim gold light that seemed to spill from somewhere high in the chamber walls. The air smelled faintly of salt and old stone, with a trace of something sweeter—like dried herbs.

For a long moment, I didn't move. The mattress cradled me in a way that made it hard to remember why I should get up at all. This wasn't my room. It wasn't even my time.

I turned my head, and the sheer size of the place hit me. Arched windows lined the stone, each one hung with heavy drapes that shifted just slightly, breathing with the sea wind beyond.

Somewhere nearby, water dripped in the silence, echoing like a clock counting off the seconds until reality caught up with me.

A round opening near the center pours a single shaft of golden light down into the room, illuminating the dust motes swirling like tiny galaxies in the air.

For a moment, I wonder if I've woken in a cathedral or a tomb.

My body feels heavy, distant. I turn my head, slow and aching, and there—just beyond the edge of the light—stand two figures. Blurred at first, as if silhouettes in a dream, until my vision sharpens and the details slip into place.

Sɪʀɪᴀɴɴᴀ.

Aɴᴅ ʙᴇsɪᴅᴇ ʜᴇʀ, a woman I don't recognize, she's tall, with pale black hair braided down her back.

Sirianna's voice is a whisper, but it echoes across the vaulted chamber as a command. "Go and tell the others she's awake."

The stranger gave a little bow and slipped off through a big arched doorway, her footsteps echoing for a second, then just gone. I tried sitting up, and wow, the pain. My chest felt like someone had dropped a brick on it. "Where... where am I?" My voice sounded scratchy and weird, as if it belonged to someone else.

Sirianna moved in closer, but her face was hard to read in the golden light.

"You're safe. For now." She sounded calm, sort of gentle?

"This is the Pharos of Alexandria in Egypt, a Sanctuary of sorts. A place out of reach from the others."

I search her face for answers, but find only the quiet certainty of someone who knows far more than she's saying.

"Why am I here?" I whisper, heart pounding in my throat.

Sirianna exhales slowly, folding her hands in front of her. "Because the light chose you, Veronica. And so has time."

I sank back into the pillows, staring at the high stone ceiling, feeling as though the weight of the whole room was pressing down on my chest. Nothing made sense anymore. Not the token. Not the lighthouses. Not time travel, or destiny, or whatever this was supposed to be.

All I felt was the hollow space where my life used to be and the gentle hum of the token still around my neck in the compass.

Sirianna stood nearby, her voice much quieter than I ever thought it could be. Almost human. "Bram brought you here after he found you... after what happened to your mother."

THE WORD MOTHER hit like a fracture running straight through me. And then it all came rushing back, the cold night air, the flashing lights, my legs giving out beneath that wide, ancient oak. Bram finds me there, curled against the roots, soaked in tears and salt and dread.

I could still hear his voice, cracked and uneven as he knelt beside me.

"SIX... Six, it's bad. It's really bad. She's gone."

He'd tried to make it sound softer, but really, how would you soften something like that?

"She... your mom. She's dead. I'm sorry, Six. I don't know how to say it any differently."

THOSE WORDS JUST SAT THERE, thick and oppressive, like the air before a storm. Even today, I would still be able to hear them humming around in my head. I pushed my hands across my eyes, as if perhaps I could just ignore it all. But that wasn't going to work. Not anymore.

I swallowed hard. My voice came out tiny, almost not even there. "There's nothing left for me here."

Bram didn't say anything. He just held me, arms locked around my ribs, as if that could squeeze the pain out. He knew some things couldn't be fixed with words.

"I need to go," *I said, and my voice came out thin and scratchy.* "Somewhere far from this. Somewhere, the shadows don't follow me. Somewhere I don't have to feel... this."

I looked at him then, really looked at him, standing there with the weight of everything I'd lost pressed into his shoulders.

"Somewhere with you, Bram."

For a second, all I could hear was my breathing, sharp and uneven, and the wind buzzing around the old oak. I waited for him to look away, to tell me I was being completely selfish or totally lost.

He didn't move away. Instead, he leaned in, close enough that I could feel the faint warmth of his breath against my ear. His voice was barely more than a whisper.

"Then we'll go," *he said. No pause. No waver. A promise shaped in a space between heartbeats.* "I know where away is. We'll get there. Together."

Something inside me—tight and knotted for so long I'd stopped noticing—began to unspool. My lungs drew in air as if they'd been empty for years. The night smelled of cold earth and cedar, the taste of it sharp on my tongue. I didn't know if it was fear draining out of me, or hope rushing in, but it left me lighter, as if my bones might float me the rest of the way.

Swallowing hard, hands trembling as I wiped at my eyes, the tears still falling even though I thought I was empty. "Then take me there. I can't stay. Every wall, every shadow... she's here and gone all at once. And it hurts too much."

Bram nodded, gentle but sure. "You don't have to stay where it hurts."

I remembered the way he'd found me, curled against the oak, shaking and broken, how he'd gotten me to my feet without a single word of pity: Just steady hands and quiet strength.

We had walked back to the lighthouse that night, side by side in the dark. No other destination, just forward.

Maybe that's all there ever is.

Forward.

THEN I HEARD FOOTSTEPS, soft but sure, echoing in the stone room. Bram. He stepped inside, smiling, and sat down next to me on the bed. The mattress sagged a little, warm under him.

He leaned in and kissed my forehead, his hand brushing through my hair, before tucking it behind my ear," he said, voice gentle and steady. "How are you?"

He was looking into my eyes. That tenderness, that tone, almost undid me.

I turned away, embarrassed by the way my face felt gritty, with the salty tracks of dried tears, and that gross taste in my mouth. "Don't get too close. I probably smell awful."

Bram chuckled, soft and real. "I've smelled worse. I Promise."

I finally looked at him, taking in the cleaner lines of his face, the damp strands of his hair brushed back, and the fresh clothes that smelled faintly of lavender and something older—stone and time, maybe.

"I'm okay," I said quietly, though it didn't feel entirely true. A little hungry, I guess. And clearly you're much cleaner than I am."

He smiled wider, his eyes catching the morning light filtering down from a slit near the ceiling. "Well, lucky for you, there's a bath waiting over there," he said, pointing to an arched side door. "Warm water, actual soap, and—get this—fresh clothes. Sirianna said she left them just inside the door.

I figured you might want first crack at feeling human again."

I looked up at him. Was he joking? "A bath? You're serious?"

"Dead serious. A huge bath. Like, basically a pool. You've earned it." He nudged my shoulder—not hard, just enough to make his point. His face didn't change. Still worried, still watching me. "And when you're ready, there's plenty of food waiting. Promise you'll stay here, for a while?"

I tried to smile. It was weak, but it counted. "Well, if there's food, then I promise."

He didn't move right away. Just stood there, letting the silence fill the room. Then he squeezed my hand, carefully, and got up.

He stopped in the doorway, talking softer but no less sure. "I'm not leaving you again. Not here. Not anywhere."

I watched him walk away, and for the first time since the oak tree, I actually thought that maybe I could stand up again.

His footsteps faded into the hall, and I whispered to the empty room, "Forward. Always forward."

Chapter Twenty-Seven

I pulled myself out of the bath feeling refreshed, but totally out of place. An attendant left a white tunic for me, and wow, it's actually not terrible. Normally, I wouldn't wear anything so flowy. But hey, it's light, comfy, and mostly modest, sleeveless, but ankle-length. Blue patterns swirl around the edges, creating little ocean waves. When in Alexandria—or wait, was that Rome? Whatever. It helps to blend in and not appear as though you've dropped out of the future.

The corridor stretches out as if I were in a museum, with marble columns and echoing silence. My bare feet pad against the polished floor, each step sending these tiny sound ripples through the space. Salt and the scent of something burnt, like sage or old torch smoke, hang in the air.

At the end of the hall, sunlight was everywhere, gold and loud, practically dragging me forward.

OUTSIDE, the hallway dumped me onto a huge marble balcony. The railings looked as though they had been sanded down by years of salty wind. Past that, the Mediterranean just went on forever, the late-afternoon sun dumping gold all over the water, making everything shimmer and squint-bright.

The air was warm but gentler out here, laced with the faint scent of salt and blooming myrrh from some unseen garden below.

A few figures stood scattered along the stone pillars—scholars, perhaps, or other travelers, their linen robes stirring softly in the breeze as they spoke in hushed tones. Some simply stared out at the distant horizon. Among the group, two familiar shapes caught my eye.

SIRIANNA TURNED FIRST, her braid catching the sun like a blackened rope. "Ah, there you are," she called, voice warm, maybe a little worried. "Feeling more yourself, I hope?"

Lyrica just smiled, with bright eyes, gave a nod, and let Sirianna do the talking.

I stepped closer to them and brushed hair from my face as the breeze tugged at my tunic.

"As much as one can feel themselves wearing someone else's clothes in another century," I said, my voice light but my heart still catching up to all of this.

Sirianna gave a soft laugh and rested her hands along the cool stone rail. "Fashion here is very simple for us women. You'll get used to it," she said, turning her gaze back to the sea. "Or maybe you won't. But either way, this view helps."

Lyrica's voice was as light and feathery as a pixie's. "This place is so enchanted. I think that it's the perfect place to exile."

Then she flashed me a smile, "But hey, what do they say? Dress for revenge, right?"

"Um... sure, Lyrica," I said, my voice hesitant, unsure. Was I agreeing, or was I just trying to keep the peace?

Sirianna and I exchanged a glance across the space between us, a quiet shrug passing between us like an unspoken joke—or maybe mutual confusion. Neither of us had any idea what to make of her, but it was easier to smile and let it slide. Our shared annoyance with Lyrica was something that we at least had in common.

"Lyrica, could you go find out how long until the feast is ready—and maybe bring us a drink while you're at it?" Sirianna asked, her tone light but edged with authority.

She gave a sort of nod, already halfway to the door. "Yes, ma'am," she called over her shoulder, sandals tapping rhythmically against the stone as she vanished inside the tower.

I WAITED until her footsteps faded into the hush of the corridor before I leaned toward Sirianna. "What is with her?" I whispered, the words barely breaking the breezy air.

Sirianna exhaled, a breath that seemed to carry more weight than sound. She stared outward, "No one really knows," she said at last. "She's... like some kind of muse or something? All about the future of music or poetry. Maybe both." Her voice trailed off like she was following a thought down some unseen road. Then she looked at me, and a tiny, crooked smile tugged at her mouth—half amusement, half something she wasn't quite ready to name.

"She claims she's part of some department of tortured poets, or was it a dead poets society? I don't remember."

I turned my gaze back toward the harbor, where strange-looking ships drifted through the water—sleek wooden hulls, faded sails, with shapes I didn't recognize, full or flapping with the salty breeze.

They slid around on the water, darting and shifting, some little and skittery, others just massive, like floating castles. I squinted, trying to make sense of it. "So... *when* are we?" I finally asked, my voice sort of drifting off as I stared at the weird scene playing out down there. Somehow, I knew the answer would only create more questions.

"This is several centuries before Yeshua, also known as Jesus, darling," She purred smoothly, "Roughly twenty-two-hundred years before your time."

I gripped the stone railing and leaned out over the balcony, my stomach dipping at the sheer drop below. We had to be ten stories up, at least. Then I turned and craned my neck to look up at the tower behind me, the structure rising even higher, disappearing into the bright afternoon sky. It stretched impossibly tall—as if dropped from a modern skyline, not a part of ancient history.

"There's no way this was built twenty-two-hundred years ago," I breathed, shaking my head. "No way."

Sirianna gave a quiet laugh, the breeze catching her dark hair. "You're not entirely wrong. Even now, the Pharos is already an ancient landmark. She's stood nearly two centuries at this point. In your time, you'd know her as one of the great wonders of the ancient world."

I frowned, the name unfamiliar. "I've never heard of this... Pharos. What happened to it?"

Her smile faded, her voice softening. "We're not supposed to reveal too much about what comes next. It can... shift or shake things up, unless you're prepared."

She paused, then leaned in, sending a whisper against the wind.

"But since you asked... an earthquake. About four centuries from now. Then the sea slowly takes away the rest."

The words settled over me heavy and cold. Nothing lasts.

Nothing lasts. Not this tower, not the view, definitely not the people who wander through its halls. That thought hit me hard, and for a second, I felt fragile inside. It made me think of my mom and also Bram.

I wrapped my arms around myself, feeling about two inches tall compared to everything, including the sky. "Where's Bram?" I said. It came out surprisingly quiet, almost as if I didn't want anyone to hear.

Sirianna made this soft sound, still staring at the horizon. "You won't find him out here. Not this close to the edge." She looked over her shoulder at me, with this half-smile, like she knew exactly what I was thinking.

"With his fatal fate being the tendency to fall, Bram's not exactly a fan of heights."

BEFORE I COULD RESPOND, Lyrica burst back onto the terrace while balancing three gold chalices in her hands.

"Here you go, ladies," she sang, offering one to Sirianna, then to me, her grin bright and maybe just a little mischievous.

"It's not Champaign, so there will be no Champaign problems tonight." She raised her cup, then lifted her eyebrows, like she was about to give us the punchline. "Let's all pretend we're on a late-night talk show and sip this."

I tried a little sip. Sweet, almost too easy. Like juice, but with something wild and kind of sneaky under the sugar. Warm, ancient, and perhaps a little dangerous.

Lyrica watched me with a look as if she knew something that Sirianna and I did not. Her eyes were all bright and sharp.

"The feast is almost ready," she said, voice dropping, like we were sharing a secret. "They're all waiting for the guest of honor, Starlight." She tipped her cup at me and did a tiny bow, grinning.

Then Lyrica wandered off toward the door, and just before crossing the threshold, she spun on her heel, tossing a glance over her shoulder, a glint of challenge in her eyes.

"Are you ready for it?" she asked, then added, "If the night gets interesting, don't blame me."

Sirianna moved away from the edge of the balcony, her gaze steady on me. "Ready or not, Six... the story won't wait."

The air felt heavier somehow, charged with something both ancient and brand new. My heart thudded in my chest as I took a step forward, legs shaky but moving just the same.

Was I ready? Not even close.

But if there was food waiting, and Bram, maybe that was enough.

I drew a breath, squared my shoulders, and followed them through the door.

With the air shifting cooler as I stepped into the shadows of the tower, and for the first time, I wondered if "ready" would ever come—because this story had already begun without me.

Chapter Twenty-Eight

The whole hallway smelled like roasted lamb and herbs, even where it was cold, and the torches flickered like they couldn't make up their minds. I followed Sirianna, my bare feet padding softly, as I tried to ignore how hungry I was.

Right before the dining hall, Sirianna stopped. She glanced down the hall, then smiled, slyly, like she knew a secret.

She gave this tiny shrug, barely a smile, just a twitch at the corners of her mouth. "Well... looks like someone's been waiting for you."

I turned. And there was Bram. He was leaning against the wall, all casual, but not really. The lamplight hit his shoulder, and his arms were folded—not in a tough way, more like he was trying to keep himself from falling apart. Half his face was half in shadow, but his brilliant eyes? Totally steady, locked on me.

The torchlight shifted, and for a moment his gaze met mine, and there it was again, that quiet openness of his eyes.

Sirianna gave me a gentle nudge, a wry smile tugging at her mouth. "I'll give you two a peaceful moment."

She left me with that thought and swept ahead toward the hall, her steps quiet but sure, leaving the two of us alone in the dim corridor.

I took a slow breath and stepped toward him. "I didn't think you'd wait for me."

He smiled, small but sure. "I'll always wait for you."

Something in my chest loosened, fragile and aching.

"I don't know if I can do this," I whispered, my voice barely holding together. "Smile. Eat. Act like I'm okay—in this place. The whole thing feels... so strange."

Bram peeled off the wall and came closer, close enough that I could feel how warm he was, even with the sea breeze trying to blow us apart. "You don't have to pretend," he said, voice low, steady. "Not with me."

Which, honestly? Made it a little easier to keep breathing.

He held out his hand, like it was no big deal.

And somehow, that was enough.

I placed my hand in his, the noise of the dining hall waiting ahead, the unknown stretching beyond that.

The chamber stretched wide and tall, lit by dozens of oil lamps glowing against the high stone walls.

The long table was crowded with platters of roasted lamb, olives, flatbread, and fruits I didn't recognize. Bronze cups bumped together as people drank a dark wine.

I sat next to Bram. Just the sight of food warmed me up and settled my nerves, at least for a minute. Across the table, Sirianna cut into a fig, her face calm but kind of alert.

"So," I said, tipping my cup and watching the wine swirl, "are all your meals like this? Candlelight, beautiful servers, and that awful feeling when the dessert trays show up?"

Bram laughed under his breath, ripping a piece of bread and

dragging it through olive oil. "Not always. Sometimes we skip the lamps."

Sirianna lifted an eyebrow, almost smiling. "And sometimes we skip dessert. Depends on the century."

I smiled, too, taking another drink. The wine felt warmer now, spreading through my chest. For a second, everything—my mom, the empty places where my old life used to be in St. Augustine—all of it seemed far away.

But it didn't last.

"In all that sleep, did you have any of your recurring dreams?" Bram probed.

"Maybe, I really don't remember," I answered honestly, thinking that the trauma over my mom may have silenced visions in my head.

Sirianna set down her knife and leaned in slightly. "If you truly want answers, Veronica, there's another way. A deeper way. Into your mind."

Bram's smile faded, his posture tensing beside me. "Are you talking about... hypnotism?"

She nodded, slow and serious. "Not, like, the parlor trick kind. More like guided dreaming. Or remote viewing, maybe. Unlocking memories or visions your brain hides, you know, to keep you safe."

I shifted in my chair. Suddenly, I was cold, even though the wine was warm in my stomach. "So, you mean... go poking around in my head while I'm asleep?"

"Not unless you want us to," Sirianna said. "But your dreams might carry clues. Stuff you could remember when you wake up, some little fragments that could help us find your dad."

I looked at Bram. His jaw was tight, but his hand was just there, next to mine on the table, steady and waiting.

"Sounds... pretty wild," I said, and yeah, the wine was definitely talking now.

"It might be the only way to get your father back," Sirianna said, raising her cup in this quiet little toast.

Several of the torches along the stone walls suddenly sputtered out, one after another, their flames extinguished as if by an unseen breath. Shadows swallowed the corners of the hall, and the glimmering torchlight that remained cast the long dining table in a strange, wavering glow. The conversation died or went to whispers mid-sentence. Laughter choked into silence. The air shifted—expectant, reverent.

I leaned in toward Bram, my voice barely above a whisper. "What's happening?"

He didn't look at me when he answered, his gaze fixed on the archway beyond the head of the table.

"Lux Aeterna is about to address the table."

"Lux... who?" My heart did this weird thump thing. Footsteps echoed in from the hallway, slow and super dramatic.

And then out of the shadows: this old guy, hunched over a carved staff. His robe, a dull or faded grey, somehow shimmered a bit, catching the firelight as he shuffled forward.

His white beard hung to the middle of his chest, and his eyes, sharp despite the lines webbing his face, scanned the chamber with the weight of memory.

He reminded me a little of Lucian—if Lucian had been plucked out of myth and dusted with more centuries. There was something Merlin-like about him. Wizardly, yes. But even more ancient. Like time had settled in his bones and chose not to leave.

Lux Aeterna stopped at the head of the table. For a second, everyone just kind of leaned in, holding their breath. He lifted one hand—not all dramatic, just a little—and started talking in this voice that sounded like he'd been telling stories forever, warm and a little rough around the edges.

"Welcome, travelers and stewards of the forgotten hours. Tonight, we break bread not just as friends or strangers, but as threads in a greater weave of time. One among us sits at this table for the first time, though her presence was written long before most of the rest of you arrived."

He looked right at me. Seriously, just turned and stared, and his eyes were kind of sad, but also not? There was this spark in them, like he was happy and sorry at the same time. "Veronica Ingram. Daughter of the once-lost but soon to be found. You are salt and light in a world dimmed by forgetting, called not merely to witness, but to preserve and to reveal. I bid you welcome. Not as a guest, but as one of us. May your questions find courage, and your courage find truth."

A hum of approval passed through the room like a gentle breeze, full of weight. The token on my chest pulsed stronger as he spoke.

I didn't know what to say. I just sat there, caught between awe and disbelief, feeling as if some invisible door had just opened before me. And that there was no going back.

As Lux Aeterna finished speaking, he offered me a final nod, then turned, his robe trailing behind him like rippling parchment. He walked with the same slow, deliberate steps, vanishing through the dark archway from which he'd emerged.

No one dared move until the last fold of his cloak disappeared from sight.

Then, with a whoosh, the torches along the stone walls reignited all at once, flames bursting to life in a synchronized blaze.

THE ROOM BRIGHTENED, but it wasn't just regular light—it was, like, illumination. The glow looked cleaner, almost gold, sharp at the edges, as if it had just been created.

"Lux Aeterna," Bram whispered next to me, like saying it too loud would freak out the stars. "You might know him by another name."

I looked over, still kind of stuck in the weirdness of it all. "What name?"

He met my eyes, super serious. "Father Time."

My eyebrows rose instinctively, unsure whether to laugh or gasp.

"He's not a legend, he is quite real," Bram said, hushed and reverent. "And if you ever see him *outside* of the Pharos, it means something on the timeline has fractured beyond repair."

A silence fell again, smaller but heavier.

THEN SIRIANNA TIPPED her chin at Bram, doing a little nod. "She's ready. We should take her."

Bram just sort of froze, his hand squeezing the goblet a little too hard. "Are you sure? tonight?"

Sirianna didn't even blink. "If she wants answers," she now stared right at me, "then this is the path."

"What path?" I sounded like a little kid.

Sirianna softened her voice. "A path into your dreams. The ones you keep having. They're more important than you think."

But to get to them, you need a little help.

Bram looked at Sirianna, brows furrowing slightly. "You're thinking... Vex?"

His voice dropped just a notch, like the name itself carried weight or risk.

Sirianna nodded slowly, her expression unreadable. "She's the only one who can reach deeply without unraveling the entranced."

Bram stood slowly, motioning for me to follow. "Come on. There's a location... a quiet place. Only a few people are aware of it— old stone, older than this hall. You'll be safe there. That's where we will find Vex."

"A special room for hypnosis, among other activities," Sirianna added with a smirk, trying to cut the tension. "Don't worry, she won't dangle a watch in front of your face or make you cluck like a chicken."

"That's only happened once," Bram muttered.

"Twice," Sirianna corrected with a wink.

Bram and Sirianna led me toward the shadows, and for the first time all night, I wondered if stepping deep into my mind meant I might not come back the same.

Chapter Twenty-Nine

I stood, legs unsure beneath me, heart thudding in my chest. My thoughts raced with the weight of what I'd just heard, and the strangeness of what was coming next.

But still, I followed them through the hall, through the flame-lit corridors, deeper into the ancient stones of the lighthouse, the wine had helped, but also I wanted answers.

Turning a dimmed corner of the corridor, the atmosphere changed—chilly, denser, as if stones were exhaling. And then, from the black immediately in front of them, a bellowing voice spoke out, low and rough, rebounding off the eternal walls like thunder in a tomb:

"Seekers! Inquiring after lost Jacob, you three!"

We all leaped, even Bram. A shape emerged out of the black, hunched over and little more than a shadow to begin with. My eyes adjusted slowly, taking in the twisted spine, the gnarled cane clutched in one veiny hand, and the long shawl trailing behind like a cloak of cobwebs.

Sirianna exhaled hard, one hand on her chest. "Vex, must you always make an entrance like an attention-seeking ghoul?"

A high, wheezing laugh broke from the old woman. "Sirianna, you old vamp of a siren," she croaked. "Of the three of you, only you should've known I haunt this space."

"How? By your wretched smell, you ancient goat?" Sirianna smirked, stepping forward without hesitation. "Veronica Ingram, meet Lunara Vex."

Vex turned toward me slowly, and I finally got a full look at her.

She was impossibly old—gray skin like dried parchment, folded and creased so many times it seemed to defy nature. Vex's silver-white hair, twisted into bulky ropes that spilled down her back, tangled with bits of bone, metal, and what looked suspiciously like a dried flower or two. But it was her eyes that stopped me cold—milky and clouded, like marbles left out in a storm. Cataracts had taken nearly all the light from them, and yet, she looked directly at me, as though she saw far more than any of us.

"Ah," she murmured, tilting her head. "This one burns bright. A flame wrapped in salt. Hmm. It's been too long," she murmured, resting her bony finger on the compass hanging on my chest for a moment.

I wasn't sure what to say.

She leaned in a bit too close. Her breath smelled like a damp cellar filled with something herbal. "You'll do," she whispered, then turned and shuffled off without explanation, her cane tapping rhythmically against the stones.

She looked at Sirianna. "She's... something."

Sirianna grinned. "She's everything we need—and more than we're ready for."

VEX LED us into a dimly lit chamber. Warm, heavy air pressed in around us, thick with the weight of a thousand whispered secrets. Only one torch burned on the far wall, casting flickering shadows that danced across rough stone. The scent of lavender and something older—dust, earth, dried herbs—hung in the air.

Against the far side of the room, I could just make out several mismatched chairs arranged in a crescent, and at the center of it all stood one peculiar seat: high-backed, reclining slightly, with padded arms and a strange metal frame. It looked half throne, half dentist's chair.

Vex moved to it with surprising grace for someone so ancient, her cane tapping softly on the stone. "Everyone, have a seat," she said, gesturing to the other chairs with a sweep of her spindly hand. "Veronica, dear, you may take the seat of seeking."

I hesitated. "That's not ominous at all," I muttered under my breath, shooting Bram a quick glance. He gave me a slight nod, reassuring, but stayed silent. Sirianna just sat and crossed her legs and folded her arms like she'd seen this show before.

Vex patted the seat, the torchlight catching the milky cloud of her cataract-filled eyes. "Come now, it won't bite, child." She gave a raspy little chuckle, like sandpaper on silk.

Reluctantly, I moved to the chair and lowered myself into it. The moment I leaned back, I felt it—an odd vibration beneath the padding, like the hum of something ancient and unseen. I shivered.

Vex moved closer, her cane lying to the side. Her hands were cool and parched as she put one on my forehead, one on my shoulder. "Relax now, Veronica," she said, her tone smoother, deeper—almost musical. "Let your eyelids fall heavy. Let the noise of the world fade to whispers. Here, in this room, there is only the air in your lungs and the thud of your heart."

I blinked slowly, already feeling the weight of her words pulling me down.

"Close your eyes, dear one," she breathed. "Sink into the water. You are a rock in a quiet pond. Unmovable. Anchored. Release."

I could hear the crack of the flash from the torch, the creak of Bram adjusting in his seat—but even those were fading away. My body was no longer part of me. My mind was cloudy.

Vex pressed her mouth to my ear and whispered, "Now, let's discover what truths lie beneath your waking mind..."

Darkness followed—not the kind that chased you down, but the type that waited, quiet and full of secrets.

THE DARKNESS WASN'T EMPTY; it moved slowly, like smoke underwater. Shapes stirred in the distance, forming and reforming.

I drifted through it, weightless, tugged by something under the surface. A current of memory? Or something else? Not sure.

A voice echoed, thin and far-off. Maybe my father's? "Six..." The nickname landed sharp, right in my chest. I tried to follow the sound. Tried to answer, but my mouth wouldn't work.

Then, through a fog, there was light.

Faint and gray, leaking through storm clouds. Suddenly, I was barefoot on a rocky shoreline, sea pounding behind me in slow motion. Cold wind stung my cheeks.

My tunic whipped in the wind like it didn't belong to me. Everything smelled of salt, rust, ozone, and something like old oil.

Ahead of me stood a tower.

It was tall and brutal in design, with stark concrete streaked by black mold; its red star had long since faded on a rusted metal plate—a Soviet lighthouse. Shattered glass littered the top lantern room, and its once-glorious beam now stared hollow and blind toward the sea. Barbed wire choked the lower levels, and graffiti in Cyrillic flaked off the battered walls. Somewhere, a steel door groaned in the wind, swinging slowly open and shut.

I moved forward as if pulled.

Then a name surfaced in my mind, *Cape... Cape Aniva.* The words didn't feel like mine, but they burned with truth. *Sakhalin*

Island. Edge of the old Soviet Empire. North of Japan. My heart thudded with certainty.

The scene flickered like a film reel stuttering.

Inside, the air was damp and cold. Rusty stairs spiraled up into darkness. A small room off to the side glowed faintly red, like a warning light stuck in eternal dusk. And there—hunched near a wall covered in maps and scribbled equations—was a figure.

I couldn't see his face, but I knew.

My father.

He was alive.

He was real.

He was waiting.

Suddenly, the air pulled backward, like a riptide pulling me away. The tower blurred, vanishing with the sea, and the mountainous rocky outcroppings were gone—

"VERONICA... VERONICA," Vex's voice was a tether, pulling me back. "Breathe, dear."

My eyes flew open.

I was back in the chair. Torchlight. Stone walls. My breath caught like I'd run a mile, heart thudding in my ears. Bram was leaning forward in his seat; concern etched into every line of his face.

"I saw him," I cried out, my voice hoarse and frantic. "My father is out there!"

Vex just tilted her head, those pale eyes blinking slowly, like she was trying to see through me. "And where does the vision come from, child?"

My hands were shaking in my lap as I looked into Vex's harsh, wrinkled face.

"Sakhalin Island," I whispered, trying to catch my breath. An old Soviet lighthouse. It's in ruins, barely standing. He's there."

The words felt like they'd come from somewhere way older than me, like they'd just been waiting for this exact moment to fall out of my mouth. The room went super still. Even the torch on the wall seemed to shrink for a second, like the whole place was holding its breath.

NOBODY SAID ANYTHING.

And then—

"HOLY CHERNOBYL!" Sirianna blurted, her eyes huge and her mouth already half-grinning.

I almost fell out of the chair. "Holy what?" I said, whipping around to look at her.

She just shrugged. "Relax, it's just a thing I picked up. A strange name that helps bring an end to an already broken empire. You'll hear that name soon enough. Trust me," she said.

She waved it off like it wasn't a big deal, but something flickered behind her eyes—something guarded. But then her expression sobered. "Cape Aniva, though... that's no joke. That place was or still is nuclear-powered.

Bram's brow furrowed. "You're saying it's radioactive?"

"It's Soviet-built, so... who even knows?" Sirianna shrugged. "That place is as run-down as the alliance it serves. An industrial wasteland, haunted by time in ways most lighthouses aren't. Just standing there, forgotten, for decades."

Her words settled on me like dust. A strange humming from my dream still thrummed low in my chest.

"I saw the inside of it," I murmured. "Rust. Decay. He's kept in this tiny room, alone. But there were other people on the island, holding him."

Vex reached over, brushing a loose strand of hair from my forehead—soft, deliberate, almost grandmotherly. "You did well, child. Your vision was clear. Now we know where he is."

"And now we're going to get him," Bram said, his voice steady, carrying the kind of certainty I needed to believe in. Fierce, even.

I LOOKED AT THEM ALL, this odd little group of time travelers and mystics, and for the first time in a long time, I didn't feel alone.

Just deeply... *awake.*

Chapter Thirty

The climb from Vex's sanctum deep in the Pharos to the top was brutal.

Endless flights of stone steps within the inner column of the tower were rough and uneven, making the climb perilous. The air grew thinner the higher we went, laced with the scent of ancient oil, charred wood, and salt. I kept looking back at Bram, who looked pale and acted like he would turn back at every step upward.

"Almost there," Sirianna said for the fourth time.

"If I fall," Bram grunted, "don't try to catch me. Just lie and tell people I died heroically."

Sirianna snorted behind him. "Dramatic exaggeration is not your fatal fate, Bram."

"Can't we just use the token *here*?" he hissed. "Like... at ground level?"

"It has to be the top," Sirianna said, not even looking back. "For the mirrors to align with the timeline. Or do you want to end up halfway inside a volcano?"

Bram didn't answer. He just kept climbing, grumbling something about how volcanoes were better than ancient staircases.

When we finally reached the summit, everything sort of fell away. To the left, the Mediterranean stretched out forever, dark and blue and shimmery, like someone had thrown a velvet blanket over the world and stitched it with stars. To the right, the desert rolled out in soft, endless waves, pale and quiet.

We stood there, right at the edge, caught between water and sand, like we could tip into either world if we breathed too hard.

We had changed back into our 1980s clothes before the transfer, wearing jeans, shorts, and t-shirts. Layers that felt familiar.

I reached for Bram's hand without thinking, threading my fingers through his. His skin was clammy, his face pale, and his wide eyes refused to look anywhere but straight ahead.

His grip? Like, iron. White-knuckle, I'm-not-letting-go, total panic mode. But he didn't pull away.

"You're safe," I whispered, leaning in so close I could basically count his eyelashes. "As long as I'm here, you're good."

His jaw did this clench thing, and his breathing was all uneven, but—I swear—a tiny smile tried to escape.

"I think I believe you," he said, except his voice was doing this shaky, almost-laugh thing.

"Good," I said, and gave his hand a little squeeze. "Because I'm not letting go."

The very top of the Pharos? Not even close to what I imagined.

At over four hundred feet up, night had settled over Alexandria, but the heavens were cloudless, full of stars that glittered as if glass scattered across black velvet.

In the center of the platform, surrounded by heavy stone railings and copper fittings, a massive bonfire roared—oil-soaked timbers crackling and spitting orange light. The flames licked the sky, casting wild shadows against the surrounding walls.

A contraption stood just behind it, somehow forged from equal parts genius and madness.

Mirrors—huge ones, cracked and curved—affixed to a rotating frame of bronze and iron. Thick lenses of bubbled, greenish glass hung like heavy jewels in a strange alignment. It looked both ancient and futuristic at the same time.

"What is..." I started.

Sirianna nodded. "Archimedes' heat ray. Or at least a version of it. Without the sun, it's harmless. But when the mirrors are tuned... Well, let's just say don't stand in front of it during daylight unless you want to be cooked like a lamb shank, or a Roman warship."

Bram stayed well back.

We approached the device slowly. I could feel the token in my pocket growing warm, as if it already knew what was coming.

"Time aligns here," Sirianna said, her voice suddenly reverent. "The lens focuses more than light—it focuses memory, history, intent. It's one of the last places the old ways still work."

I took out the token. It pulsed faintly, similar to a heartbeat.

"You ready?" I asked Bram, half expecting him to turn around and bolt back down the stairs.

He swallowed hard. "Just... do it quick."

I stepped up, clutching the token in both hands. The bonfire light bounced off it, throwing wobbly shadows all over the top of the tower. I shut my eyes and tried to find that link I'd used before—that shimmery tug between time and place, that odd pull on my brain.

"Take us to Sakhalin Island," I whispered. "To the Lighthouse. To my father."

The token got hot, fast. The mirrors above our heads started to hum, vibrating just a little, as if they'd heard me and were waiting.

The fire crackled louder and became even hotter, as the air grew electric, like the moment before lightning splits the sky.

Everything slowed.

The stars bent and blurred.

And we vanished from the Egyptian air.

WE LANDED HARD ON A COLD, green linoleum floor—the kind you'd expect in a run-down hospital or forgotten government building. The air was stale, tinged with the scent of rust and sea salt, and for a moment, everything around us buzzed with static and disorientation.

Twisted iron girders arched above us in a warped skeleton, the remains of something once grand. We were lying at the center of a shattered framework—roughly the size of the great lens back in St. Augustine—but this one was fractured, missing huge chunks of its once-precise glass. Jagged shards clung stubbornly to the rusted metal, and what remained of the lens was stained and clouded with age. Broken. As if someone rolled it down the nearby stairs.

Around us, the space resembled an old office, but not one anyone had worked in for years. Paint peeled in long strips from the walls. A broken rotary phone hung off its cord nearby, and the once-white blinds over the windows were yellowed and brittle. The smell of mildew clung to everything. This was no ancient wonder, no golden past. This place was exactly like Sirianna described: an industrial wasteland.

SIRIANNA SLOWLY SAT UP, brushing linoleum grit from her pants. She glanced around at the rusted metal, broken lens, and peeling paint, then leaned toward me and whispered, "Charming. A lighthouse designed by Soviet despair."

It was daylight, but not the kind that was good.

The sky was so flat and gray it looked like someone had sucked all the color out of the world. I just stood there, kind of numb, and then suddenly there was this total, frantic explosion overhead—a fury of frantic wings. Bats! Not just a few, either. Hundreds. They shot out from the rafters, a whole blizzard of flapping and squeaking, right above my head.

No warning at all. Bats everywhere. They zigzagged through the rusted beams, like a bunch of living shadows, all tangled up and shrieking and wild. The noise was insane, like someone dumped a blender full of dry leaves over us. I'm pretty sure I screamed.

I ducked without even thinking, heart pounding, and buried my face in Bram's chest. He wrapped his arms around me right away, steady and strong, holding me tight while the cloud of furry leathery bodies swept past. I could feel his steady heart thudding through his shirt, and I clung to him even tighter as the bats funneled through a busted window with this creepy, perfect precision, disappearing into the pale afternoon.

"Our arrival must have spooked them," Bram whispered, his breath warm against the top of my head. He didn't let go.

I peeked up at him, startled by how calm he sounded, but grateful for the anchor.

"I've had worse welcoming committees," Sirianna muttered, brushing her hair from her shoulder like this was just another weekday.

We climbed carefully out of the shattered lens, its jagged edges and twisted iron groaning faintly as if protesting our weight. My Converse All-Stars hit the linoleum, and I brushed myself off, streaks of rust and dust clinging to my t-shirt and shorts.

THE COLD AIR WAS BITING. We definitely hadn't dressed warm enough, and my teeth chattered as I crossed the room to the nearest window. Or, well, the place where a window used to be. All the glass was gone, just a jagged metal frame. I leaned into the opening and was instantly blasted by a gust so cold that it made my eyes water. It smelled sharp and salty, like the ocean, and I sucked in a lungful, grateful for something that didn't reek of mold and rot.

Down below, waves slammed against rocks, all white foam and

spray. There was a second island out there, too, smaller than this one, just a hunk of stone sticking up from the gray water. I rested my fingers on the window frame. The metal was so cold it stung, and when I exhaled, my breath hung in the air like a little ghost.

"You said there were others here?" Bram's voice came from behind me, quiet and serious.

I stayed facing the water. I didn't want to turn around. Not yet.

"I sensed them," I said, still staring at that far-off island and the flat, dead horizon. "They're keeping my father prisoner."

No one spoke for a second. The only sound was the wind, whining through the empty window.

"I saw him," I said, lower. "Shackled up. Just for a second. Then I heard footsteps, someone walking toward him. But I woke up before I could see who."

Sirianna stood, straightened her cloak with a snap, and muttered, "No one's expecting us here. Not without a gravitational wave."

Her voice echoed slightly in the cavernous, ruined space, adding an eerie chill to the already bleak surroundings.

Bram tried one of the doors lining the hallway, the handle creaking as it gave way. It opened to reveal only a narrow, dusty, and forgotten utility closet—but inside, hanging from a hook, was a long, heavy military jacket—faded green canvas, worn at the cuffs, with brass buttons dulled by time.

He pulled it down gently, brushed off the worst of the dust, and turned to me.

He just came up behind me and draped it over my shoulders, his hands, like, hanging there a little too long. "You're shivering," he said, concerned, looking at me like he was trying to figure something out.

I glanced up, hugged the coat tighter, and tried to smile. "I'm a Florida girl," I said, tucking my chin down. "This kind of cold should not be normal."

His mouth twitched, but he didn't answer. He just stayed there, right next to me, basically blocking all the wind leaking in through the busted window.

"Where do you think he is, Six?" Bram asked, his voice barely more than a breath beside me.

I stared down the dark corridor stretching ahead of us, the stone walls swallowing the dim light. The air felt heavy—as if the whole place was holding its smelly breath.

"I don't know," I said, shaking my head and staring at the floor. "How big is this place, really?"

Bram let out a breath and looked around, like maybe the walls would just tell him. "Too big. And way too quiet."

Sirianna edged forward, stopping right at the spot where the light just sort of fizzled out. "If he's captive, then someone's watching him," she said, voice all flat and serious. "So, we have to get their attention. Then see how many there are and where they show up from."

I swept my eyes around the chamber's rusted iron walls, wide shadows, and old debris forgotten in corners. That's when I saw it: a rusted metal garbage can tucked behind a broken bench, thick, dented, and stained.

I walked toward it, heart pounding, and placed my hand on the cold rim.

Looking back at Bram and Sirianna, I gave a single nod.

"Then maybe it's time to make some noise."

Chapter Thirty-One

Bram didn't even pause.

He grabbed the garbage can with both hands, and the metal rattled a bit as he hauled it up the stairs. He tried to keep his movements quiet.

"Wait, are we sure about...?" I tried after becoming hesitant.

He shot me a look, eyes wild. "You wanted noise," he said, and kept going.

He reached the steel landing above, then, with a grunt, hurled the can to the next flight. It clanged against the walls, flipping, crashing, crashing again. The sound roared through the hall as the metallic beast began rolling down the iron steps.

Then he turned and bolted down, his shoes slapping the steps in perfect rhythm with the thunder he'd unleashed.

"Now!" Sirianna hissed, grabbing my wrist and pulling me toward the narrow closet door tucked under the stairs.

We dove inside, heartbeats hammering in the dark. The air smelled like old pine cleaner and dust, the same tiny space where

Bram had found the coat. We barely fit—shoulder to shoulder, breath to breath. I could feel the token vibrating against my chest, as if it were just as afraid.

A moment later, Bram burst in after us, yanking the door shut behind him.

Outside, the garbage can slammed to the ground. It echoed up the walls, like the whole building might rattle apart. We froze.

Somewhere above us, footsteps could be heard. Not Bram's. Not Sirianna's. Not mine.

Something—or someone else.

On the other side of the closet door, the silence grew dense, as if it were waiting.

Footsteps. Slow, heavy, one at a time. Coming down the stairs.

Each step seemed to vibrate through the steps above and into my spine. Sirianna's hand tightened around mine in the dark. Bram didn't move, barely even breathed.

The footsteps reached the floor.

A pause.

Then the unmistakable sound of boots crunching glass or metal.

Whoever it was had found the can.

Clang.

Someone nudged it with their foot.

Clang. Clang.

The steps seemed to circle it, slow and suspicious.

Bram reached for the latch.

I opened my mouth to whisper something—*wait, don't*—but the door was already cracking open, just an inch or two. He leaned in, his eye pressed to the narrow gap.

The dim blue light from the stairwell spilled into the storage closet like a trickle of moonlight, not enough to see their face, but enough to catch the glint of something metallic.

A ring on their hand.

A weapon at their side.

Bram's breath caught as he watched the figure lean down to examine the can more closely. His grip on the edge of the door trembled—not in fear, but readiness.

The stranger stood upright again, still facing the can, dropping a cigarette from his lips. Totally unaware of the three hearts pounding just feet away.

Then, with a scuff of his boots, he turned and began ascending the stairs again—slow, cautious, unconvinced.

Only once the last footfall faded did Bram carefully open the door and lean into the cold, exhaling through gritted teeth.

"We've got their attention," he whispered. "Now we find out where they are."

Sirianna stepped out after Bram, silent and sure. I followed, heart hammering in my ears. We all looked up the stairwell, shadows curling around each step.

"Are we supposed to follow?" I asked, not really wanting to know.

Sirianna just nodded, already heading off.

I groaned and looked up. The stairs twisted forever, like a nightmare.

Behind me, Bram made this noise, "Ugh. More stairs?"

Even though my stomach was twisting in knots from nerves, I almost laughed.

So we started up, one step at a time, trying not to slip, the metal rattling under our shoes.

Each turn in the spiral narrowed the light, tightened the air, and pulled us deeper into whatever truth waited above.

AT THE FIRST LANDING, the spiral sort of spilled out into this weird, skinny space with two heavy wooden doors—one on each side. Dust hung in the air everywhere.

Bram reached for the nearest door, fingers just brushing the iron handle. He turned it slowly. Locked. He crossed to the second one and tried again. Nope. Total dead end.

"He climbed higher than this," he whispered, stepping back, eyes flicking up, up, up.

He didn't wait. He just started up the next flight, shoes scuffing on the metal steps. We went after him, hearts thumping, each step a little higher, the spiral squeezing in around us, nerves tight and jumpy.

Someone was up there.

The steps got narrower the higher we went. The walls pressed closer, and it got dark, as if any light was being sucked out of the stairwell.

Then, halfway up, I heard it: a weird humming noise, low and off-key, drifting up from below.

WE FROZE.

THE SOUND GREW LOUDER, closer. Someone was coming. And not just someone—whoever it was was humming. Cheerfully.

I peered over the railing. A figure appeared below, wearing headphones connected to a cassette player clipped to his belt. He carried stacked trays of food, clattering metallically with each step.

A meal.

Bram's eyes met mine, big and startled. Then he looked over my shoulder to Sirianna, who was already spinning around, checking the cramped staircase for somewhere to hide. There was nothing. No door. No cut-out in the wall. Just more stairs, curling up, and the footsteps of someone bringing food, getting closer.

"We're trapped," I whispered. My heart raced.

Bram shook his head, jaw set. "No, we're not. We just haven't figured it out yet."

But we all knew—whoever was climbing would see us in seconds. And there was nowhere to hide.

The humming grew louder, closer.

Then, a figure emerged around the curve of the staircase. A man in dull gray clothes, balancing two metal trays in his hands, oblivious. Headphones rested over his ears, and a faint, muffled beat of music leaked through—a song from some forgotten mixtape.

He didn't see us until Bram moved.

BRAM LUNGED FORWARD WITHOUT A WORD, planting his foot square in the man's chest. The trays went flying, clattering against iron steps, mashed potatoes, and something red splattering like blood, and the man let out a startled yell as he tumbled backward.

Down he went, limbs flailing, crashing hard against the unforgiving metal steps. The noise echoed through the tower like a bomb had exploded.

THEN, a heavy door on the landing that we were all on burst open with a bang.

A man stepped out, gun drawn, eyes wide. He wore a blue insulated vest and had the rugged look of someone used to being obeyed. His gaze zeroed in on Bram and me.

"Don't move!"

But Sirianna *wasn't* where he expected.

She'd pressed herself into the shadows in his blind spot beside and almost behind the open door—silent, waiting.

It happened so fast. She lunged, caught his wrist, and the gun went off—a ricochet with a bright spark tore against the iron. They were tangled, jammed up on the landing. Sirianna tried wrenching the weapon sideways, shoving his arm against the wall. He tried to throw her off, but she was quicker, meaner, her reflexes quick and sharp.

"Get the gun!" Bram yelled.

I just stood there. I couldn't move. My legs were cemented. My ears were still ringing.

Another crash—Sirianna slammed the man's arm against the wall again, this time with a sickening *crack*. He screamed, the gun dropped, clattering to the metallic non-skid floor.

Bram dove for it, skidding across the landing as Sirianna landed a final blow, elbow to jaw, dropping the man in a heap.

Everything went quiet. The handgun, now in Bram's possession, was smoking.

Sirianna straightened up. She was breathing hard, hair in her face like she'd run a mile. She yanked her cloak back into place and looked up and down the hall, eyes thin and sharp.

"So much for shadows and whispers," she said, kind of under her breath, but it still sounded mad.

BRAM TURNED AROUND, still holding the gun, with both hands. His knuckles were white.

He looked from me to the man curled on the ground, bleeding and shaking.

"How many people are in this building?" Bram asked, his voice trembling—not with fear, but fury barely contained.

The man winced, clutching his side. "Just... just me and Levi. I swear. There are only two of us."

Bram stepped forward and planted his boot right on the guy's busted arm. He let out this howl from the pain that didn't seem human.

"You're lying!" Bram barked and leaned in, like he wanted to grind the truth out of him. "Who else is here?"

The guy twisted around, squirming. "Okay! Okay, there's another one!"

"Who?" Bram snapped.

The guy sounded like he was going to pass out. "The... the asset.

That's what they call him. So, yeah. Three."

Bram didn't so much as blink. "Where is he?"

It felt like the whole building was holding its breath, the air getting tight and weird.

"He's... he's two landings up," the guy said, voice all shaky. "Room sixteen. Please. Just let us go."

I LOOKED AT THE STAIRS—JUST two more flights. The numbers on the doors kind of ran together as I spun around towards Bram.

"Keys!" I yelled, stepping right up to the guy. "He's locked in! Give me the keys! Now!"

The guy flinched like I'd slapped him. He reached for his pocket, slow and scared.

Bram didn't budge. "No sudden moves," he said, gun steady.

The guy finally fished out a ring of keys and slid them across the floor. They scraped and clattered across the landing.

I grabbed them and took off for the stairs, not even bothering to fix my coat. It slipped off my shoulders, but I barely noticed. Cold air hit my arms. I just kept running.

I only felt the burning in my legs and the pounding in my heart.

Up one landing. Then another.

I found the door marked 16—faded paint, rust at the hinges. My hands trembled as I tried the first key, then the next. The third clicked. I shoved the door open.

THE ROOM WAS dim and cold, a single barred window letting in slivers of pale light. And there—slumped against the wall, wrists shackled above his head—was my father.

"Dad..." My voice broke, barely more than a whisper.

I scrambled across the room, knees smacking the floor, landing hard right next to him. His head sort of rolled my way, eyes all swollen and puffy, barely able to focus. There was this awful bruise, dark and ugly, stretching across his temple, and his lips were split and dry, like he hadn't had water—or hope—in forever.

He squinted, blinking slowly. "You're... You can't be real," he rasped, voice all scratchy and weird.

"It's me," I said, hands shaking as I reached for his arm, just to make sure he could feel it. "It's Veronica. It's Six."

The name hung in the air. His eyes fluttered, trying to clear the haze—a pause. Then something in him shifted.

"...Six?" His voice cracked around the word like it might shatter him. "My God, it's you... You're older."

Tears slipped down my cheeks as I fumbled with the keys, fingers clumsy. "I'm here. We came for you... With the Collective. You're free."

His arms trembled in the shackles. "I thought I'd imagined your face so many times... I didn't know if I'd ever see you again."

Finally finding the right key. "You're coming with us, Dad."

The last shackle clicked free, and his wrists—red and raw—fell into his lap like they'd forgotten freedom.

Just saying it—*Dad*—opened something in me I hadn't realized was still locked. The tears came fast, warm, unstoppable.

His eyes got watery when he looked at me, like really looked at me, and then his arms came out, shaking. We crashed into each other, squeezing so hard it was like I could erase all the years we'd missed, just by holding on tight enough.

"You're here," he said, his voice muffled in my hair, and he sounded totally wrecked, like he didn't even believe it. "I've imagined this moment so many times... but I never thought it would actually happen."

I leaned back, just a little, so that I could see his face. Still, my dad, even with the bruises and everything. Still him.

"Are you okay to move?" I asked, wiping my cheek with the back of my hand.

He nodded, then laughed softly, breath catching. "With you here, yes. I could walk through fire."

I helped him to his feet just as Sirianna stepped quietly into the room. She paused in the doorway, arms folded, her eyes taking in the scene with something like reverence.

"I'll give you two a moment," she said gently, and for once, her voice no longer held a sarcastic or caustic tone, only respectful.

My dad leaned into me while we stood there, both of us kind of wobbly but at least not totally lost anymore. The silence was thick, almost like it meant something, except for the waves somewhere way off, crashing every so often. Then Sirianna said, real low but with a sharpness, "Jacob... this should have never happened."

My dad turned her way, slow, with this crooked smile that barely moved his bruised mouth. "Sirianna. You're a sight for sore eyes."

She came closer, arms crossed, eyebrows all scrunched up. "Well, your eyes definitely look sore," she shot back, not even pretending to be nice. "When you two are done, we've got a lens to catch."

That made my stomach tighten again. I looked around. "Where's Bram?" I said, maybe too loud.

Sirianna started to answer, but my dad cut in first, locking eyes with me. "Bram is here too."

Sirianna actually smiled, which was seldom the case. "He's getting a couple of guys ready for a voyage," she said. "He'll be ready when it's time."

A FEW MINUTES LATER, we were all together on the rocky, jagged shoreline with Bram. The wind whipped at our clothes, sea mist curling around us like breath from some ancient god.

Out beyond the rocks, a rowboat moved steadily across the dark water—two figures inside, with one of them rowing haphazardly, absent of any grace or rhythm.

Bram watched the boat in the distance with quiet determination.

"Where are they going?" I asked when the wind died down for a brief moment.

He shivered for a moment, not taking his eyes off the boat.

"They'll return here soon. I told them that when they no longer saw us, they could row back."

He paused before tossing the gun into the ocean.

"They're not travelers. Dorian was paying them, mostly with vodka, cigarettes, and bad promises. By the time they get back, we'll be at the Pharos," Bram said. "Is everyone Ready?"

I turned to look at the ruined lighthouse as we walked toward it. The Aniva lighthouse, with its crumbling bones silhouetted against the bruised sky. It sat hunched over the rocks like something modern but broken, yet still keeping its vigil at the end of the world.

WE HAD TRAVELED to the ends of the earth to find my dad.

Chapter Thirty-Two

We stayed at the Pharos for three days, letting the world spin without us.

My father needed time; his body was weak, and his voice was barely more than a whisper. He slept more than he spoke. Whatever they'd done to him at the Avina lighthouse, it had taken more than his strength. It had stolen years and light from his eyes.

Whenever he would awaken, he asked simple questions, "Where are we? Are you safe? What year is it?"

I answered what I could. But I never mentioned Mom.

That truth about her sat between us like an unlit torch, heavy and waiting. I'd look at his face, thinner than I remembered, and think—not yet. Not while he's healing. Not while I'm still trying to believe he's really here.

The Pharos became a strange kind of home.

Sirianna kept herself busy in the chambers downstairs, probably plotting her next time-warping takeover. When I wasn't checking in on Dad, Bram and I drifted through the empty halls, pulled along by the quiet and by each other. We spoke in low voices because anything louder felt like it would shatter the fragile calm that we were trapped inside.

Sometimes, when the sea breeze slipped through the cracks in the ancient stone, cool against my skin, he would reach for me, and we kissed. Softly at first, as if we weren't sure we were allowed. Then, deeper, slower, the two of us, trying to memorize the feeling of each other in case time pulled us apart. Each kiss was a secret- stolen, breathless, aching with everything we hadn't said.

For once, we weren't running or plotting. And for a little while, that felt like enough. However, certain things waited for all of us on the other side of the world—timeline events that demanded our attention. Things that tugged at my thoughts even as we rested beneath the ancient stone blocks of the Pharos.

I wasn't sure I could even call St. Augustine *home* anymore, not after everything that had happened. The place I left behind felt like a shadow of a life I no longer fit inside. But that didn't change what needed to happen there.

Most importantly, my mother's and Meridian's bodies needed to be recovered, honored, and laid to rest. The thought of it twisted something deep in my chest. I hadn't told my father yet. I didn't know how. Every time I looked at him, frail and trying so hard to rejoin the world, I swallowed the words like stones. *Not yet,* I told myself. *Let him have a few more days of not knowing.*

But the dead will not wait forever.

According to Bram, those who travel across time must have a burial at sea. Something about the pull of tides over time, the way the ocean keeps secrets that soil cannot. It was a sacred act, older than any of us, older than the factions. A final kindness. A way of letting go and letting them return. And soon, we'd have to go back and face it.

I found Dad standing alone on the limestone balcony, framed by morning light and the slow shimmer of the Mediterranean.

The water below looked all glassy. Little reed boats just drifting around, silent, like leftovers from some ancient world. I cleared my throat and tried to sound normal. "Dad? You're up... you're feeling better?"

He turned, slowly. The bruises were still there, all purple and ugly, but his smile was the same as ever, warm and kind of crooked, like it always used to be.

"With you here?" He came closer, moving carefully. "I feel stronger already. Just knowing you're safe..." He stopped, searching my face. "I kept dreaming I'd see you again. I'm looking forward to seeing St. Augustine. I just want to go home."

The word 'home' made my chest tighten. I grabbed his hand, squeezed tight, trying not to lose it.

"Dad... there's something I need to tell you."

My voice trembled. "Mom—she... she died. It was an accident. A freak accident. Or at least I keep telling myself it was an accident. Just over a week ago."

I stepped into his arms, and he held me, gently at first, then with the urgency of a father who thought he might never hold his daughter again.

"I know," he whispered into my hair. "I felt it right away. The whole world just kind of froze."

Dad and I just stood there, not talking, barely breathing, and it was like we were locked together in this bubble where clocks didn't even run. I could see it on his face, heavy, the quiet things that he always carried, the kind of stuff he'd never actually say. Maybe it was about Mom, or perhaps beyond that, it was about his past traveler experiences.

I held onto him, finally letting myself feel all of it. The years we'd lost. The time that got shattered. The ache of her being gone.

"I didn't get to say goodbye," I said, my voice barely there.

"She knew you loved her," he told me, his words heavy, like it hurt to say them, but he needed me to hear it. "That... she always knew."

So we stood there, side by side on that old balcony, two people patched together by what we'd lost, stuck together by love, just watching the sea.

"DAD..." I started, careful, watching the way he stared out at the water, like maybe he could see something I couldn't. "You know we can't stay there, right? In St. Augustine. I mean... I've been gone for a week. No note, nothing. You've been missing for years. Everyone already thinks you're dead."

He didn't look at me, just kind of nodded, his jaw tight. I could see it hit him, all at once.

"I know," he said, a little softer. "St. Augustine was... it was a great place to watch you grow up. But that version of our lives? It's gone."

"There's nothing left for us there now but questions we can't answer and a pain I don't know how to carry in daylight," I said mournfully.

He turned to face me then, the weight of the years etched into the lines around his eyes. "Yes," he said, voice hoarse. "When we return... to take care of your mother's affairs, to say goodbye properly... We'll have to be cautious. Quiet. Low profile. Just doing what needs to be done."

I nodded.

"We can't go back and pretend it's all normal," I whispered. My voice cracked. "We're not the same. I'm not the same. The city's not the same. She's gone. We'll go back, but is it home if she's not there?"

Something flashed in his eyes—a quick, bright, watery thing—but his voice stayed steady, almost stubborn. "No. We'll never be the same." He stopped, like the words were actually painful to express. "But we're still here. And for now... that has to be enough."

I leaned into him, the ocean breeze catching my hair. For a

second, we just stood there, two ghosts from different times, holding on to whatever was left.

BRAM, Sirianna, my father, and I stood beneath the great lens of the Pharos once more. The air shimmered with energy, ancient stone humming beneath our feet. With the token in my palm and all hearts aligned, we made the light smearing transfer, time folding in on itself, until the fire of the Pharos of Alexandria dissolved, and we were back beneath the shadow of the St. Augustine Lighthouse.

Lyrica had tried to come along, of course. She twirled her way into the chamber with a cryptic smile and a suitcase full of riddles, and her own style of chaos. Thankfully, the Collective had other plans for her. A mission as a muse, creating strange inspiration into the dreams of a future artist, somewhere near Reading, Pennsylvania. She vanished in a flash of glitter and dramatic flair, leaving only a faint perfume of lavender and something she called Wonderstruck.

MY FATHER and I settled quietly into the old Coast Guard barracks near the lighthouse. During the day, we stayed tucked away, hidden from curious eyes. But when night fell, we ventured out into the sleeping city. We walked through the cobblestone streets like shadows, watching the moonlight dance across the bay. Our city, frozen in time, caught between several centuries.

One night, two strange things happened at once. The sky was moonless, the air thick with the scent of diesel and something sweeter —honeysuckle maybe, or decay. My father and I walked through the half-lit hush of a Florida night toward a run-down gas station, its flickering sign buzzing with the sound of an anxious insect. We went in for snacks—something stupid and normal—and that's when I saw it.

THERE IT WAS. My face. Staring back at me from the side of a milk carton.

A LOW-RESOLUTION PHOTO, grainy and printed in a washed-out, dotted black and white.

Like a ghost from a poorly remembered dream.

My name.

My age.

Missing from St. Augustine, Florida, since June 12th, 1985.

I couldn't breathe. My throat clenched. I thought I might cry— or scream. But before either could happen, a low murmur drifted from behind the counter. A television was playing, the volume just high enough to catch a calm and serious voice.

FROM THE NIGHTLY NEWS SHOW, *Nightline.*

"...A rise in Satanic activity and the disturbing uptick in missing children across the southeastern United States..."

AND THEN MY face appeared again. Larger now. There, on the screen, mixed with static.

MISSING SINCE THE GRUESOME, yet unexplained, death of her mother, Marsha Ingram. Along with another teen, her classmate Dorian Novus, who also vanished that same week.

A SNAPSHOT of Mom and me filled the screen—one I hadn't seen before, which made it worse somehow. I looked happy in it. She did too. Then it cut to a black silhouette. Dorian. No photo existed. Just a featureless shape where his face should be.

THEN JENNY UNSNER POPPED UP, blinking into the camera with her frizzed-out hair and that ridiculous pink sweater vest as if she were auditioning for a daytime soap.

"Veronica got weird after Dorian showed up," she said, *her voice sounding similar to a town gossip girl. "There were rumors that he was into Satanic stuff. Like, you know, real rituals. That guy creeped out all the girls, except for Veronica."*

Which was rich, coming from the girl who practically melted when he looked her way.

THE SCREEN CUT AGAIN—TO a local detective, his badge catching a glint of fluorescent light.

"Marsha Ingram's death... might've been accidental," he said, *not sounding convinced, "but we haven't seen anything this brutal since Athalia Lindsley's murder in '74. That's how quiet this town usually is."*

I LEFT the Doritos on the counter and slipped out the door, the bag crinkling faintly in my shaking hand before I let it fall. I didn't wait for Dad. I turned away, not wanting to see the cashier's eyes flick to mine and register the match.

Because the girl on the milk carton wasn't a ghost.

She was me. Still breathing and still bleeding. Still mourning the loss of Mom and Claire, all I've known here, in this town.

And I would always have to remain missing.

Chapter Thirty-Three

Dad and I hung around the marina at night, keeping to the shadows just beyond the Bridge of Lions. The masts of the sailboats rocked gently in the dark, their shrouds clinking like wind chimes from weathered ghosts. It felt like we were haunting the place more than planning a heist, two fugitives watching the tide and waiting for the right moment to steal a sailboat.

That was our job: to steal a boat. Not the kind of father-daughter bonding I'd ever dreamed about, but here we were.

While Bram handled the more delicate matter of claiming Meridian's body with the correct paperwork and signatures, Sirianna had forged a mountain of documents to take care of my Mom's.

According to the files, Marsha Ingram had generously donated her body to science—specifically to the University of Florida's College of Medicine. A convenient fiction, neatly typed, forged, and notarized by a Collective agent at the Pharos posing as a notary.

Sirianna was born to walk through locked doors and leave chaos smiling in her wake. She didn't ask for favors, no. She made people *want* to give them. With lips like sin and eyes that whispered secrets, she could unravel a man with a glance and stitch him back together with promises he'd never remember agreeing to.

She didn't just charm; she *removed* resistance.

Of course, she was the one sent to the coroner's office for my Mom. No one else could've pulled it off.

Still, to ensure a smooth transaction, they studied the clerks' schedules carefully, circling the best target, a mid-level male employee, one with just enough authority to stamp a document and just enough loneliness to let Sirianna do the rest. Divorced, most likely. Tired. Vulnerable in the way men don't admit until it's too late.

For the visit to the coroner's office, she wore a charcoal gray pencil skirt that clung just below the knee, as if it held secrets. Professional enough to slip past suspicion, tight enough to make hearts falter. Her blouse was a silky off-white with a plunging neckline that hinted rather than revealed, the kind of fabric that shimmered slightly under fluorescents, catching the eye without seeming to try. She had the forged donor form folded in her purse like a loaded gun.

A fitted blazer cinched at the waist gave her an air of authority, but it was the heels—sleek black stilettos- that turned her into something cinematic. Every echoed step was a slow countdown, a reminder that she was in complete control of the room.

She'd pinned her raven hair just high enough to bare the curve of her neck, that vulnerable place just below her ear—but left a few strands loose, like she wanted someone to notice. Around her wrist, a gold bracelet with a single dangling hourglass charm—just enough to catch the light when she reached for a pen.

Her lipstick? Crimson. Not red—*crimson*. Like a promise or a warning, depending on how close you stood.

And her perfume was something floral and ancient, like orchids blooming in a thunderstorm.

Ten minutes later, she walked out with everything she needed: a stamped release form, a flustered clerk, and not a single trace of doubt behind her.

Sirianna never lied.

She just made you forget the truth.

And the truth was too tangled to tell anyway.

TONIGHT, our part was simple: wait for the tide, choose the right boat, and vanish like phantoms on the Matanzas waterway.

The boat we had been eyeing for days was a sleek, double-masted schooner named *Solstice,* moored just south of the marina near the ancient coquina seawall. She was nearly fifty feet of polished wood and regal stature, her hull gleaming under the moonlight like a forgotten relic of some royal fleet. One of the largest vessels in the bay, she carried an air of entitlement—as if she belonged wherever she sailed, unquestioned and untouchable.

Dad said that was the beauty of it. "Something that bold," he told me, eyes scanning the rigging with something like reverence, "you don't sneak around with her. You glide out like you own the tides."

He was sure we could take her through the drawbridge without raising suspicion. If we timed it right, we could move her smoothly and steadily through the open span of the Bridge of Lions, and no one would question a thing.

The tide was creeping in, lapping quietly at the barnacled pilings beneath the dock. In the hush of early twilight, we slipped aboard a gray inflatable dinghy tethered low and hidden in the shadows, well out of sight from the harbormaster's shack at the far end. The only sounds were the creak of ropes and the soft splash of paddles slicing the dark water.

We didn't speak.

With practiced quiet, we paddled toward the *Solstice,* moored near the breakwall, its silhouette barely distinguishable from the horizon. One by one, we climbed aboard like ghosts—or pirates—keeping low, alert for any movement or watchers.

I moved quickly to the helm while my father raised the anchor with a controlled grind of chain. The engine coughed once, then purred to life, low and stable. We eased away without lights, steering south along the inlet, the salt wind sharp against our skin.

The old hospital loomed ahead along the old bayfront like a relic from another time, its crumbling facade catching the weak glint of moonlight. A more modern hospital was finishing construction further down shore to the south. We cut the motor way before reaching a narrow pier, letting the current guide us in.

There, under a flickering sodium lamp, Bram and Sirianna waited beside a white van, their expressions unreadable in the dark.

As we drew closer, they moved in tandem—no words exchanged—wheeling out two long cardboard crates from the back of the van, the kind that didn't need labels.

No one had to ask what was inside.

THE *SOLSTICE* GROANED beneath us as she eased away from the dock, her hull scraping the silty bottom with a low, teeth-gritting sound that sent a jolt through all of us. For one tense moment, it felt like we might run aground before we'd even truly begun. But the tide was on our side, lifting us inch by inch, freeing the boat from the waterway's muddy grip. With a gentle lurch, we finally broke loose and slipped silently from the shallows into deeper water, gliding toward the open current.

"Hold the wheel steady," Dad said, cutting the engine and nodding toward the helm.

I remained in place, heart thudding with a strange mix of nerves and exhilaration. The dim red glow of the ship's compass lit my hands as I gripped the wheel.

Bram and Sirianna moved fast, their shadows darting across the deck in the moonlight. Dad was right there with them, all three working together to unwrap the booms and haul up the sails. The canvas snapped open with a soft pop and filled up, the Solstice shuddering as the wind caught hold. The mast groaned. Ropes pulled tight. Suddenly, we were gliding forward—not with gas or diesel, but with the old magic of wind and bravery.

The Solstice tipped, just a little, leaning into the breeze as we slid toward the dark arches of the Bridge of Lions.

Dad flicked on the navigation lights: green on one side, red on the other. Little dots glowing in the dark, like eyes. Then he hit the VHF radio, twisting the dial, flipping through the static, listening for anything—a ping, a voice, anything at all.

But there was just static.

The radio hissed and popped until Sirianna's voice came through, smooth and sharp, like she was used to being in charge. She pressed the mic right near her mouth.

"Soltice requesting passage, Bridge of Lions, do you copy?"

A pause. Then a groggy voice replied, "BOL copies. Stand by."

The night was totally still. Then, out of nowhere, this massive horn blared—a deep, mechanical thing, like a foghorn, sound bouncing off the water, making my heart jump. Up ahead, the drawbridge started moving: gears grinding, red lights blinking everywhere, the two sides lifting slowly, like some mechanical monster opening its jaws.

Solstice rocked under my feet. Bram was messing with the sail when all at once the wind kicked in, shoving us forward so hard I almost lost my grip. My dad stood right next to me at the wheel, just calm, like always. He leaned in, voice steady and close: "Keep her straight. Line up the bowsprit with that red beacon out there, see it? That's your thread. Just hold course. Let the wind do the rest."

I nodded, but my hands wouldn't stop shaking.

Every muscle in my body was tight with focus.

The green and red lights of the bridge reflected off the water like shards of stained glass, rippling with our approach.

I could feel the weight of history in that moment, with the power of the ship beneath me, the bridge towering above, and the stars blinking through the thin veil of fog.

I was steering us forward, past the columns that had watched ships, storms, and secrets go by. But nothing like this.

We slipped between the rising spans, and I swear I didn't breathe. Wind whipped at my hair, the deck buzzed beneath my shoes, and my pulse pounded way louder than the sails overhead.

Then we were through.

I let out a slow breath, staring at the open water ahead, knowing something was different now. The girl who'd passed through one side of that drawbridge wasn't the same one coming out the other side.

WE ROUNDED the southern tip of Anastasia Island, the Solstice's bow slicing straight through the dark water. I kept my hands tight on the wheel, steering us toward the mouth of the inlet.

The channel narrowed, flanked by marsh grasses and the silhouette of dunes to the starboard side, with the buildings of Vilano Beach lining the port side. Then the land on both sides fell away entirely, and we slipped, quiet and smooth, into the open Atlantic.

The ocean greeted us like a secret being unwrapped, vast, calm, and endless.

The sky was, like, black velvet, with stars everywhere, all twinkly and gorgeous, like they were trying to say something nobody really understood. The sails pulled tight, snapping and popping, catching every bit of wind, and we kept moving—not super fast, but steady, like the ocean was finally ready for us just to go already.

I kept the bow pointed dead east. The Solstice remained heeled a bit, taking on the southwest breeze, but the compass didn't even twitch. Behind us, the shore just kind of melted away, fading into the dark, until it was gone.

Shore lights blinked off, one after another, swallowed up by the night, until just a few were left, scattered like stubborn fireflies.

UNTIL THERE WAS ONLY ONE.

WAY BACK, the St. Augustine Lighthouse was still there. Its beam swept the water every thirty seconds. Slow. Steady. Like a pulse. A light or heartbeat, maybe. Mine. Or Bram's.

Then he came up behind me. The deck creaked under his boots. I felt him before I heard him—a quiet warmth folding into my space, like the tide coming home. His hands slid over mine on the wheel. Warm. Firm. Steady. The boat steadied. So did my heart.

"You're a sailor," he said, voice low and right next to my ear. "Or... maybe you're a sailor's dream."

His breath brushed my neck. I smiled, couldn't help it, something fluttering crazy in my chest.

I turned my head just a little, enough to see him out of the corner of my eye. Moonlight caught the soft edge of his jaw.

"Then I hope the dream never ends," I whispered.

He didn't answer. Just let the silence hang, thin and perfect, between us.

AS THE NIGHT WORE ON, I noticed my father and Sirianna pulling down the jib at the bow of the boat, the sail whispering as it folded in on itself. Then my father turned to the mast and began lowering one of the mainsails, hand over hand, the canvas groaning gently as it came down.

I stepped forward, puzzled. He caught my glance and gave a faint, solemn nod.

"Cardboard will not take them to the deep," Dad said, all serious. "Canvas will."

At the stern, near the rail, those two long boxes just sat there, waiting.

I leaned against Bram, soaking up his warmth.

"Whatever's out there," I said, quieter now, "I want to face it with you."

The stars above kind of shimmered, as if they agreed.

THE LAND VANISHED, and the darkness got deeper. We drifted between two infinities: water below, stars overhead, just floating in that place where time goes soft and anything feels possible.

The cartons were just there, side by side, big red letters stamped across them: Human Remains. Sirianna crouched down, peeled back the lids, carefully. Inside: bodies, already wrapped in thin, white shrouds. Nobody said a word. They didn't have to. You could see it in the way their hands moved, slow and heavy, like every inch hurt.

Together, they folded the thick, salty canvas over the bodies, wrapping them up in an ancient-offering style.

As my father tied the rope slowly, precisely, looping it around each husk as if he were knotting a part of himself into the ritual.

The endless and black ocean churned patiently, waiting to take them home, as we all sat adrift watching for first light.

Chapter Thirty-Four

The sky was starting to take on that beautiful bruised color, kind of pink and copper smeared together over the edge of everything. It made the dark feel softer, like the night was finally letting go after hanging on for way too long. We were standing there at the back of the Solstice, not moving, the water all glassy and the sails drooping, like even the ship was too sad to bother.

Bram stepped up, and the sunlight caught the water behind him so he looked like he had this gold outline, almost fake, like something from a movie. His voice was hushed, like he was trying not to wake the boat or something. "We return Meridian to the sea," he said, eyes locked on the bundle, all wrapped up tight in sailcloth with the ropes neat and careful. "A traveler not just through time, but through truth—through sacrifice, and through secrets too heavy for most men to carry."

He stopped talking for a second. His jaw clenched up, and the wind did this little shivery thing, tugging the last star away, like it was time to go.

"He walked where few dared, across fractured timelines and forgotten centuries. Meridian saw the world as it was, and as it could be," Bram said with reverence.

Sirianna bowed her head beside him, her dark hair flowing in the breeze. My father stood with one hand to his chest, the other resting on the gunwale.

"He died doing what we all hope to do," Bram continued, voice thickening, "protecting someone else's future. And for that, he lives on."

He looked down, his eyes glinting in the new light. "The hourglass sands never cease, always overturned. And when it resets, Meridian will find his way back. He always has."

The wind sighed as they lifted his body, wrapped it in canvas, and weighted it with the sail that had once carried us through time.

The sun rose a little higher, painting the waves with gold.

We said nothing for a long time. Then Bram stepped back as Sirianna and Dad lifted the shrouded form with care, and with one final prayer, released it into the deep.

THEN DAD STEPPED FORWARD NEXT, his weathered hand briefly brushing over mine for strength. The sunrise caught the edges of his face, softening the lines of grief etched into him. When he spoke, his voice trembled, not at all from weakness, but from the weight of memory.

"She wasn't a Traveler," he said slowly. "Not in the way the Collective defines it. Not in the way I am. Or Six. But in all the ways that matter, Marsha lived as one."

He looked down, swallowing hard. "She moved through time the way only a mother can—with love and patience. She raised our daughter with a heart full of stories. She made banana pancakes on Saturdays, sang off-key in the car, and somehow always knew the exact right moment just to sit next to you and say nothing at all."

He paused. The wind tugged at the sails, the sea swelling under us, steady and slow.

"She didn't know about gravitational waves. Or Tokens. Or the weight of the timelines hanging on our shoulders. But she knew how to love. How to forgive. And how to build a home with just her hands and her heart."

His voice cracked then, just slightly. "I should've told Marsha that I loved her more often, but I didn't. I should've told her everything, but I couldn't. Even in the darkness of her days, of my disappearance, she knew something was coming. She always had that sense. And I have to believe that she will reach us again."

He turned slightly, eyes scanning the water.

"She's not gone. Only traveling a different path for now. And when the waves pull back and the hourglass is turned, Marsha will be there. No longer a memory, but as a Traveler."

He stepped back, brushing a tear from his cheek.

And as if on cue, the sun broke out fully over the horizon, gilding the waves in gold and making the sea shimmer as it held the edges of another world.

The sail-wrapped form of my mother was silent as Bram and Sirianna lifted it together, solemn and careful, as if afraid to break something already gone. Morning light left long streaks across the deck of rose gold, as the sea below waited, still and endless.

With a quiet nod from my father, they released her. The weight of the canvas and rope gave her form and dignity as she descended. And then—*rip*, the water broke tight around her, not a splash but a sudden, slicing sound like a seam being torn open. The sea took her without question, folding around her and pulling her under with reverent finality.

I clutched the rail, fingers trembling.

I had thought I'd already said goodbye. On the shore. A hundred times in the silence of my thoughts. But watching her vanish into the deep, swallowed by the very ocean that had always sung around our home, I felt the goodbye settle into my bones. It wasn't loud or dramatic. Just real, as if the tide is pulling something precious out of your hands before you can hold on tighter.

She was gone. But not lost.

"I'll find you again," I whispered. "No matter how long it takes. Across time... or through it."

CUTTING ACROSS THE ATLANTIC, the Solstice sailed westward, the wind tugging at the remaining sails. My hands gripped the large wooden wheel, guiding us steadily toward the lighthouse, its tower a pale needle rising above the horizon. The sun had climbed high enough now that the beacon had flickered off, but the silhouette of the lighthouse still stood watch in the distance.

And somewhere past that, out on the land, was Dorian.

Bram and my dad hustled across the deck, tugging on ropes, adjusting the sails, trying to catch the morning wind. With every bump of the boat, the shore got closer.

The coastline started to look like itself again: that skinny arm of dunes and scrub brush my dad always called Conch Island.

"It's not even an island anymore," he'd say, with a laugh. "And no one has ever seen a single conch there. Just this stubborn strip of land, holding back the ocean in front of the lighthouse. They say it was named after a legendary fisherman nicknamed 'Conchy'."

We'd decided it would be best to run the boat aground there. Conch Island was technically part of the state park, close enough to town that the rightful owner could retrieve the Solstice without much trouble. No damage done, aside from a few missing sails.

WE DISEMBARKED from the Solstice one by one, the hull gently kissing the sand as the tide eased us into the shallows. The old schooner creaked softly behind us, sails lowered, its work complete. Bram splashed into the knee-deep surf first, boots sloshing, then turned to help Sirianna and my dad steady themselves. I followed last, barefoot, the cool water sucking at my ankles as we made our way onto the beach.

The sand was soft but sticky, clinging to our soaked clothes as we climbed dunes of pale sea oats, sand, and crushed shells. At the top, the view opened up, and the narrow cove lay before us, calm and glistening in the morning sun. On the far side, a half-mile away, we could see the weathered roof of the Navigators Grill and, behind it, the familiar silhouette of the lighthouse rising above the canopy.

But the strip of water between us and home shimmered, as if tempting us to a challenge.

"We could swim across," I offered.

"Or we hike three miles through snake-infested park trails," Bram said flatly, raising a brow. "Which sounds exactly like something I don't want to do barefoot."

My dad squinted at the horizon. "Tide's going out, so there's less water, and the current's not bad. It's a straight shot if we stick together."

Sirianna smirked, already knotting her hair atop her head. "Let's not overthink it. I've been through much worse in a skirt."

I laughed, despite myself, and nodded. "Then it's settled. We swim."

We looked back one last time at the Solstice, noble and still in the morning light.

THEN, side by side, we stepped into the water, the mangroves closing in like crooked fingers around us. The air smelled of salt and decay, thick with brine. Beneath the surface, the water was murky and warm, concealing a bottom of deep, sucking muck that clung to our ankles and tried to pull us under with every step. Each stride forward was a fight, the shoreline ahead glinting with promise beneath the watchful eye of the distant lighthouse.

We pressed on, waist-deep, then chest-deep, until there was nothing to do but swim for it. The current tugged at us with invisible hands, and the silence on the surface was eerie, with only our labored breaths and the occasional cry of gulls above.

The opposite shore details came into view, coquina-laden, sunbleached, scattered with fragments of shell and bleached driftwood. We pushed through the final stretch, my limbs burning, lungs raw.

AND THEN IT HAPPENED.

My foot came down on something jagged, and pain shot up my leg like lightning. I screamed, a sound ripped straight from my core, as I fell forward, instinctively throwing out my hands to catch myself.

Another wave of agony tore through me as both palms met a hidden bed of razor-sharp oysters. The edges bit into my skin, shredding flesh, warm blood mixing with saltwater. I cried out again, louder this time, the sting so sudden and searing it stole the breath from my lungs.

Bram was beside me in an instant, his hands gripping my arms to keep me from collapsing further. "Six! You're bleeding—don't move!"

"I—I didn't see it," I gasped, trembling as my sliced skin overwhelmed everything else. "It's in my hands—my feet—I can't..."

My father and Sirianna rushed toward us, the water splashing as they closed the gap, faces etched with worry and urgency.

And just like that, the final steps home became a desperate scramble, not just to reach the shore, but to keep moving through the hurt, through the blood, toward safety.

I stumbled onto the shore, gasping, tears streaking down my face as the saltwater mixed with blood dripping from my torn feet. Every step was agony—sharp, stabbing, hot—and by the time I collapsed onto a jagged slab of coquina, I was trembling from head to toe.

The sea breeze caught his hair just enough to make him look as if he'd walked out of someone's dream. Bram's eyes darted over my leg, jaw all tight, breathing tight. "Ugh. Oysters," he said, and dropped to his knees in the sand. Then, not even thinking about it, he yanked off his white t-shirt in one fast move. Even with every-thing hurting, I couldn't help but notice how strong he looked in the morning light, chest broad, arms flexing as he ripped the shirt into strips.

"You know," he said with a soft smirk. "This is where we first met." His eyes flickered up to meet mine as he gently wrapped the first foot.

I let out a shaky laugh, "You're ridiculous."

He didn't answer right away—just focused on wrapping my second foot.

He finished up, brushed this little piece of hair off my forehead, and looked at me. Like, super gentle. Barely even talking.

"I've got you, Six. You're not doing this alone."

And for a second, the pain faded, not just from the bandages, but from him. The way he looked at me, even with stigmata-like wounds on my hands, I didn't feel so torn or broken anymore.

WE CROSSED the empty lot outside Navigator's, the pavement all cracked and warm in the morning glow. My father and Sirianna moved ahead, not saying anything, their shadows stretching out in the early sun. Bram hung back with me while I hobbled along; every step became kind of a big deal.

Salt air stuck to my skin, mixing with sweat and old memories. My feet, all bandaged up, throbbed.

My chest felt hollow- carved out by everything lost and every-thing found.

Halfway through the lot, I faltered. The burning, stinging sensa-tion on the soles of my feet was too much.

Without asking, Bram slipped his arms around me and lifted me off the ground. I let out a breath I hadn't realized I was holding as I melted into him, my head resting on his shoulder, my side resting against his bare chest, and my arms moving around his neck. I let my eyes slip shut for just a moment.

He carried me through the quiet hush of the Live Oaks, their gnarled limbs arching over us in a cathedral of shadows.

Across the empty street, the lighthouse just stood there, sort of hunched in the gold of early morning. No longer flashing, just there. As if it were waiting. Or watching. Or both.

And when I finally stepped onto the crunchy gravel at the edge of the lighthouse, it all just kind of hit me: the pain, the grief, the whole weird miracle of being back here. So I let myself cry. Not because I was sad, but because it felt good to let go.

I had crossed oceans of time, followed whispers through ruins and dreams, and now, I was home. Or what once was home.

Chapter Thirty-Five

Bram set me down at the bottom of the lighthouse steps, his hands staying on my arms a second longer than necessary. The sun hit his face, and he sort of smirked, like he was about to say something ridiculous.

"If I carry you over the threshold, Six," he said, flicking a piece of hair off my forehead, "I'm pretty sure that means I have to marry you. You know, tradition."

I couldn't stop grinning before calling out, "Dad!" I yelled way too loudly. "Bram has a really important question for you!"

Bram made this low groan and shook his head, still smiling that crooked smile.

My dad turned around, as if annoyed, eyebrows up. "What?" he said, obviously confused.

I waved my hands in the air and managed a chuckle, "Nothing! Never mind, Dad. Just keep going."

He gave us both a suspicious glance, then turned back towards the second set of granite steps.

Bram leaned in close enough for only me to hear. "You're impossible."

"And yet, here you are," I whispered back, grinning.

Sɪʀɪᴀɴɴᴀ ᴀɴᴅ Dᴀᴅ's bare footsteps echoed against the stone as they watched where they stepped. Bram offered his hand to help me up, and I took it, though part of me didn't want to move just yet.

I glanced down at myself—my clothes still damp from the swim, my hands scraped, my feet aching. Everything felt sticky, sore, and salt-stung. I winced as I flexed my fingers.

"I feel so gross," I muttered. "First thing I'm doing when we get back to the Pharos? A hot bath".

Bram looked at me with this crooked half-smile—like he wasn't sure if I was joking or delirious, but he was going to go with it either way.

"Maybe let someone check your hands and feet first," he said gently, his voice quieter than usual. "You've been through hell, Six."

I glanced at him. Honestly, we both looked wrecked—like we'd been run over by a bus.

"Fine," I whispered, and managed a half-smile. "But after the bath, I want food. Real food. Something salty. And then I'm sleeping for, like, a week."

He nodded, way more serious than I expected. "Deal," he said, voice low. "But only if I get the room in the Pharos next to yours."

Wʜᴇɴ ᴡᴇ ꜰɪɴᴀʟʟʏ sᴛᴇᴘᴘᴇᴅ ɪɴᴛᴏ the lighthouse, it felt like walking into the ruins of a memory—dusty and strange and familiar all at once. Like the place had been waiting for us to come back, whether it made sense or not. I had literally never been in here, not in the morning, not with all this insane light pouring in. The hallway for all its decay was, like, blinding, and it made every single patch of chipped paint, every brownish stain, every sad little sign of neglect totally obvious. The oil house smelled like rust and something moldy, and there were bird feathers and, ew, little rodent droppings everywhere.

"Home sweet home," I muttered, making a face at the mess.

Bram leaned in, almost a little too close.

"I've seen worse," he whispered. "Besides... with a little work... Okay, a lot of work, this place could still shine."

I looked at him, the glint in his eyes, the way the morning sun caught the dust swirling in the air.

Before tiptoeing, the soles of my feet barely even touched the cold stone. I slipped down the dim hallway and into the rotunda. The air was chilly and somewhat damp, with a peculiar tang of rust and old salt, but it actually looked cleaner than it had last time, not so much like a dungeon, more like a place that just didn't get a lot of visitors. Still, it was super echoey. You could practically hear history dripping down the walls.

Bram was already going up the spiral stairs, his hand just barely skimming the iron rail as he climbed. He looked like he had a mission or something. I followed, careful to step only with the balls of my feet on each skinny stair, moving slowly and quietly, letting the cool metal chill my toes. The whole staircase twisted up like a seashell, shadows flickering every time we passed a window, getting brighter and brighter as we wound our way toward the top.

By the fifth landing, Bram and I caught up with Dad and Sirianna, both leaning slightly on the railing, catching their breath. The sunlight slanted through the narrow window, illuminating the flush on my father's face—and the sly, almost secretive grin on Sirianna's lips.

Wait. *Was she... my father?* No. No way. My brain was just making mischief out of the thin air up here.

"Youth has its privileges," Dad said with a wink, gesturing for us to go ahead, his tone half-amused, half-conceding defeat to the climb.

Bram smirked as we slipped past them, and I gave Sirianna one last curious glance before heading upward. Whatever was going on—or *wasn't*—I was going to have to keep my eye on them.

As we reached the seventh landing, I looked up—and my breath caught in my throat.

"**Bram!**" I screamed, but it was already too late.

Dorian came crashing down from above, a monstrous shadow, leaping from the eighth landing across the chasm.

His boots slammed into Bram's chest, knocking him off balance and hard against the brick wall. The sound of bone meeting stone cracked through the stairwell. Bram collapsed onto the iron grate, gasping, dazed.

Dorian was on him in an instant, straddling him with the fury of a man possessed. His fists rained down in brutal, relentless arcs, cracking against Bram's jaw and temple. Bram's head bounced against the floor with a metallic *clang, thud, clang*—each impact more sickening than the last.

I screamed again and charged toward them. Blood was already leaking from Bram's mouth.

"Get off him!" I cried, throwing myself onto Dorian's back, clawing at his face. My fingers tangled in his hair, yanking hard, but he roared and reared up like a beast.

With one savage jerk of his shoulder and a snarl, he flung me off as if I were a rag doll. My back hit the iron railing before I landed on the unforgiving floor, my head smacking hard enough to explode stars in my vision. The world tilted. Sound dulled. My ears rang. I gasped, blinking blood through the blur. I saw Bram.

Through the haze, I saw Dorian's hand fumbling at his belt. He pulled the dagger—but Bram kicked it clean from his grip. It clattered across the landing, spinning wildly before stopping by my shaking hand.

Bram wasn't down.

Groaning, battered, he clawed his way to the railing, dragging himself up inch by inch. His hand gripped the iron, white-knuckled, his other arm cradling his ribs. His face was pale with pain—and something more.

Terror.

Because just behind him was the drop. Open air spiraling seven stories down the tower's hollow center.

My vision pulsed, blood dripping from my temple as I picked up the blade.

Dorian looked around for the knife before turning to see Bram rising.

With a howl, Dorian lunged—and slammed into Bram's chest, shoving him back.

Bram's bare feet slid.

The iron rail dug into his lower back as he teetered on the edge, arms windmilling, the black void yawning behind him.

"No!" I yelled, scrambling up.

Bram's eyes locked on mine for a split second. His lips parted— terror written across every line of his face.

This was his nightmare. His fatal fate... Falling.

DORIAN DIDN'T SEE me rise behind him.

With a scream that came from somewhere deep in my chest, I threw myself onto him, plunging the dagger into his face. Straight into his left eye.

He shrieked with a terrible, gurgling howl and thrashed, his blood spurting across the floor, hot and wet. In the confusion, his hand yanked at my chest, fingers catching the compass. The chain around my neck snapped, and the compass flew.

It bounced once, then twice, and finally rolled off the edge.

I lunged, my hand grasping at empty air, but the compass disappeared into the darkness below.

"**No!**" I cried out.

Below us, I heard a voice—"*Got it!*"—and saw my father's outstretched hand catch the compass just before it would've bounced down the iron stairs, the token up for grabs.

I heard Bram slump back onto the cool landing floor.

DORIAN WAS blind in one eye now, screeching in agony, blood pouring from the ruin on his face. He tried to bolt, stumbling blindly toward the edge.

He missed the top step entirely.

His foot hit air and he went tumbling, flailing wildly, howling like a banshee as he crashed down the iron stairs, hitting every railing, every corner on the way. A trail of crimson followed his descent, painting the walls.

At the fifth landing, he staggered upright, swaying drunkenly, one hand over his ruined eye.

He passed my father and Sirianna, who had just reached that level, both staring in horror.

"My eye!" Dorian wailed as his echo reverberated inside the tower. "You stupid bitch! I'll kill you all!" His voice cracked and echoed as he vanished into the depths below, the sound of his boots fading into the distance.

SILENCE SETTLED OVER US, broken only by my ragged breath and Bram curled up on the ground, groaning beside me.

Bram lay sprawled across the iron steps, his chest rising in shallow, ragged breaths. Blood streaked his temple, and for a terrifying moment, I thought he might be unconscious—or worse.

Then he stirred, groaning as he rolled to one side. He braced himself on the railing, the metal rattling faintly beneath his weight.

I dropped beside him, heart pounding, hands trembling as I brushed the blood and sweat from his face. His eye swelled shut—his bottom lip split.

He looked like hell.

"Six," he croaked, voice all gravel and weirdly... grateful? "You saved my life. You know that, right?"

I just lost it. Tears everywhere. I put my hand on his face—even though it was bloody and bruised. "Two burials at sea in one morning is enough," I whispered. "I couldn't lose you, too."

Someone shuffled behind us. Dad stepped up, holding the compass. It looked rough. All scratched up and not shiny at all.

"This belongs to you," he said, real quiet, and sort of tucked it into my hand. "You kept it safe. It brought you to me."

I wrapped my fingers around the cool metal, nodding. The weight of everything pressing in at once—grief, relief, pride, love. All tangled up.

"She did it," Bram repeated, louder this time. "She took him down. By stabbing him in the eye."

"Six, you've become one bad little bitch. And trust me, I know bad." Sirianna smirked, standing a few steps below, cloak torn, her dagger still drawn, eyes scanning the stairwell. "But that won't be the last we see of him," she said darkly.

BRAM REACHED for my other hand, his grip warm and steady despite the tremble in it. Our fingers interlaced.

The battle was over...for now. We were bruised, breathless, still standing.

I clutched the compass to my chest, its pulse steady beneath my fingers, like it had never truly left me.

The storm had passed. The girl who was supposed to break did not.

I had crossed time, survived betrayal, and stared into the dark.

And when it tried to take everything from me,

I didn't let go.

I didn't lose myself.

I found her.

Chapter Thirty-Six

Some who vanish are only finding their way.

I've learned that now, standing beneath the immense stone arches of the Pharos, where time folds like waves and lighthouses burn like stars. It's beautiful here, ancient, mysterious, and alive with whispers from past millennia. This place is a reminder of how far I've wandered, but it isn't home.

HOME SMELLS like magnolia and jasmine, combined with the salt air clinging to your skin.

Home sounds like gulls arguing over scraps behind a bait shop.

Home is the groan of the Bridge of Lions rising at dawn, and marveling at the architecture once across.

Home is St. Augustine.

I miss it more than I thought I would.

SOMETIMES I CLIMB to the highest point of the Pharos, just before dawn, and I look west, toward the place where my lighthouse still stands. I imagine it waiting, its beams sweeping over the Atlantic like a song, steady and faithful.

Bram teases me, says I've gone soft. But he knows. He misses it too.

MY DAD'S RECOVERING—SIRIANNA'S back to scheming. There are duties here, things to learn, histories to protect, and assignments to accomplish. Responsibilities I never asked for—but will take on anyway for now.

But part of me is already gone. Part of me is walking the cobblestone streets barefoot after a storm, with the scent of rain and pizza in the air. Part of me is climbing the iron stairs of the tower with Bram right behind me, breathless and brave.

Another part of me is still at the edge of the inlet, steering the Solstice past the drawbridge, through the darkness, toward whatever came next. For so long, I existed as a kitten, but in a city of so many lions, I left as one.

I know I'll return.

The light calls to me.

And when I answer, I'll come back not as an apprentice, but as something more.

Not just a daughter.

Not just a traveler.

But a keeper of what matters most to us all.

Time.

Truth.

And home.

IT WAS the kind of early evening that felt out of place in Florida.

The sky hung low, a flat expanse of cold silver cloud stretching to the sea. The trees along Red Cox Drive stood twisted and still, their bare limbs clawing at the pale light. Wind hissed through the cedar branches, whispering secrets or warnings that no one would hear.

A MAN STEPPED out onto an open sports field behind the elementary school. He moved with calm purpose, his trench coat swaying behind him like a curtain drawing shut. The coat was long and dark, but not new—creased at the collar, dulled at the seams. In one hand, tucked close to his body, was a rifle. Its polished barrel reflected only a sliver of that colorless sky. He kept it low, partly hidden against his side by his coat.

He wore mirrored aviator glasses, though the sun was nowhere to be found.

He stopped at the corner of Red Cox and Santa Monica Avenue, where the sidewalk had long ended further back. A place where the locals drove by and tourists rarely traveled. The gusts began to become sharp off the distant dunes. He stood in the cold hush of early December, staring up between and above the Oaks.

Up at the lighthouse.

The dark tower stood against the sky like a monument to something holy, something sacred. The lens at the top is rotating, but not yet illuminated, holding on like a frozen breath waiting to exhale.

The man raised the rifle, his trench coat snapping slightly in the wind as he lined up the sights.

But he didn't fire.

Not yet.

INSTEAD, he pulled the weapon away from his face, exhaled slowly and deliberately, reaching up to remove his sunglasses.

His left eye was missing. In its place, a ruined mess of flesh and scar tissue, pulled tight like melted wax. It had never healed right. It never would. The lid grafted shut like a warning.

His remaining eye was cold, blue, unblinking.

He raised the rifle again and exhaled. No shaking. No hesitation. Just gravity and decision.

THEN HE PULLED THE TRIGGER.

A SINGLE CRACK split the air; a sharp punctuation mark against the silence of the coastal neighborhood. Birds scattered from the trees like ashes torn from a firestorm. The sound echoed, rolled, and vanished over rooftops and dunes, swallowed by the Atlantic.

A FLASH OF FRACTURED LIGHT.
The lens atop the lighthouse shuddered.
A hole, with cracks blooming outward across the prisms.
The man stood still, expressionless.
Waiting.
The wind rose.
Rain began to fall.
Then the light clicked on.
A flicker. A stutter. Then a beam—dim in places, splintered at the edges.
But still shining.

NOT COMPLETELY DARK.

Acknowledgments

This book exists because of the support of more people than I could ever properly thank. For years, I stared at blank pages, wondering if I'd ever get here—and I wouldn't have without the belief and encouragement of so many along the way.

To my parents, who have been supportive of all of life's endeavors and decisions with little judgment. Always ready to help pick up the pieces when things went wrong, and sometimes things have gone wrong, even and especially into adulthood. Not everyone has that kind of lifetime love and support, and I am grateful for them both.

To my wife Ashli, whom I too often underestimate and don't appreciate enough. She provided support and assistance with final edits to ensure continuity, punctuation, and grammatical accuracy. Self-published authors often lack a budget for professional editing. Leaving it to a spouse to find all the errors in one's project is usually both highly effective and affordable. Thank you.

To the many writers and creators on social media who freely share their advice, ideas, tips, and experiences on fiction writing, self-publishing, and marketing, who have been helpful along this journey.

To my friends and colleagues who were ARC readers, thank you for taking the time to read the work of a first-time author. Your feedback, encouragement, and excitement shaped this story in ways I'll always treasure.

There are the staff and volunteers at the St. Augustine Lighthouse & Maritime Museum who have shaped my passion for historic preservation and lighthouses. For their guidance, patience, and knowledge, I will always be grateful.

This book is a love letter of sorts to the historic community of St. Augustine, with over 460 years of recorded European and American history. Its architecture, stories, and spirit make it an almost magical place. And although I did not grow up here, St. Augustine has become my home, and it always will be.

And finally, **to you**, the reader holding this book in your hands: thank you for stepping into *Of Time and Light*. I hope these pages bring you a little wonder, a little hope, and perhaps a reminder that time, both the past and the future, is worth looking into.

Thank you for supporting an indie author in the vast and talented community of self-publishers.

The Author

Citizen J. Edwards lives with his family in St. Augustine, Florida. *Of Time and Light* is his debut novel.

More information on future works can be found at:
https://www.cjeauthor.com